FUTURE PERFECT

By Michael Foy

What's been said about "Future Perfect"...

"Foy has written a clever work that speaks loudly to our times and the troubles of our own making that we're in. If only our current world had a protagonist like his. And possibly it does, but maybe we won't know until each subsequent piece of our situation has been nestled into the next convolution.

Anyone aware of how the Russian nesting dolls work--with several figurines, each smaller one fitting into the next larger size—will see in them an analogy to the unusual and innovative structure of Foy's work, a complex yet perfectly logical, interwoven fabric that can only be understood in its entirety, once complete.

Foy, a former engineer, has put an engineer's imagination, and then some, into this extraordinary and tantalizing tale.

Whoever enjoys a puzzle and some innovative science along the way will appreciate what Michael Foy has created with this material. The novel works both on the level of an intricate brainteaser and on the level of sheer moment-to-moment intelligent entertainment.

Kudos to Foy for his complex and alluring work and for this character who changes as we watch and as he begins to figure out the broader, and broader, and broader view."

G. Miki Hayden, author of 2004's Edgar Award Winning "The Maids" in "Blood on Their Hands" by Lawrence Block and Writing the Mystery: A Start-to-Finish Guide.

"Future Perfect"

ISBN 0-9747256-1-7

Published by ZoomBook Press, Printing & Publishing

ZoomBook™ and ZoomBook.com
are a part of GizMo Systems, Inc.

Visit us on the World Wide Web at:

http://www.zoombook.com

He who controls the past commands the future.
He who commands the future conquers the past

- George Orwell

Prologue

With each orbit, the satellite mapped the planet's surface, down to the smallest patterns of dry, cracked earth used as input for the device's calculus in projecting future topography. Since the satellite was rendered invisible by its shielding engineering, mankind remained totally ignorant of it and its surveillance. Thus concealed, the miniature, exotic circuitry labored to fill a memory capacity of trillions of gigabytes. But, in addition to this earth's geography, the satellite kept a memory location for the actions of every sentient being detected. Soaring over the mesas of the southwestern United States, the strange probe located one such target life form: a man lying immobile.

Part I

Reawakening

Chapter 1

The man came to groggily and spat dust from his lips. Opening his eyes, he slammed them shut again in reaction to the blinding sun. He tried once more. Squinting, his eyes eventually adjusted and he tentatively viewed an unending landscape of scrub brush and cactus. Then he began to rise, but recent injuries racked him with pain.

When a tickling sensation on his leg propelled his attention to a huge spider crawling across his blue cotton pants, he sat up explosively and knocked the insect off of him. The bug scurried away, but the man's violent movements made him grimace with new pain to his head.

What's next? he wondered in irritation while wiping dampness from his brow. As he brought his arm down, he noticed that his shirt sleeve was stained red and he checked to see where the blood might be coming from. Eventually touching his head with care, his fingers found a wound caked with his own vital fluid and speckled over with desert dust. A dried carmine smudge covered the rock that had apparently been his pillow for some length of time.

While the man tried to remember his fall, he was startled by the deep throaty snicker of a palomino stallion that stood not twenty feet away. The animal was outfitted with a full saddle, including an inviting canteen. At the horse's feet lay the tattered remains of a trampled snake, no doubt the reason for the fall, the man realized. With the mystery solved, he forced himself to his feet, heading for the promise of badly needed water.

The feathered shaft of an arrow struck the ground where he stood, vibrating from its impact and startling him. Six war-painted Pawnee rode hard in his direction, shooting more arrows that he had to dodge while sprinting for his horse. In mid-stride, he remembered his belt with two full holsters, the bottoms tied around his thighs. Surprising himself with a gunslinger's style, he drew a six-shooter with his right hand, turned and fired on the Indians who were fast closing in.

They'll feather me with arrows before I can get to my mount.

Have to fight them off. His first shot missed, but he didn't panic. The second struck one of his attackers in the shoulder, knocking the brave off his mount just as another arrow nearly hit his own horse's leg. *Got to hurry!* He fired another errant shot but then found the range and dispatched three with ease. He discarded his empty gun back into its holster, barely getting the other weapon out before shooting one of the two remaining Indians, point blank.

The last warrior, however, knocked the white man down, dislodging the gun from his grasp and causing him to hit his injured head on the ground with a jarring impact. He fought to maintain consciousness while the painted savage pressed a plumed spear onto his throat. *My six shooter...can't get my hand free to grab for it.* The Indian, sitting across his opponent's middle, bore all his weight and energy on the spear handle trying to crush the wounded man's windpipe. With his strength eluding him, the gunfighter struggled against the slighter Indian, whose leverage came from the dominant position. Pressing this advantage, the savage fought fiercely, sweating from a Mohawk strip on the back of his head. This and the adornment of feathers and ear pieces identified his tribe.

Time to act. Abruptly, the man brought his knee up into the kidney area of the brave's back, weakening the Indian's resolve. With the pressure on his throat relieved, the traveler twisted the spear out of his enemy's hands and in the same motion awkwardly pounded his fist directly into the painted face. *Now if I can just reach my gun. . . Got it!* Shot at such close range, the last savage blew backward to land with a sickening thud on the hard, dry ground.

Finally victorious, the gunman breathed heavily from his exertions, and, all threat eliminated, lay back on the ground to relax while massaging his throat. His rest did not last long, however, for something on the horizon caught his eye. On a nearby mesa, smoke rose to the sky at regular intervals. He could not read the signals, but assumed the worst. He was obviously a trespasser and still in danger, so he forced himself to mount his steed, then headed in the opposite direction from the smoke.

At last swilling the cool contents of the canteen, the injured rider allowed his cream-colored horse to take the lead. Oblivious, until his thirst was quenched, he finally became aware of his errant path as sun-bathing lizards scurried away from the horse's hooves. Unfamiliar with the territory, however, he decided to trust the animal's instincts, while groggily clinging to the saddle. Through the swirling mists of his mind's confusion, he viewed his progress from above, as though he were outside his own body.

And then in the briefest of flashes his mind's eye withdrew its perspective, moving upward at a dizzying speed till he and his horse shrank to a mere point. He saw the desert's boundaries and nearby towns. But they too disappeared into the distance. Still ascending, he perceived the curvature of the earth and ultimately the entire planet as if from a high orbit. Startled, he jerked to awareness, trying to comprehend such a vision. The earth had been laid out before him from an altitude many hundreds perhaps thousands of times greater than the highest known flight of any hot air balloon he'd ever heard of.

He pondered this mightily, but fatigue soon forced him to a half-wakeful state again. Forgetting the vision for the moment, he considered another uncanny perception, which was of impending jeopardy. He had some sense of a warning from he knew not where, yet he longed for the challenge ahead. Somehow he knew he was different, and, subconsciously, he inventoried skills that others might covet.

For all that, he struggled to remember why he wanted to come West. Although he was rugged enough to handle the frontier, the tall man's muscles now ached with fatigue; his short, black hair was matted from a feverish sweat and red-rimmed green eyes stung from the dusty trail. The fight had taken more out of him than he had realized. His head bobbed as he fought to stave off the sleep that would rob him of his vigilance. If he didn't find shelter soon, he would make easy prey for any new band of marauding Indians.

At length, the silhouette of a small township appeared against the setting sun. As he rode toward a small house on the outskirts, a young, dark-haired woman picked up her long skirt and ran out to meet him. The look of concern on her face was evident even at a distance. I must look like hell, he thought. Up close, the man sleepily noted her appearance. Her conservative dress sported a lacy border that ringed a high neckline. Only her forearms and a pretty, yet hard face were exposed by the ample garment. This and a look of iron determination gave the girl the appearance of a typical frontier woman.

She called to him. "Jamie, what happened?"

The question took him off guard. "That's my name?"

He fell off the saddle in a faint.

Chapter 2

Jamie opened his eyes, half expecting to see a blinding sun above. Instead, he stared up at a ceiling from a comfortable bed, a situation infinitely more desirable than the desert awakening a few hours before. Or *had* it been just a few hours ago?

He lifted heavy legs onto the floor, prepared to stand, but the pain in his head made him change his mind. Putting his hand to the spot that hurt, he felt a wrapping there, but before he had a chance to examine it, the door opened and the woman he had met earlier came in with a tray. Seeing the food made him realize he was hungry.

"Good afternoon, Jamie. I thought I heard you rustlin' round in here."

"You know me?"

She paused, obviously taken aback. "You don't remember who I am?"

She stood in front of him allowing her features to be scrutinized. In full daylight, Jamie realized she was a slim woman in her late 20s, who moved with an athletic ease.

"You met me at the edge of town yesterday. You called me `Jamie'."

She appeared confused. "Well, that's what you said your name was when you rode in the first time."

"The first time!" He had no such memory.

"Yes, a few days ago." She gazed at him with uncertainty. "We talked at the saloon for several hours. You drank a lot of whiskey." She hesitated. "I suppose that much liquor'll addle one's memory a mite but at least you remembered to leave a nice tip. Anyways, my name is Lilah Petrov and I'm pleased to meet you again, Jamie."

"Jamie? I don't remember that name. But I can't come up with a better one. I suppose that bump on the head did disturb my memory." He smiled painfully.

"What happened to you, anyway?" After setting the tray

down at the foot of the bed, she eased into a broken rocker by the pine dresser, as if trying not to attract too much attention to herself.

"I'm not exactly sure. The first thing I knew, I was waking up in the middle of nowhere, bleeding from the head. While I tried to get my bearings. I was attacked by some hostile Pawnees."

"Never mind. Some coffee with lunch should make you feel better." Her face lighted with a pleasant smile.

"Lunch? What time is it?" He had forgotten to even wonder about the time.

"A quarter of two. Are you late for something?"

"Well no. I guess I can't think of anything." He took a sip of coffee and looked around the room. The furnishings were unremarkable: the bed with brass headboard that he sat on, a bureau of drawers with a wash basin and pitcher on it. The rocker in which she had settled in a patch of sunlight streaming through a curtained window. "Where am I?"

"In a room above the saloon." She glanced outside, as if to make sure.

"And my horse?"

"Tied to a hitching post right there. Poor thing was dying of thirst. I paid a local boy to bring him to the watering trough and brush him down. It's a fine thing, letting him carry you that distance without water."

"I had other priorities. How did you get me up here?" Healthy though she looked, she didn't appear capable of hauling him around.

"I had some neighbors bring you here in their wagon. It wouldn't be proper for you to be seen at my house."

"That was your house at the edge of town?" He scratched his fingers across the stubble of a days' old beard.

She nodded her head.

"What town is this?"

"This is Ute."

"New Mexico?" He supposed he'd heard of it. He must have. Yet he felt strangely dislocated. For a second, the picture he had seen of earth from a distance flashed into his mind.

"Uh huh."

Jamie attempted to stand again, but the pain in his head forced him to remain in place. Squeezing his eyes and clenching his teeth allowed him to cope with the waves of discomfort. Coming to his side, Lilah gently helped him lie back down in bed.

"You slept from last evening until now. I was worried, so I had the doctor check on you. He'll want to know that you're awake. He fretted that you had a concussion after he saw that bump on your head." Her eyes went to his wound and his bandage.

"Not a concussion, just amnesia."

"What?"

"Loss of memory." He was willing to accept that his name might be Jamie, but anything else from the past was out of reach, in a haze. The pain in his head made trying to concentrate and remember impossible.

The girl just frowned and moved the tray closer to him on the bed. He ate hungrily and the grits and eggs did make his head feel better.

"So we talked when I first rode into town?"

"Yes, you seemed to be enjoying the show. And the whiskey. I often talk to strangers like yourself who might come back and spend more of their silver."

"Are you a barmaid, Miss Petrov?" Nearly done with eating, he took the time to examine her again.

"It's Mrs., but please call me Lilah. No, I'm the bartender." Her tone was almost without emotion.

"Hmm. That's an unusual profession for a woman."

"Not when you own the bar," she said, again with little emphasis. "I inherited the place from my husband. He was killed."

"Oh, I'm sorry. Was it recently?" He finished the toast spread with preserves and wiped his mouth with the linen napkin she had thought to provide.

"Several years ago when the town was a bit more lawless. Now, thanks to the new marshal, Ry Hobbs, things are a lot quieter around here." Although the feeling didn't make it into her voice, her eyes flamed with a quiet anger.

"Outlaws killed him?"

"Out in the street in broad daylight. But if they hadn't done it, I would've gotten around to it myself." Her cheeks had gone red with whatever emotion she strove to hold in check.

Jamie raised an eyebrow. After a moment, she started to explain. "What better calling for an alcoholic than a saloon owner? Or so Mitch must've thought. He drank everything in sight--his way of coping. People hated him, he said, for being the privileged son of Russian immigrants. Then, about two years ago, he took to beating me. I went to the preacher for help, but Reverend Oakland didn't believe me even when I showed him the bruises. Maybe he just didn't want to know about it for fear of getting involved. Anyway, I had no one to turn to. I was trapped. Then one day a group of drifters solved my problem. I didn't see the gunfight but I was told that Mitch got a little too brave and got shot for his trouble. After that, a new marshal came and set things right for the whole territory. Now that we have a town with laws, the saloon is a thriving business, thanks to me."

"You're an admirable woman." He truly saw her as such. She had lived under a great deal of hardship and had not only survived, but had succeeded.

"Oh yeah? Even after wishing my husband dead?" She retreated from where she had stood and turned her face from him.

"You did what you had to do. Where I come from, we admire strong women."

She looked at him again with interest. "Really? Where is that?"

"I don't remember exactly, to tell the truth. Maybe you could help me recall. At the bar, did I tell you what I was doing here?" If he had the energy, he would sit up again, but he couldn't quite muster it.

"I guess you really can't remember. Let's see, we talked about the show and how much you liked my girls. Then we started to talk about this town. You asked how were the people. Did it have a sheriff? Stuff like that. Nothin' that interestin'."

"Did I do anything unusual while I was here?" Because he knew that something, some purpose had driven him to this place. He felt impelled toward a mission he couldn't quite recall.

"Not that I saw. You just rode in early and said you'd be leaving that evenin'. What did strike me as odd was that you dressed like a gunslinger but didn't act like one. You were very polite." She smiled shyly, not the business woman or the barkeep, but just a girl.

Several hours after their fruitless conversation, Lilah again rapped softly and opened the door to Jamie's room. She looked surprised to find him up and dressed. "Should you be out of bed?" she asked.

Jamie had turned from gazing out the window. "I feel fine now, thank you. That lunch and coffee really did me a world of good."

"You do seem a lot stronger. Your color is back, too. Just to be safe though, I've brought the doctor to take another look at that head wound."

The doctor entered the room, greeting his patient with an amazed expression on his face. "My, my, we are a quick healer, aren't we? How's your memory, son?"

"Still bad, I'm afraid."

"I'm sure it will come back in time but now I'd like to change the dressing and examine that contusion." The doctor considered Jamie's appearance. "You look strong enough to walk to my office. Do you mind? I have better facilities across the street."

"No problem," replied Jamie, grabbing his hat.

Jamie took in the details of the room as the doctor slowly

placed the cold metal stethoscope over several locations on his patient's chest and back. Typical doctor's office, Jamie thought. A glass-front cabinet containing several bottles was the major furnishing, along with the examination table Jamie sat on. The doctor's bag rested dutifully by his side on the table.

"Breath deeply," ordered Dr. Collins, listening carefully.

Collins was in his mid-fifties by Jamie's estimate, medium height, and thin, with a ring of gray hair going from temple to temple but avoiding the top of his head. Not a very formidable opponent, considered Jamie, who surprised himself at thinking in those terms. The doctor completed his inspection and began to take the dressings from the wound, but with the last wrap removed, he abruptly paused, as if in shock.

"Anything wrong, doctor?"

"No, everything looks fine," denied the physician as he quickly rewrapped the area with fresh cloth. "You're a lucky man, Mr. McCord."

Jamie grabbed the medical man's arm. "You recognize me?"

"No, that's what Lilah called you," blurted the doctor, a little frightened.

Jamie released his hold at once. "Sorry, doc. I guess I was hoping that someone would fill me in."

"That's okay, son. Maybe seeing your personal things will spark your memory. I'm afraid I had to cut away your clothes to dress the wounds. But I salvaged everything else."

Collins walked to some storage shelves and brought back a box, inside which Jamie discovered his guns, belt, a small notebook and a few other small items. He withdrew a coin purse from among the objects and extracted a silver dollar, offering it up to the man who had cared for him. "Will that cover my bill, doc?"

"And then some, but I must tell you, your life was never in danger. I just helped the healing process." After his conscientious explanation, the doctor reached out and accepted the payment made. He then watched his patient slide off the examination table and inspect his belongings. Jamie could tell from the doctor's posture that he had a certain curiosity about the box's contents.

Opening the notebook, Jamie viewed several pages of random dots and lines with unrecognizable symbols at the bottom of each page. The symbols were a form of mathematical calculation unknown to current science, he believed. But he knew of them, could interpret their very sophisticated nature... or at least he used to be able to. He replaced it in the little wooden chest and examined the other items, eventually getting to the object that seemed to most excite the doctor's concern--a pen.

"What's that?" blurted out the doctor.

"It's a pen," answered Jamie, by reflex more than memory.

"I've never seen one like that before. What's it made of?"

"Plastic."

"Plastic? What's plastic?"

"It's a material . . . ." The words trailed off as Jamie stared at the artifact. Wait a minute, he thought, this thing is somehow out of place. *Where does it belong? Why can't I remember?* He struggled against the boundaries of his mind for a long while before giving up. No use forcing the memory now, since he knew it would come when he attained full recovery. He tossed the item to the doctor, who awkwardly caught it.

"Have a souvenir," said Jamie as he smiled and exited the building.

As soon as Jamie left, another man entered the examination room. In his forties, with salt and pepper hair, formidably built and dressed in cattle rancher's clothing, he had an incongruous but authoritative military bearing.

"For a man who has no idea who he is, he seems rather in control of himself," the stranger commented to the doctor.

The doctor nodded, evidently unsurprised by his new visitor's sudden appearance. "He appears to be a remarkable man." The doctor glanced sideways at his visitor. "I thought you were going to Phoenix today."

"I've already been and back. I just had to brief some of the brass on our progress."

"Oh, yes. I forgot you have... what did you call it? A harrier jet?" The doctor looked at the stranger more directly.

"Something like that. Anyway, why were you so perplexed when you removed the bandages?"

"Because the wound was gone." The doctor's eyes took on a strange light.

"How do you mean 'gone'?" The man heard the doctor's words, but without comprehending.

"When I examined him yesterday, he had a deep laceration in his skull along with widespread contusions. The injury was so bad, I literally feared for his life, considering the little equipment I have here. Now, not even twenty-four hours later, he's completely healed. You'd never know he had a wound. Anyone else would've been flat on his back, yet he's strolling around as if nothing had happened." The medical man shook his head, in disbelief at what he had seen.

"What did he give you?" questioned the other.

"He said it's 'plastic'."

"Let's have a look."

Jamie crossed the street on his way to the hotel, when an explosion from behind tossed him to the ground. Quickly recovering, he looked back at the doctor's office now in flames. What could have caused that? Jumping up, he ran toward the fire. A bucket brigade was already forming. but too late to save the life of Dr. Collins.

Chapter 3

The burned-out carcass of the doctor's office smoldered against the setting sun. Shadows from the dead structure reached across the street, the townspeople avoiding the evil touch of them. That evening, some boys explored the building, the adventure made even more appealing because of their parents' disapproval.

Inside, they found the burnt wood blackened and moist, its unpleasant odor going unnoticed in their excitement. Awed by the many devastated rooms, the four of them separated to better investigate. Jeremiah, the youngest, found the doctor's office with shattered glass on the floor, and ash still dripping slowly off the ceiling. Marveling at the destruction, he wondered if the doctor had suffered much in his last moments. Remembering the covered bodies taken out, he tried to imagine their grisly appearance. Strange, he thought, that the other body hadn't been identified.

Unperturbed by the mystery, Jeremiah crunched rubble on the floor as he continued to scavenge for something of value. Nothing worthwhile revealed itself until he turned to leave. There by the door lay an object apparently undamaged by the fire. The thing looked like part of a pencil. Bending down, he excitedly brushed the soot from his discovery. Everything else in the house was blackened by the heat. This wasn't even scorched. The odd piece was perfectly white, like ivory.

"Hey guys come here. I've got something," yelled Jeremiah while disassembling his find.

The footfalls of his friends converged on his location.

"Would you shut up," hushed Matt upon entering the room. "We're all in big trouble if anyone finds us here."

"Yeah, but look what I've found." He held up the pieces of his prize--an ivory-colored white case in one hand and the interior of the thing in the other. The boys clustered about him and observed the device with awe.

"Let's see," cried Matt. He ignored the plastic case and examined the interior. With his own attention now drawn to it, Jeremiah noticed shiny metal flakes in a strange pattern visible through a transparent encasement.

Jamie lay on his bed with fingers intertwined behind his head. Staring at the ceiling, he tried to make some sense of the events since he had awakened in the desert, but the uncomfortable head wrapping interfered with his concentration. Apparently, in his haste, the doctor had wrapped the damn thing too tightly. Jamie reached up to relieve the pressure but as the outer layers loosened, the inner ones also fell away. Damn it! Jamie took the opportunity to personally assess the damage. What the hell? He felt through his scalp for several moments yet couldn't locate any scar tissue. Turning up the oil lamp, he went over to the small mirror on the dresser and examined his scalp more closely--but a visual inspection also revealed nothing.

The injury that had pained him when he woke in the desert was completely gone. Why hadn't the doctor told him? While he pondered the matter, someone knocked at the door. Somewhat annoyed, Jamie unlocked it to find Lilah standing in the hall. He would have turned anyone else away. "Hello, Lilah."

"You're looking better than ever. I'm so glad." She had a bottle of whiskey and two glasses. "Like to drown your sorrows?"

"My, but you are a forward wench, as they used to say." He hoped she understood that he was only joking and she wouldn't take offense.

She ignored the comment, entered the room and sat on the bed. Jamie closed the door behind her. "Do you blame yourself for what happened to the doctor?" she asked in a soft tone.

He looked at her sharply. She'd made a very astute appraisal of his mood and he realized that there was more to this woman than her simple appearance indicated.

"Well, it was a bizarre coincidence, don't you think? I can't help feeling that I should've known something to save the doctor's life."

"How do you mean?"

"He asked me about a pen I had in my personal belongings. He had never seen one like it before. It had self-contained ink and was made of plastic."

"It was made of what?" She put the glasses down on the bed and began to measure out the whiskey.

"He had the same reaction. Haven't you ever heard of plastic?"

She shook her head.

"I obviously had and it seems this knowledge is out of place." He bit his lip. "I fear that his death had something to do with that pen."

"Why do you think that? The doctor had a lot of fancy concoctions in that cabinet of his. He told me once that if they weren't handled just right, some could be downright dangerous." She presented him with one of the glasses and poured again.

"You mean like ether?" He sipped from the glass and nearly coughed at the strength of the alcohol. Letting it burn down his throat, this time he was the one who took the rocking chair.

"Yes, that does sound like one of them. How did you know about that?"

"I just did." He sipped again.

"Maybe you're a doctor too?" She gazed at him probingly and placed her own glass to her lips.

"No, I don't think so. Or at least it doesn't sound right."

He looked at Lilah sitting on the bed and sensed something different about her tonight. He couldn't figure if it was her mood or attitude, but she was definitely creating an atmosphere. What was it? Why did she seem so intriguing to him now? Her apparel was no different, although closer fitting. Her hair was the same, but more neatly in place. She was also made up and wearing a scent.

After a few moments of contemplating her, he eventually caught on to the subtle yet obviously studied movements of her body, rife with suggestion. Could he allow this distraction with all that was on his mind right now?

"It's going to be a hot one tonight," she commented as she removed her boots. "Hey, you're not even sweatin'."

"Who's minding the bar this evening?" he questioned her.

"Every now and then I rely on my workers so I can take a break."

He rose and poured both of them a tot more of the whiskey, then resettled himself on the bed next to her, where his attention was seized by her intoxicating scent. His eyes, drawn to the bottom of her dress, noted it climbing to her knee. Very fine stockings covered the exposed, shapely calves.

"I like your nylons." His voice came out in almost a whisper.

"My what?"

"Nylons." He pointed to her stockings.

"Oh my stockings. You do talk strange by times, Jamie McCord, but thank you for the compliment. They're from Paris and it took a pretty penny to bring them here. Would you like to touch? They're silk, you know."

"You've never heard of nylon, either?"

Again, she just shook her head.

"Plastic and nylon. These words must be clues to my past."

"Maybe we should find out who else knows about them," she suggested, her glittering eyes on his face.

"Right! But whoever they are, I've got a feeling they're not in this small town." His train of thought vanished when he looked at Lilah once again. Her subtle sensuality finally overpowered him. Her leg, still invitingly extended, drew his caress.

"Your touch feels so cool, that's nice. Please don't stop," she cooed.

Her dress and, soon, the quaint undergarments fell to the floor. Lilah quivered as the soft wetness of his lips caressed her perfect bosom. The sensation made her try to respond in kind but Jamie gently resisted her attempts. Covering her entire body with his teasing lips, Jamie hastened to the fiery climax. A little while later, he assumed a similar prone position beside her.

As he stared at the ceiling, his mind wandered. Somehow, the passionate sensations triggered an image of a green lushly forested landscape. Scanning with his mind's eye, he looked down a gentle slope to a shimmering sea. A bright sun glinted off its surface, a surface pleasingly broken by small white caps. Halfway to the horizon, a boat sped along, yet its sails were non-existent. A steamship then. On further inspection, though, Jamie noticed in awe that the peculiar hull didn't touch the water directly. The sleek multi-cabin craft hovered above the surface by a means unknown. The boat was a yacht, a plaything for someone of impossible means… or was he having some kind of weird fantasy? He shook his head.

So preoccupied, Jamie only partly acknowledged Lilah's return affections but after several moments of warm nuzzling, he drifted back to the pleasantries at hand. Completely naked, every square inch of his body tingled in anticipation. The warm wetness of her lips stole up and down his being in a decadently teasing manner. The steady rhythm of her attentions slowly built, causing his muscles to alternately spasm and relax. For the first time since he had awakened in the desert, he felt hot, even though the day's heat had long passed. Lilah's rhythm plateaued maddeningly, making self-control impossible. His composure finally failed him utterly.

At length, as he lay with his eyes closed, relishing the afterglow, his mind conjured the memory of another woman.

Lilah noticed his expression. "What's the matter?"

"I think I just remembered someone I used to know."

Lilah understood at once just what he meant. "Was she pretty?"

"Yes, very."

She got up from the bed abruptly and proceeded to get dressed. Jamie realized that her feelings were hurt.

"Sorry, Lilah. I was surprised by the memory."

"That's all right. I understand."

Clearly she didn't, but he couldn't be concerned about that now. A shred of his past had revealed itself and he had to recapture that memory.

Chapter 4

Still wearing dust from the trail, the bounty hunter didn't waste a moment tracking Jamie to his room. The saloon was dark and quiet as he limped upstairs, his gun drawn and at the ready. He opened the door.

A paraffin oil lamp turned low provided only a feeble glow, putting him at a disadvantage. Holding his breath, he probed the bed with the barrel of his gun and found it empty. Almost relieved, he blew out the lamp, seated himself in a chair facing the only door and waited. After a while, a conversation filtered in from the hall. The ambusher prepared himself. The sounds ceased just as an arm wrapped around his throat and a hand forced his gun from his fingers.

"Damn it, Jamie! How the hell do you do that?"

Indeed, Jamie had entered the room from the open window through the window in the hall out of some compulsion he could not explain. His eyes had adjusted to the darkness in an instant, allowing him to easily overcome his pursuer. The move possibly had saved his life and might provide a clue to his identity, since this man obviously knew him.

Quickly, Jamie tied the intruder's hands behind his back and walked around the chair to relight the lamp. His captive was a large man in his early thirties, wearing a West Point jacket and a Union Army hat.

"I tried to teach the technique to you a long time ago but you were too stubborn to learn," Jamie fished. He didn't want to reveal just yet that he had amnesia.

"Bullshit! You weren't interested in teaching us nothing. Your only care was turning a buck." The intruder was scornful.

"Other men were making a profit out of the war. Why shouldn't I have?" Jamie paced in front of his prisoner.

"I knew it. I figured you had the gold all along." The stranger appeared mad enough to spit.

"I didn't say anything about any gold," Jamie denied.

"You didn't have to. You've as much as admitted it."

"Assuming I have this gold, am I correct in thinking that you want part of it? Or maybe all of it?"

"I wouldn't touch your stinking gold myself. You've made enemies in the Confederacy. And they don't take kindly to people stealing from 'em. The South is planning to rise again and they want what's theirs."

"Then you're their agent come to get it from me. Why are they so sure I took it?" Jamie continued to dig for information.

"Well, who the hell else would've stolen it? You were responsible for getting the stuff from Richmond to Shreveport. You were the only outsider in the group. All the others were loyal Confederate officers, who thought they'd hired a dependable scout."

"I see the plan. Richmond was about to fall and they didn't want their gold reserves falling into the hands of the Union Army. So they paid a scout, me, to get them safely to Shreveport, skirting Union forces."

"'Cept you and the gold never got to Shreveport. The only thing I haven't figured was how you got hundreds of pounds of gold away from a company of soldiers when you had only one horse. It took six mules to carry that shipment."

"Doesn't sound very likely, does it? Have you considered that the so-called loyal Confederates abandoned their cause and buried the gold somewhere along the trail?" Actually knowing nothing about the situation, Jamie followed the logic of the matter

"I sure did. That's why it's taken me so long to come after you. I looked into every last one of them. And none of them is living high off the hog. If they had the gold, they wouldn't be mining coal or picking cotton or those other things. The thief's got to be you. Somehow you figured a way of getting those bags away from the others."

Jamie stared at the stranger a moment, trying to evaluate him.

"Why you looking at me like that? Have I changed that much?" asked the man, unnerved.

"What do you call yourself these days?"

The bound man laughed. "Jamie, you know I was never one for those aliases. Couldn't keep the names straight. Not like you, anyway. I'm still the same old Cliff Conroy. How about you?"

"So do you have your six mules for the gold?" Jamie continued to stare, speculating on where this drama would lead.

"I'm just supposed to bring you back alive."

"So they could interrogate me about the missing gold? I don't think I like that idea, Cliff. I like the West. I'm thinking of staying."

"It doesn't look like the West likes you. I heard you had some Injun trouble and the doc had to patch you up. Maybe saved your life. Why'd you kill him?"

"You assume a lot, my friend. Tell you what. Why don't you enjoy the hospitality of this inn while I figure out what I'm going to do with you?" With that, Jamie gagged the man, picked up his own meager possessions and departed, leaving his uninvited guest tied to the chair.

Downstairs, in the kitchen, Jamie found Lilah recovered from the unintended insult caused by his reminiscing over a past love interest. He told her what had just happened.

"Apparently I've got the Confederate Army chasing me for gold that this Cliff fellow thinks I have." He stood restlessly in appeal to her to help him sort out this confusion.

"And do you have it?" She tidied at the cabinets, avoiding facing him.

"I honestly don't remember, but it doesn't seem likely. I supposedly spirited away several hundred pounds of the stuff from some Confederates, which wouldn't have been easy for one man."

"How much would that be in greenbacks?" Her back was still to him, but he could hear the curiosity in her voice.

"I don't know, but does it matter? How could I have possibly carried that much gold across the country? And if I did take it and stashed it somewhere in the South, I'm not about to go back and get it, in light of what Cliff tells me."

"Cliff thinks you have it here?" She continued her task of straightening the jars of sugar and spices.

"Not exactly, but he says I know where the gold is. Still, I'm inclined to think he believes I carried it to somewhere close by." Jamie felt exasperated by the situation.

"How does he think you could carry the gold that far?" She picked up a towel and wiped down the wooden countertops.

"I don't know. He's not that bright."

"Where is this Cliff now?" Her glance at last took him in, in a friendly fashion.

"Tied to a chair upstairs."

Jamie and Lilah walked back to his room, Lilah obviously buoyant about the prospect of gold.

"Well, if nothing else comes of this at least he knows you. You could ask him about yourself," she suggested.

"Trust me, I want to. But something in the back of my mind stops me. He's definitely not a friend and I don't like the idea of telling him about a personal disadvantage. Plus, I don't think he'd believe me anyway."

"I suppose you're right. But he doesn't know me. Maybe I can find out some things, without tipping him off that you forgot who you are." Once again, she showed herself to be a clever woman.

They opened the door and turned up the lantern. The ropes that had bound Cliff to the chair were in several pieces on the floor. But the man himself had vanished.

"Damn, he got away," Lilah blurted out angrily.

"Don't worry. He won't get far."

The full moon swathed the dry plain in a ghostly light, the low cactuses casting long shadows in Cliff's path. He rode his Appaloosa hard eastward, anxious to be paid for completing his mission's first phase, contacting Jamie McCord. He regretted not having the convenience of his mobile phone but his orders were very strict about this, for fear of compromising the mission. Intent on reporting, though, he allowed his horse's footfalls to lull him into a pleasant fugue.

Abruptly, the animal stopped, jarring Cliff back to awareness. The horse shook its head up and down and lifted a hoof toward its nose.

"What's the matter, boy?"

The mount turned white-eyed and in an explosion of activity launched Cliff into the air. He landed hard on his side but had no time to grimace. Lurching sideways, Cliff barely avoided a lethal flurry of flying hooves. Concluding its frenzied fit, the horse galloped out of sight while Cliff watched helplessly. Testing his leg, he found walking a painful chore and realized he wasn't going to catch up to the dumb animal. His only choice was to head back to civilization.

Cliff limped back into town, intending to secure another horse. Heading for the livery stable, he made sure to cling to the shadowy areas. An eerie wind blew a tumbleweed across his path just as a banging shutter made him jerk around. But after what seemed like an inordinately long time, he reached his destination--safe. The barn was unlocked, so he entered and quickly shut the door behind him. Peering out the crack between the doors, he watched a while to see if he'd been noticed.

Satisfied that he had remained unobserved, he turned to the dark interior and waited a moment for his eyes to adjust. The only light came from chinks between the wall planks and the loft opening above the front doors. Straw littered the floor where several horses were tethered in the stalls. The smell of the place was unpleasant, but he would soon grow used to it. Starting to shop for his new mount, he stopped at every berth, examining each animal, until one of the more spirited steeds had to be quieted. This one he would take.

When he searched for a saddle, some shapeless phantom struck him from above. Fear constricted his stomach as he wildly threw his fists. Out of the gloom, a returning fist materialized and found his jaw. Soon after, Cliff woke to recognize his attacker. "You?" he grunted in astonishment.

"Howdy, Cliff. Hope there are no hard feelings over that bump on the head," soothed Jamie.

"You son of a bitch," cried Cliff. "You locoed my horse, didn't you? You were expecting me back here."

"I guess I know you all too well. Which one were you going to steal? That mare over there?"

"You know it was the stallion. You saw me from above."

Just then, another man, tall with a couple days' growth of black beard, entered the stable, his unhurried approach accompanied by his chinking spurs. His long coat didn't hide a belt full of bullets or gun holsters that were tied to his thighs. He had a sinister look in his eyes that made Cliff flinch, and his eyes fell to a star-shaped badge on the man's chest.

"Is that enough to lock him up?" asked Jamie of the marshal.

"Yeah. We don't cotton to horse thieves in this town," said Marshal Ry Hobbs to Cliff. "Get up!"

Cliff's half-hearted effort to stand was too slow for the marshal, prompting Hobbs to grab him by the hair and force him to his feet. Pointing a gun at Cliff's face, he turned to Jamie." Thanks. I owe you for this."

"That's okay, marshal, seeing him behind bars is thanks enough."

The sarcastic tone apparently infuriated Cliff, who attempted to charge at Jamie. Instead, the marshal checked the angry outburst, hitting Cliff across the face with the butt of his gun. Blood leaked from the Confederate soldier's nose.

"We'll finish this later, Jamie," Cliff threatened as the marshal roughly dragged him away.

Chapter 5

The sun was high and the town was well into its daily activities when Jamie strapped his holsters to his thighs in preparation for exploring the streets below. He could hear the pounding coming from the blacksmith shop as the craftsman beat a horseshoe into shape, a familiar clamor definitely, although he somehow felt he hadn't heard it in a while. The belt routine, too, seemed like second nature to him, the movements indicating his proficiency at handling weapons. Maybe he should test his abilities.

Jamie walked to just beyond the edge of town for an unobstructed shooting range. Before he started, though, he opened his shirt and let the sun beat down on him, reveling in the early heat of the day. The outdoor warmth and air filled him with a sense of well-being, dispelling the cold, clammy feel he had while inside. Must be some lingering effects from the fall, he thought. Conversely, he noted the townspeople shunned the heat, drawing their shades and remaining indoors.

He shrugged his shoulders at their strangeness, then proceeded with his gunmanship test. A low, flat cactus provided a platform for the stones he placed atop as targets for his shots. Stepping back twenty paces, he took careful aim and fired three times in rapid succession, disintegrating the rocks into much smaller pebbles. Hitting the mark had been easy. On a whim, he shot off the thin needles protruding from the cactus. Again, the bull's eye had been no problem for him. Next, he placed a stone on top of the cactus, stepped back twenty paces and turned his back on the target. Wheeling around as quickly as he could, he fired at the piece of granite, hitting it dead on.

This is reflexive. I've done it before, yet it doesn't spark any memories. What am I, to possess this ability? Not farmer or rancher. Maybe a soldier? Cliff knows something about me. How can I get this information out of him without letting on about my amnesia?

It was somehow instinctive for Jamie not to reveal any weakness to strangers, so with the intention of taking Lilah's suggestion about Cliff, he walked back through town, toward her house. Indeed, she could be very helpful in wresting information from the ex-Confederate.

Outside the general store, some Indian squaws on their way to shop provided a distraction. Most of the townspeople shunned the Redmen, except for the proprietor, whose only concern was sales and profit. Jamie, on the other hand, viewed these visitors curiously, noting their unusual attire. The three women sported braided pony tails hanging down from the back of their floppy hats. Colorful ponchos draped their upper torsos and partially covered their pants. Four male children, ranging in age from about five to eleven, clung to their mothers.

As Jamie casually scanned the group, his eyes lit on one of the women. The look she returned was such an odd mixture of awe and recognition, it stopped him cold. The squaw quickly turned away and entered the store with the other women, while leaving the children outside to wait.

The young Indians glanced sideways at the passersby in obvious fear of being noticed. Three men went over to the children, one man purposely teasing and eventually shoving a child to the ground. The youth did not say anything, attempted to get up but was knocked down again. The oldest boy came to his brother's rescue, only to receive the same treatment. His unintelligible protests caused the white men to jeer and laugh.

Hearing the commotion, the Indian woman who had recognized Jamie ran out of the store and shoved the offending white man from behind. Caught off guard, the man fell to the ground while his companions simply laughed. When the ruffian regained his feet, he drew his gun, but the weapon jerked itself right out of his hand. Wheeling around, he sought his attacker.

Jamie stood nearby with smoking pistol and a half-smile on his face. One of the other bullies drew his weapon on Jamie, but received a bullet in the shoulder for his effort. This was much more fun than shooting at rocks. Holstering his six-shooter, Jamie walked toward the ill-bred rowdies when the third man made a sudden movement to decoy Jamie, while the one who had bullied the Indian boy drew his other gun.

In less than the speed of thought, Jamie redrew his Colt and shot the bully in the chest. Almost instantly, the man collapsed to the ground--dead. A white crowd gathered around the scene, along with the rest of the Indians now out on the wooden sidewalk. Jamie reached the corpse at the same time the marshal arrived. Ry Hobbs bent down to confirm the kill and glanced back up at Jamie with a frown.

"They were having some fun at the expense of those Indians. I tried to help them but he drew on me," Jamie explained.

"I saw what happened, but, you know, my life was a lot easier before you came to town." Marshal Hobbs straightened and looked again at the fallen man and then at the two others. "Lilah will be glad, I suppose." Hobbs picked up on Jamie's confused expression. "You didn't know? These are the men who killed her husband."

Jamie gazed at them again. The wounded one was in no condition for any more hostility and the decoy seemed too scared to attempt anything else. In any case, the marshal's deputies had the matter well in hand.

"Marshal, do you need me for anything else?" asked Jamie without breaking eye contact with the Indian woman he had just saved.

"No, not now, but stick around and try to stay out of trouble. I may want to ask you some questions later on."

"I've got no reason to go anywhere."

Jamie took the two steps to the wooden sidewalk where the Indian women and children stood quietly. The object of his stare avoided eye contact. He forced the issue. "You know me," he said, as much a question as a statement.

The woman evidently understood English and nodded, swallowing hard.

"From where?"

She pointed to the horizon and Jamie's eyes followed her finger--to nothing ahead. He continued to look as though force of will would put something there. Nothing appeared but a mesa well in the distance. He turned back to the woman. "You mean that mesa?"

She looked at him with an expression of uneasiness. "I go,"

she said abruptly and started to leave.

Jamie caught her arm, leaned close and whispered in her ear. "Who am I?"

The girl began to tremble, her eyes rolled back and then she fainted. The other women, watching, caught her and laid her down. She recovered shortly but her companions helped her stand and hustled her away. Jamie started to follow when someone grabbed his arm. "Lilah!" he exclaimed.

"Had enough excitement for one day?"

Dazedly he looked after the Indians for a moment before replying. "Yeah, I guess so."

"Then let's get out of here," she said and led him to her house.

Lilah poured two cups of coffee and brought them over to the kitchen table where Jamie sat, still pondering the Indians. With the cup in front of him, he broke out of his reverie. "The marshal said those were the men who killed your husband."

"That's right." Today, she had reverted back to being a woman of little expression, quite a contrast to her passion of the evening before.

"You seem indifferent."

"I've put that messy business well behind me. When Mitch died, I grieved for him in spite of what he had put me through. He was my husband. You don't live with a man for as long as we lived together and not have some feelings. I hated his killers but realized the favor they'd done us both. Maybe now Mitch is at peace with himself as he never was in life. And I now know that's why he drank, although it's still hard to forgive the beatings. But I eventually forgot those times." She paused as if fighting to keep control. "And now I'd rather not be reminded."

"I understand."

They both sat in silence. Finally Lilah spoke. "You shot two of them? You must be pretty good with a gun."

"I practiced this morning," he admitted.

"Most people practice for years. You've probably handled a gun before to get that good." She sipped at her coffee and seemed to be mulling over his situation.

"That's what I was trying to find out. It felt very familiar to tie my guns around my thighs. So I decided to see what I could do."

"You know, the marshal ties his holsters around his thighs. Maybe you're a lawman?" She seemed encouraged by the idea.

"Maybe. Let's see. What have I found out so far? I'm good with a gun, I'm familiar with materials no one else has ever heard of, someone has accused me of being a thief and the Indians know me."

Her puzzlement showed. "Is that why were you talking to those Indians in town?"

"One of them recognized me. I had to use my gun to save her from being killed."

Lilah jumped up. "Why did you let them go?"

Jamie took Lilah's wrist and gently forced her to reseat herself. "Because the Indian girl who knew me fainted when I asked her who I was. She was too afraid to be of any help."

"So that's why she was on the ground. Maybe she thinks you're their Great Spirit."

"The great spirit?"

"Once when I was a little girl, on the trail west, my family stayed with a group of Hopis. During our visit, the Indians celebrated some kind of pagan holiday. At night, we could hear them howling at the campfire. Their shadows flickered on our walls. It made dad afraid. He said to stay out of sight but this only made me more curious. So when no one was looking, I sneaked a peek. And what I saw I'll never forget. They were all dressed up in animal hides decorated with feathers and jewelry. Most either smoked or ate something I found out was called peyote. They were crazy out of their minds. Others beat drums, while the rest chanted and did wild dances around some kind of idol. The smoke from the fires was so thick I couldn't see it clearly but I think it was a mock up of a white man."

"A white man? The Indians were worshipping a white man? Are you sure?"

"The face was painted white and it wore clothes like us. Not a feather on him. Anyway, the chief stood over all this in the most decorated clothes. When some Indian women were touched by him, they passed out. Later, they told me that it was fear of the spirits that made them faint. Fear of their own medicine man, who I thought was chief. To them, he holds the power of life and death. To anger him is to invite disaster in their culture." She was excited with the idea that she had found the answer for him.

"Hmm. Maybe she thought I was a medicine man. But why me?" Jamie was at a loss for a logical explanation.

"I guess at one time she saw you do something. Like a miracle,"

"Now what could that have been?"

"Maybe you had a lot of gold?"

Jamie frowned. "I need more information. Do you know where her tribe is?"

"They were Hopi Indians. My bartender says they have a village a day's ride to the north."

"That's the same direction as the mesa she pointed to."

"The mesa?"

"Yes. When I asked her where I came from she pointed to it. Something is vaguely familiar about that direction, but I can't remember what. I'll probably have to go there to find out for sure."

She rose from the table and got the pot of coffee from the potbellied stove to pour them each a refill. "Do you still want me to talk to Cliff?"

"Yes. That's why I was coming over. He's the best lead I've got right now. Do you mind going over to the jail and talking with him alone?" His eyes appealed to her to help him out.

"I'd be happy to, but why alone?"

"If I'm there he may wonder why I don't answer your questions about me. You should pretend that we haven't talked."

"All right, I can do that." She smiled.

"Thank you. Now may I ask you a question?"

She smiled again. "Sure, what is it?"

"Why are you helping me?"

"It's the Christian thing to do. And can't you tell that I like you, Jamie McCord?"

They both smiled this time, as she took his hands in hers, but he wondered what strange destiny might eventually separate their paths--something not connected with the world that she knew.

The rooster had not yet crowed when Jamie got out of bed quietly, allowing Lilah to continue sleeping. He gathered his clothes and dressed in the other room while deciding what provisions he would take to the mesa. Wondering how long he'd have to wait for the stores to open, he looked at his wrist. There was nothing there. Why had he done that? He had expected to see something, something that would have told him the time. Jamie furrowed his brow as he concentrated, staring at his wrist, forcing up fragments of memory.

"A wrist watch!" He checked his outburst, remembering that Lilah still slept. But the watch... It told the time and could be worn on the wrist. It wasn't something that had moving hands, either, like the bulky pocket watches of the townspeople. It was . . . what? Digital! He used to own one but where was it now?

After thinking about this for a few more minutes, he realized that the wrist watch couldn't be manufactured with the techniques of the day. Several contradictions in what he knew kept jumping out at him; gaps between what was possible here and now and what was possible somewhere else kept coming to the forefront of his mind. Jamie knew that eventually all the pieces would fit together but he had to keep searching to prompt these memories.

Leaving Lilah's house, Jamie looked off in the direction where the Indian woman had pointed. Streaks of cloud patterns occupied the morning sky and the sun cast its early rays over the miles of dry scrub brush this side of the mesa. An unremarkable formation, yet something about the mesa drew his eye, something subconscious that felt more familiar the longer Jamie thought about it. Here was another memory that eluded him.

Lilah reacted differently to Jamie after her meeting with Cliff. Anxious for her report, he had to pry the information from her as she chose her words carefully while timidly keeping her distance. If he hadn't run into her she might've avoided him completely, he realized.

"So what else did he tell you?"

"He said you both were bounty hunters, that you're a dangerous man with a gun. And ruthless when it comes to money."

"And you believed him?"

"Cliff said he limps because you shot him in the leg and stole his $500 bounty. He showed me the wound."

Jamie tried to imagine himself doing such a thing. He couldn't decide if he could or not but realized the idea didn't bother him either way.

Lilah continued. "During the war you made money off both sides. All you cared about was profit."

"A mercenary?" Could he have been such a man? Perhaps.

"He said you're using me like you've used everybody else. That made me wonder. Have I been too trusting? For all I know, you know exactly who you are." She blushed and gazed at him with some degree of concern.

"What purpose would it serve for me to pretend I have amnesia?" His eyes held hers, communicating the truth of his situation.

"I don't know. I just know that you scare me now." She pulled out of their intimate exchange and cast her glance down toward the ground.

"Well, I feel bad about that. But the rest doesn't particularly bother me. All I care about is regaining my memory. I'll be riding north tomorrow after I finish gathering supplies and check in with the marshal. Do you want me to settle up for the room now?" He was stung by her unexpected reaction to him.

Staring bewilderedly, Lilah didn't answer as Jamie placed a few silver pieces in her hand and walked away.

Given free reign by the marshal, Jamie stowed the last of his supplies in the saddle. Tightening a strap, he saw a figure running toward him, back-lit by the rising sun.

"Wait!" she shouted. Lilah came closer.

"Well, good morning. I didn't expect to see you today." He tried to keep the hint of bitterness out of his voice.

"Yes, I know. I'm sorry about last night. After you left I got to thinking about what Cliff said. I guess it just didn't make sense to me that the same man who would save Indians from white men would be a ruthless killer." Her face was flushed with the effort of catching up with him and she glowed with emotion.

"That could have been selfishness, you know. When I saw that the Indian woman recognized me, I had to save her." He wanted her to think well of him, but at the same time, he wanted to be entirely honest.

"You also took my side when I told you about Mitch. That told me you are a fair-minded man." She gazed at him earnestly.

"You're an attractive woman. I might've had ulterior motives."

"Oh. Are you trying to tell me you are what Cliff says you are?"

"I'm trying to tell you I don't know." Despite himself, he reached out and took her soft hand in his.

"So you want to protect me from yourself." She smiled.

"Yes." He released her abruptly and continued with his preparations.

"I've known some desperadoes in my time and even if you are one, I believe you wouldn't harm me." She touched his shoulder.

"And that's good enough for you? A belief? You don't mind the possibility that you might be in the company of a ruthless killer?"

"If my husband had been a bushwhacker instead of a wife beater I'd never have stopped loving him."

Jamie turned and stared at her a moment and then couldn't help his smile. Taking hold of her hand again, he embraced and kissed her. "I'll see you when I get back," he whispered.

"You're riding north alone?" She clung to him.

"Yes, why not? The Hopis are friendly, aren't they?" He stepped away. Anyone might see them and he didn't wish to harm her reputation.

"If you have to ask, then you can't be from around here. Or else you just don't remember. During the war, the tribes had the run of the West. We were overrun and saw firsthand their hatred of us. They killed and tortured. Even the women and children weren't spared." The expression in her eyes went dark and he saw memories of a hard time in them. "In the three years since the war ended we've gotten back U.S. Army protection, although we're still a long way from being safe. But you're right about the Hopis. They're a friendly group. It's Red Cloud's men who aren't and they're all over the place. Those six Indians you fought might've been Sioux or Cheyenne as easily as Pawnee. The bloodthirsty savages are fighting the cavalry to a standstill. You never know when they'll attack."

"Nevertheless, I have to go. The keys to my identity are there. And I'd rather risk my life trying to recover it than sit around not knowing." He tightened the saddle once again, although he'd just secured it the minute before.

"Will you at least consider a scout who can guide you through safe trails," she begged.

"I thought you said that Red Cloud's men were everywhere. How can there be any such thing as a safe trail?"

"Some trails are safer than others."

"Obviously, I'd like to avoid trouble. Where do I find this scout?" He looked around as if he might spot him here and now.

"You've been talking to her," Lilah announced.

"You?" He was completely astonished. "I can't let you go on

a dangerous trip like this. Besides, you said you didn't know where this village is."

"I don't. exactly, but I can get you to within a few miles of it. You can't come from a frontier family and not learn a few things. I was twelve when dad took us on the trail West. Camping out is no stranger to me and if you have the belly for it, I can take you."

About to protest, he realized that he wanted her with him-- maybe, in fact, for more than protection. "How can I turn down such a gracious invitation? I guess I've just hired myself a scout."

"Good, it'll take me an hour or so to get ready. You wait in the saloon and I'll have Kelly, our bar maid, whip you up some breakfast." Her eyes were soft and Lilah gave him a pretty smile.

Chapter 6

Jamie ate heartily, finishing his last bite just as Lilah reappeared. Again, she captured his eye by accentuating the tight curves of her body with the close fit of her clothes. Her gender was obvious. She wore her hair in a pony tail and with her shirt tucked into her buckskin pants she reminded him of a character he had once read about, Calamity Jane. Anyhow, her practical outfit reassured Jamie about her trailblazing abilities.

"Are we ready?" asked Lilah.

"Sure are. Let's go."

At least the company would be good, Jamie thought as they mounted their horses and rode north. Tethered behind them, another mare carried the supplies. Lilah's idea for the additional horse greatly increased their range. Already she had proved her worth.

Barely an hour outside of town, they entered rough hewn lands. Gullies appeared, some of them big enough to hide three horses and two riders from sight. Twenty-foot walls rose around them as they entered one such passageway, the cliffs presenting jagged faces. This raw land was magnificent and something in Jamie's nature demanded he take the time to appreciate it. Lilah, however, was oblivious to the landscape, concentrating only on finding the most efficient way forward. Finding another gully just wide enough for single file, she led them down it. The lower elevations she sought out reduced the chances of their being seen, but if they were attacked, he realized, they would be in an almost indefensible position. He galloped up beside her when the gully widened.

"We're easy pickings down here if they find us," he shouted over the clatter of the hoof falls.

"Shhh! Do you want to get us killed?" she pleaded.

He was caught dumbfounded. The tough talking Lilah was afraid and it surprised him. "You mean I shouldn't have made so much noise?" He lowered his voice.

"Not unless you want to lose our scalps."

"I'm sorry. I didn't realize. . ."

"Never mind being sorry. Just be quiet." They rode silently side by side until the gully narrowed again, forcing Jamie to drop back.

Several hours later, Lilah explained that if attacked on level ground or here in a gully, the two of them wouldn't stand much of a chance, anyway. The logic seemed sound, given that roaming bands of Indians usually didn't travel in small numbers. Now with each passing hour, he sensed Lilah's increasing worry, a concern that was contagious. The same hoof falls he had been oblivious to at the start of their journey suddenly echoed off the walls of this newest gully with deafening rapidity. Lilah rode at a brisk pace but despite her obvious competence and the sunny blue sky, Jamie's foreboding didn't abate.

Eventually, the gravel cliffs gave way to gently sloping prairies with seas of tall wild grass spreading to the horizon. The scent of growing things filled the air, a sweet smell to Jamie and one that he relished.

Shadows lengthened as sunset neared. The route Lilah selected obviously favored safety over speed, but Jamie had hoped to be farther along by now. The two set up camp after dark and Lilah hung blankets to block the fire light. "These won't make us invisible but it'll be better than nothing," she told him.

After a good trail meal, they lay alongside one another on their makeshift beds.

"So why is this Red Cloud so feared?" queried Jamie.

She looked at him, astonished but after a moment seemed to realize that Jamie would have no way of knowing the answer. "Red Cloud is the chief of all the Sioux and Cheyenne Indians. He's one of the few--if not the only--Indian to fight the U.S. Army to a standstill."

"What does he want?"

"His land! And he doesn't want soldiers or white settlers on it. You know, before the forts were built here, there was peace. The generals told Red Cloud that all we wanted was to pass through. But then the army came, built forts and settlers flocked here to till the lands protected by the soldiers. Daddy sympathized with the Indians. He used to say that their way of life was being taken from them. Anyway, Red Cloud declared war. And his men have fought like devils since then."

Jamie lay on his back and tried to read the stars in the sky. "Would Red Cloud attack unarmed settlers?" he asked.

"Yes! He claims the army has done the same to them."

"I see. But he'll eventually be defeated," Jamie pronounced.

"You sound so sure. What makes you say that?"

"I just sense a certain inevitability about it." He did feel certain and didn't know why. An odd tingling in his brain told him that history had already, long before, decided the outcome. What was wrong with him?

Behind Lilah, some motion caught his eye. Something covered in shadows slithered toward her, its tongue darted in and out tasting the warm air. A rattler! *Can't let it harm Lilah.* His expression caused her to turn around. *Damn! Shouldn't have let on. Hope she doesn't startle it.* But Lilah saw nothing and looked back at him in confusion. Bolting upright with his gun out, he reached over her and pounded the head several times with the butt.

"What'd you see?" she asked, startled by his actions.

"Nothing. Just a rattlesnake wanting to join the fireside chat."

She grabbed a piece of kindling to defend herself, turned around again and only now saw the dead thing.

"You saw that in the shadows?" she asked, amazed.

Jamie had not only identified but had accurately struck the snake's head.

"You've got keen eyesight," she marveled.

"I guess it was just the angle I was at," he retorted as he flung the dead creature away.

"Probably attracted by the heat of the flame."

With that, Jamie noticed the motion of the tall grasses

swaying in the cool breeze. The temperature had dropped and a chill seized him, making him realize something else about himself. He preferred hot weather.

In the morning, they mounted up and pursued signs that Lilah recognized, indicating that the Hopis were close. In less than two hours, they located the encampment tucked away in a group of flat-rock outcroppings and almost in the shadow of the mesa. Jamie and Lilah rode into the village.

This place was exactly as Jamie imagined, perhaps even remembered. Smoke rose to a cloudless blue sky from the top of teepees. Women dressed partially in white settler garb tended to the children. Men in the center of the village skinned a buffalo. Taking all this in, Jamie occasionally caught someone's eye only to have his gaze rebuffed.

"They're afraid to look at you, Jamie. Are you sure you haven't been here before?"

"No. I'm not sure. That's the trouble, isn't it?"

Dismounting, they led their horses by the reins toward a group of elders who were speaking Hopi. Jamie didn't understand but was impressed to hear Lilah answering them.

"What did they say?" he asked.

"Looks like you have been here before. They bid welcome to the great white medicine man."

"Me! A medicine man? Are they sure?"

Lilah translated the query for the Indians. The foremost red man frowned and asked another question.

"He asks if they've offended you. And wonders why you don't wish to recognize them? I think you better pretend, Jamie. They may be friendly, but it won't do to make them mad."

"All right, tell him I was just testing him. Our friendship is renewed."

Lilah translated. The chief smiled reassuringly and signaled to someone behind the group. The elders parted to reveal four young braves, one stationed at each corner of a blanket they carried. The cloth contained a pile of large stones and was laid gingerly, almost reverentially, at Jamie's feet. The tribe stared at the white couple in their midst, obviously expecting something from Jamie. Lilah asked the chief what they wanted and Jamie could see she was startled at the response.

"They want you to make flour out of the rocks."

"Flour out of rocks?"

"They think you can do it."

Jamie smiled at the chief and then at Lilah but there was no humor in either pair of eyes. *Simple Indians. I must've tricked them before and now they expect me to do it again without my memory.* Lilah's eyes pleaded. *What to do?*

"Tell them they must pass a test of faith to prove worthy of the great spirit's generosity."

She hesitated.

"Go ahead, tell them."

She translated. The chief looked confused.

"Tell them that in a half moon they will have no wants, if they abide by my wishes."

Lilah again translated. The chief spoke in subdued tones to the other elders before responding.

"He doesn't quite understand it," she told Jamie. "But he asks what they have to do."

"Great! Tell them they have to reintroduce me to everything from my other visits. Then they shall have food aplenty."

"Can you keep that promise?" she fretted.

"I certainly hope so. Maybe I'll remember how I did it before." He smiled, but he was doubtful as well.

Worriedly, Lilah conveyed the optimistic promise, prompting broad smiles from all within earshot. The happy group surrounded Jamie, wanting to touch him. Some tried to talk to him in Hopi. After a few moments of this, however, the chief dispersed the crowd. All returned to their business except an Indian maiden who escorted Jamie and Lilah to a teepee. Buffalo hides covered the floor for sitting and several blankets made up the bedding.

"Do you mind spending a couple of weeks here?" asked Jamie.

"Why not? It would just be like camping."

"Lilah, there is nothing for you here, you know. You're free to go anytime you like." Perhaps he had asked too much of her when he'd invited her on this uncertain venture.

"Are you telling me to go?"

"No. Nothing like that at all. I'd love you to stay. I just don't want you to be uncomfortable or afraid."

She came over and put her arms around him. "I've decided to see this thing through."

"I was hoping you'd feel like that. These Indian women don't altogether appeal to me." Jamie slowly unbuttoned the back of her dress.

The next day, the Indians showed Jamie VIP treatment as they cheerfully vied for his attention. He patiently listened to stories of his prior visits and it seemed everyone had something to say. Lilah often struggled to translate for several at once as they tried to shout over each other. During the course of the day, Jamie heard numerous contradictions in what were certainly some exaggerated tales.

That evening, the celebration in honor of the great white medicine man's arrival represented a welcome respite to the day's activities. Traditional Hopi dances, games of skill and of course peyote, an intoxicant and hallucinogenic derived from the native cactuses, marked the festivity, the latter responsible for the more erotic dances.

In spite of the day's efforts, Jamie experienced only the faintest sensation of memory. He would have to try again tomorrow. When the tribe retired in exhaustion to their teepees, Lilah and Jamie sat under the stars, savoring a few moments to themselves.

Jamie worked on the notebook that had been among his personal possessions from the doctor's office.

"What have you got there?" asked Lilah, peeking over his shoulder.

"Just indulging in a hobby of mine."

"The writing just looks like dots and lines to me. What does it mean?"

"Well, the dots represent stars. The lines between them define known constellations or groups of stars. You see this group? That's Sirius, the dog star constellation."

Jamie pointed to the sky showing Lilah the true location of what was represented in his book. She looked from the book to the sky several times.

"What are those symbols at the side of the pages?"

"Those are dates and calculations to help me locate certain objects in the sky."

"Objects in the sky? What's so important up there?"

An excellent question. What is so important up there and why do I want to find it? No wait. It's not want, I need to know the location of something. Something that's critical for me. . . to be in contact with.

The satellite completed yet another orbit, an orbit unchanged by any new directives. The artificial intelligence device came as close as a machine could to wondering at the recent absence of communication. Simulated emotions had prompted independent action in the past and once again justified their addition to its design in calling for a self-diagnostic. The result confirmed optimal performance in all systems. The problem had to be at the source. The overseer had stopped transmitting. But why? There was no indication, as had been given in previous eras, that silence would be coming. Silence, however, defined most of the satellites existence and it didn't overly analyze the possible causes. It would continue to wait--for waiting was what it did best. Its patience was eternal. It had to be.

Several days later, the re-indoctrination continued, still without any major breakthroughs. At noon, some young braves showed Jamie the art of arrow making. He was intrigued by the skill but the lesson did little to spark his recollection.

"Jamie!" Lilah ran toward him, breathlessly trying to talk." The old women. They just told me something... I think you'll find interesting. You see that mesa over there?" She pointed to the same one that the Indian girl from town had indicated.

"Yes."

"They say it's haunted. The Great Spirit guards it and no tribesman is permitted near. Many scouts have tried to explore it. But they don't come back if they get too close."

"What does an Indian superstition have to do with me?"

"You're the only one who's been there and returned!"

Jamie looked toward the mesa again, trying to conjure the memories he knew he should have.

"So do you recognize it?"

"Something is familiar about it. But just vaguely."

"Maybe we ought to get a closer look?"

"Yes, I'll go tomorrow."

"Good," she agreed. "I'll gather some provisions."

He shook his head in the negative. "I'm going alone. I don't want to endanger you anymore."

"I see. So you'll go off by yourself and leave me alone with a tribe of savages." She pretended to be indignant, but he could see right through her act.

"You'll have to do better than that. These Indians won't harm you."

"All right then, what about the Sioux who would wipe out this tribe and me with it?"

"Good point. O.K., you can come. But you have to agree to stay back if I ask you to."

"Agreed."

That night Jamie gazed at the brooding mesa, massive enough to eclipse most of the full moon. Silently defiant, the rocky outcropping ignored his stare, its black shadow casting a threat on the village. He strained to remember his earlier trip there as a cool breeze laden with an ominous warning caused him to shiver. What keys to his past were there, if any, and why did the mesa fascinate him so? Tomorrow, he was going to find out.

Chapter 7

Lilah stole out of the teepee while Jamie slept, walking her horse to just outside his hearing range. She mounted and rode with secret purpose, eventually bringing the horse to a gallop.

The moonlight cast a shadow from the mesa engulfing Lilah. She rode around the base looking for anything unusual, anything she could point to for Jamie, so he might test his memory. Directing the horse up the steep gravel slopes, Lilah approached the shear rock wall, inspected it and discovered nothing unusual. Disappointed, she dismounted, unpacked a kerosene lamp and lit it, ignoring the danger of being seen by hostile Sioux. Encircling the rock, Lilah probed the smooth surface and halfway around found a deep crevice whose rear wall was lost in darkness. She entered it holding the lantern high, but eighteen feet in found that the back wall was missing even the tiniest oddity. Cursing, she turned to leave then jerked her head back around when her mind's eye belatedly recognized a familiar pattern.

What she saw was only faintly discernible in the rock, but it had been there all along yet nearly invisible. Bringing the lamp close, the light revealed a man . . . and, still, not a man for he was made of the same gray material as the mesa. She froze, as petrified as the apparition in the light. What she had found was a rough, angular statue.

But unlike any statue she'd ever seen, this one moved toward her.

The morning sun streamed in through the open top of the teepee, the resultant warmth on Jamie's face awakening him. Turning over, he realized Lilah wasn't beside him now. The shadows on the teepee walls indicated that the morning activities had begun outside. He resolved to face another day attempting to recover lost memories. Parting the buffalo hide, he exited the teepee and found the village bustling with the business of the tribe.

Lilah, however, was nowhere to be seen. Unconcerned, he stretched, yawned and only then noticed that her horse was missing. She wouldn't have gone to the mesa alone, would she have? His blood ran cold. She sure as hell would've!

Jamie caught the arm of a passing squaw. "Where's Lilah?" he demanded.

The girl just smiled and moved her hips in a provocative way. Damn it! he realized. She doesn't understand. He grabbed her more firmly. "Where is Lilah?"

Confused and frightened, she referred him to an old man, a former chief sitting nearby. The man was hard of hearing, but he spoke English.

"Where is the white woman?" Jamie asked.

"The white woman called Lilah is safe." The chief said this with remarkable certainty. Jamie relaxed and looked the old chief in the eye waiting for some other morsel of wisdom. Instead, the man just motioned for Jamie to follow him. As they walked, the chief introduced himself. "I am Two Eagles."

"I'm Jamie McCord."

Without any further exchanges, they reached the location that Two Eagles intended, a small plateau surrounded by natural rock walls. There in the middle sat a large rock, a very crude headstone but the inscribed letters were readable.

IAN McCORD
1802-1864

Jamie walked to it, stood over it to make sure he had read the plaque correctly. He pored over the letters digesting their significance, yet still struggled to accept what he supposed. "My father?"

"Your great father. He was honored in our tribe. He provided food from where there was none. The others expect the same from you. They don't understand that skills are not always passed from father to son in the white man's society."

"They may indeed have been passed down to me. I don't know. I can't remember anything before nine days ago," clarified Jamie.

"I believe you are an honest man. If you say you lost those memories, I believe you, although I've never heard of such a thing." The old chief gazed at Jamie with a calm benevolence.

"What was my father like?" Jamie wondered out loud.

"I don't know. But they say he was tall and well formed. Much like yourself."

"You never met him?"

"No. How could I? He was your great father."

A non-sequitur that told Jamie nothing. The babblings of an old man? "How do you know that Lilah is safe?"

"Because things are not what you've been led to believe. She is safeguarded by her own sort." His look was a kind one.

Jamie grew concerned, beginning to doubt the old man's sanity. "Where is she?"

"I don't know. But she is safe." There was that assurance again.

"You seem to have a good command of English. And yet some of your meaning escapes me. How do you mean she is safeguarded?"

"I'll explain. But let us go back to the village. Spirits from another world people this place. We should not linger here any longer."

As they walked, Two Eagles talked--or maybe he rambled. "Each of us, we are born into this world and have to move through it. Something different motivates each person. Those without any driving force in their lives wither and die. The Indian's way of life has been taken away by the white man. For us to survive, we have to adapt to the white man's driving force. Many of my people feel that this is bad, but I think progress must be good. The old ways have to fall to new, better ways in spite of lost knowledge. We are forced to share our land with the white man since his ways are stronger. We can't compete until we learn those ways. Only then will our people reclaim their dignity and live in a community that benefits us all."

The old chief paused and touched Jamie on the arm. "You

are moving to relearn your place in this world. But this is incidental to your real purpose. Your real purpose is like no other white man's. I can't say if your path is a good or bad one. But you must be given the freedom to live as you have to. At least until someone either stops you or helps you."

The chief's speech comforted Jamie. Two Eagles seemed to have everything in perspective and Jamie sensed he had something very important to reveal.

On the way back to the village, Jamie considered the chief's unconditional friendship. The old man understood the reasons for the impossible promises Jamie had made to the tribe and, more than any white man had, he showed empathy to Jamie's plight. Jamie drew comfort at the prospect of a newfound confidant.

Back in the village, Jamie offered the chief his hand as a gesture of peace and goodwill. Two Eagles shook it with surprising strength, but when Jamie made eye contact an arrow appeared in the old man's neck. Arteries spouted blood, as the chief fell to the ground clutching his throat in agony. Time slowed while Jamie drew his gun and shot the chief through the temples to stop his suffering.

Several hundred yards away, a Sioux started to cock his bow for another shot. He never completed the task. A hole appeared between his eyes due to a well-placed bullet fired from Jamie's gun.

More arrows flew toward Jamie, one embedding itself in his calf. Buckling momentarily, but with his adrenaline flowing, Jamie ran to the cover of a Conestoga wagon that the Hopi must have traded for. Behind this shelter, he examined his wound and discovered the point of the arrow lodged against bone.

Tearing his shirt for a tourniquet, he assessed the enemy's strength. Twenty Sioux fired upon the village now with rifles. With their surprise attack underway, the need for silent arrows had passed. Cunning bastards!

The Hopi ran around in confusion, the normally peaceful people panicked by the thought of conflict. Amid the gunfire, a woman wailed at the side of the fallen ex-chief with no concern for her own safety. Fascinated by this, Jamie momentarily forgot his pain and the ongoing assault. Even though he'd only known the man for a few short hours, he would miss the old Indian, too.

He was not given time to reflect on his loss, as another arrow brushed his sleeve and thudded into the ground under the wagon. They must've circled to the other side with those damn arrows again.

Jamie clenched his teeth and pulled the arrow from his leg. Tears escaped down his cheek as a throbbing ache replaced the sharp pain. Blood stained his pant leg and ran inside his boot, so he hastily tied a makeshift tourniquet just above the damaged area.

Finally, some stouter Hopi returned fire, although only with arrows. Their good aim yielded nothing, however, since the Sioux concealed themselves well, probably having hidden overnight behind the sparse cover. They outflanked and outgunned the Hopi and would inevitably prevail, but in spite of this the Hopi fought bravely. What else could they do?

Jamie reloaded his guns and formulated a plan. Armed and ready, he jumped out from under the wagon and grabbed one of the careening horses. Using the animal as a shield, he leaned well to his right, out of the line of fire and of sight. The Sioux didn't notice, as the horse, one of dozens, whisked him through their own lines. Behind one flank of the attacking warriors, he let go of the horse, falling into a minor depression in the ground where he made himself as small as possible. Bringing out both guns, he took stock of the enemy. *Clever Sioux, but I'll bet you didn't expect this. Hmm, eight of them. Surprise will have to account for a lot.*

Firing, he felled three with his first three shots and the others turned around too late to save two more. The remaining three tried to protect themselves against assault from both front and back. Now the battle became one of attrition. Which side would be the last to stand?

Bullets exploded into the ground around Jamie, while he fought to stay low in the shallow burrow. The Sioux had found the range and were getting too close. He rolled to his left as rifle fire hit the spot he had just abandoned.

Jerking his head up, he fired three shots in rapid succession. Another Sioux fell and Hopi arrows took care of the last two of this contingent, who had forgotten their vulnerability to attack from the tribe. With his work done, Jamie ran back into the village, zigzagging so he wouldn't get hit by errant shots.

As his line of vision permitted, he spied some Hopi shooting from the cover of the Conestoga wagon. He dived the last couple of feet to join them, but they ignored him, too busy returning fire. They undoubtedly realized what he'd done but even without the threat from the rear, their efforts claimed only a handful of the frontal assault.

Looking around the wagon, Jamie replaced his spent ammunition, just as he noticed a flaming arrow being aimed at their flammable cover. *No you don't!* Almost without thinking, Jamie aimed and fired. The Sioux archer pitched face forward down the rocks with a hole in his chest, his bow and arrow still aflame.

The conflict raged on for what seemed like hours, decaying into something of an impasse with both sides shooting bullets and arrows in answering volleys, but resulting in no more and no less than a continuing exhaustion on each tribe's part. Jamie determined that he would have to break the stalemate by taking it on himself to breach the enemy's flank. He quickly reconsidered, however, after hearing an unexpected volley of violent gunfire. The surprised Sioux were suddenly caught in a crossfire. They panicked, fearing an ambush by superior forces and wasted no time retreating amid pursuing shouts of defiance from the Hopi. Jamie recognized their benefactor. It was Lilah.

"Where the hell have you been?" he grunted when she finally arrived by his side.

Her proud smile vanished at the rebuke. "I just saved your bacon, mister. I don't deserve that tone."

"You're right. What I really wanted to say was thank you. Now, where the hell have you been?" He added a note of sarcasm to his pique.

"Over there," she said, angrily pointing toward the mesa.

"Over there? Didn't it occur to you it could be dangerous? I can't believe you went off by yourself especially after what the

Hopi told us. Why'd you do it? No, don't answer! It's gold fever, isn't it?" He stared at Lilah in accusation.

"Well, why not? Do you think I want to run that damn saloon the rest of my days? I'd like something different out of life. Maybe do some traveling. Europe, maybe Paris. Is that so bad?" She spoke defiantly.

"No, that's not bad. It's the obsession that's bad. Obsession for gold has destroyed many lives. People looking for something that may not even exist. Look at what's happened to you already. You've left your own business unattended. For all you know your workers could be stealing you blind." Truth to tell, he had been rattled at not finding her this morning, worried before the fight to the point of being ill. And to think, she had been off seeking riches. That thought made him more irritable still.

"I can trust 'em." She crossed her arms in front of herself, as if to fend off his words.

"Do you know that for a fact? Or is it convenient to believe it while you hunt for gold? Here's another question for you. Let's assume you can trust them, how do know you can trust me? You're taking big risks with someone you hardly know. Are you sure you're prepared for the worst case?"

"I don't know. Maybe I'm not," she replied. Her arms dropped and she was almost in tears.

"Well, it just so happens, you can trust me. But mind you, the gold isn't my top priority." His heart softened, seeing her that way.

"But what if it's there? Won't we take it?" she asked with a little less spirit of rebellion.

"Yes, we'll take it. And you can have an equal share. I have no use for it."

Lilah embraced him as the Indians watched.

By the end of the encounter, in spite of the unexpectedness of the attack, the Hopi had suffered surprisingly minimal losses. In a tribe of about sixty, five were dead and three were injured, the poor Sioux marksmanship ruining their chance at a massacre.

When the couple walked back to their teepee after helping the tribe, Jamie noticed that Lilah was limping.

"What happened to your leg?"

"Oh that. A statue almost fell on me at the mesa. I twisted my ankle trying to get out of the way. I'm sure it's fine."

"Statues at the mesa?" He raised his eyebrows.

"Yes, statues at the mesa." She seemed to smirk.

"What did it look like?" And, he wondered, was it a key?

"Wouldn't you rather hear about my ankle?" She displayed the limb in question ever so slightly.

"You said it was fine. Now what about the statue?" Not that he didn't notice the ankle.

Lilah frowned but answered his question. "The thing was old, not in very good shape. Part of it crumbled when it fell."

"No matter about the gold, we'll definitely have to get a good look at that. I can't imagine statues in this wilderness. The Hopi make fetishes, not statues. "

Lilah noticed that Jamie was having trouble walking, too. "Why are you limping?"

"Oh, I took one in the calf back there." The wound burned a lot less than it had at first, but a slight ache was still present.

"My God, it looks terrible," she intoned, noticing his pant leg and boot liberally coated in blood. "We're at least going to have to clean the laceration."

In their quarters, Jamie stretched his injured leg out on the hides. His bloodied clothes stuck to his skin so that Lilah had to cut the pants away with a hunting knife. As she requested, a Hopi woman brought a jar of water. Gently, Lilah cleaned the wound but as more of the skin was exposed, she ran her hand over the calf with a bewildered expression. "Where did you say you were hit?"

"Right where your hand is. In the side of my calf."

"Jamie McCord, you're nothing but a big sissy. There's hardly a scratch here. You must've got someone else's blood on you."

Jamie sat up to look, confirming Lilah's observation. Only a small cut. The sight of it seemed strange to him and yet the healing was somehow expected. "I pulled an arrow from that spot not two hours ago."

"In the heat of battle, the mind can play tricks. The arrow head just grazed you."

"I guess you're right," He furrowed his brow, not quite accepting her statement.

Jamie pondered his existence while staring at a bright moonlit sky through the top of the teepee. Some enigmatic formula had governed the events since his awakening in the desert and he realized the equation had too many variables for him to solve without a healthy memory. On another level, however, he sensed some hidden force trying to manipulate him to its own ends. Could such an odd perception be based in reality? He wrestled with the feeling, knowing this sense of being a pawn in a game was something else he would have to contend with.

For now, he knew enough to abandon such distracting thoughts in favor of the business at hand. In preparation for the upcoming mesa exploration, Jamie willed himself to get to sleep. He rested fitfully, though, as frequent dreams denied him the repose he sought. His mind's eye viewed a flurry of blurred and fused images that eventually resolved themselves into a scene. He saw himself waking up in a desert . . .

The sun blinded him and his head ached as Jamie inhabited the dream image of himself, reliving the events from a few weeks before. Blood that had flowed freely during his unconsciousness matted his hair. He felt the deep gash in his skull and a sense of danger gripped him when he remembered the imminent attack. Trying to prepare, he moved as if submerged in molasses. As expected, the Pawnees bore down on him, but this time, at least, he didn't waste precious moments running to his horse. Jamie, immediately yet slowly, pulled a gun from its holster and took aim the instant that their arrows sped toward him. In the arrows' mid-flight, though, Jamie's mind's eye shifted. He now observed himself outside his body, struggling to take aim at the savages. Abruptly, this image, too, transformed.

He was in the doctor's office having his wound dressings removed and, true to the actual events, Jamie noted the doctor pausing. Dr. Collins was looking at the exposed wound in some confusion.

"Anything wrong, doctor?"

"No, everything looks fine," said the doctor, quickly rewrapping the area with fresh cloth.

Again, the scene shifted, this time to Jamie's room above the bar. He unwrapped his own bandages and felt through his scalp for the expected scar tissue. There was none. Turning up the lamp, he looked into a small mirror but, as before, his inspection revealed nothing at all. The deep laceration, only a day old, was completely healed.

Now this scene faded, giving way to the inside of the teepee. Lilah hovered over his blood-soaked leg. "Jamie McCord, you're nothing but a big sissy. There's hardly a scratch here. You must've got someone else's blood on you."

As before, Jamie only found a small cut.

One more scene shift. His mind's eye whisked him off to another location, a dense forest where a gunfight ensued. Several uniformed men pursued and shot at a lone, fleeing figure. Jamie tried to recognize the man and or his aggressors. Their uniforms were neither Confederate nor Union. The colors were mixed in riotous blotches. Splashes of greens, grays and blues flashed in a crazy, random pattern as if some berserk painter mistook their clothing as his easel. The hunters brandished rifles but these were no Winchesters; the weapons spewed bullets faster than a Gatling gun.

The lone figure also carried a firearm that resembled no six shooter Jamie had ever seen. Like a cross between a gun and rifle, it had a long handle and the barrel tapered down to a nozzle that sprayed several rounds of ammunition in an instantaneous burst. With this gun, the man held his own but the soldiers were maneuvering toward him, gaining ground all the time. Their uniforms blended into their surroundings so well that they were hard to see.

The thought struck Jamie hard and, suddenly, he realized that was exactly the purpose for the random colorations. These devilishly cunning men had raised soldiering to a deadlier art than he could have imagined in his wildest nightmare. The revelation that someone would go to the trouble to perfect these kinds of lethal advantages was frightening.

The killing specialists approached the man's position, but miraculously the object of their chase had disappeared. Jamie, rooting for the man, followed his progress as he ran through the forest without a sound. Breaking this silence, a beating noise overheard grew louder with each passing moment.

The man stopped, looked skyward to see an impossible sight. A metallic dragonfly hovered over the trees, creating a deafening sound that issued from a single, rotating blade on top. The object's bulbous front reflected the cloudy skies but as it turned, Jamie could see men inside the thing, operating it. A vehicle, he conjectured, but one far more complicated than even the most sophisticated locomotive. As the fugitive looked upon it in awe, a hail of bullets escaped its underside, hitting him directly. When the runaway twisted in a spasm of pain, Jamie recognized himself, which triggered the dream to end like a burst bubble.

He woke in a sweat, remembering the futuristic gunfight in vivid detail. Did the dream represent a genuine memory, or an unrealistic fantasy manufactured by his own frenzied mind? Filing it away, he tried to analyze the earlier scenes. A common theme throughout all of those struck him forcibly--a remarkably fast healing process. He recalled a part of his existence since before the accident, providing him with the only reliable clue he had so far about his past.

Chapter 8

An unusual summer rain prolonged their trek to the mysterious mesa, gouging muddy quagmires in the dry earth. Despite the downpour, he and Lilah rode comfortably in their waterproof rain gear. Anxiously, Jamie prodded the horses on, his dreams whetting his appetite for more information about his past. No less anxious, Lilah had her own strong motives for hurrying to the rock formation, her lust for gold causing Jamie to reconsider her loyalty and why she was here.

Peering through the droplets that continuously trickled off the brim of his hat, he fixed his gaze upon the mystery-shrouded mountain. Thunder and the sound of cascading water interrupted his concentration as the storm center grew near. Bolts of lightning approached the mesa, one magnificent burst eventually hitting it with enough power to create an aura.

The rain flashed to vapor after hitting parts of the mesa that had been superheated by the strike's intensity. Coerced by millions of volts, protons and electrons flowed to certain material structures alien to the native rock. Now almost petrified, these materials formed circuits, circuits that could have been energized by microvolts in another time but today took megavolts to function, and for only the briefest instant at that. Within that instant, however, a living semiconductor recognized that a pair of planetary natives approached. The male and female rode four-legged beasts and were obviously not the advanced ancient enemy it had once eliminated.

Triggered by the human presence, though, the biochip terminated its start-up routine in favor of a higher priority. No matter their impotence, these humans were natives, lethal enemies who had to die. The ancient device uselessly vibrated in its attempt to move before it realized its petrified condition. Immobile, it transmitted a command to fire its radiation weapons, but too late. That single, brief, life-giving charge had been exhausted.

"Wow! Did you see that?" marveled Lilah.

"Yes, I haven't taken my eyes of the thing since we started."

"I've seen some lightning in my day but that beats all."

"It certainly was magnificent but . . . ."

"But what?"

"But it seemed like, just for a moment, it was aware of us." Jamie knew that was a crazy thing to say.

"The lightning was aware of us?"

"No. I meant the mesa." He turned to see Lilah staring at him with concern. "Scared?" he asked.

"Are you starting up with that again? I've never been afraid of doing what I had to do. Especially with such a big stake at the end of the trail. I must admit, though, the trail does seem different today. A little more solitary."

"Well, fear or not, I just hope you're not disappointed. We don't know for sure that there is any gold." For himself, he didn't care. The idea of the gold barely touched him, in fact.

"And we don't know there isn't, either. Maybe the statue will give us a clue." She stared ahead.

"Ah, yes, the statue. I'm very interested in seeing that."

"You sound as if you don't believe me," she challenged.

He urged his mount carefully forward, through a pool of water collecting on the path. "I believe you saw something. I just can't figure who would build it. The Indians certainly don't sculpt any manlike figures. And I don't see why any white man would put a statue there."

"Well, there's one there just the same. You'll see." She shook the water from her head to no avail.

The rain let up as they reached the mesa's base. Lilah at once led Jamie to the moving statue within the shallow cavern. In the dim light, he, indeed, found the crumbling remains of a man-sized figure. Jamie conjectured that its builders, whoever they were, never intended the likeness to be perfectly detailed.

He leaned down for a closer look while Lilah went to fetch a lantern. Too eager to wait, Jamie conducted his investigation without light. Through the broken fragments, he could see a hollow interior. Inside, various petrified objects were fixed in place except for one loose piece. Jamie reached in and grabbed it when a scream brought his head around.

Running out, he spied Lilah in the grasp of Cliff Conroy while Marshal Hobbs stood idly by, waving his gun. Jamie perceived at once that Hobbs had masterminded the situation.

"Let her go, Hobbs!" demanded Jamie.

"Oh, do you remember me now? No? Then it's true. You really don't know me. I thought you were playing some kind of game. But you weren't acting, were you?"

Hobbs turned to Cliff. "This means he probably doesn't remember where the gold is, either." Cliff stared stupefied at the lawman, whereupon Ry Hobbs drew his gun and fired, without hesitation.

Cliff Conroy sank to the ground, shot through the chest. As he fell, he attempted to draw his own gun but another shot from Hobbs, this time in the head, stopped Cliff forever. Lilah, frozen in horror, didn't take advantage of her momentary freedom. Hobbs looked back to McCord while keeping his gun trained on Lilah, but with reflexes that surprised even himself, Jamie drew and shot the marshal's gun right out of his hand.

A quick man as well, Ry Hobbs was already leveling his other gun at Jamie. Hmm. Now that was a stupid move. Didn't he realize Jamie would have to kill him to protect himself? Jamie started to squeeze the trigger, but stopped. Recovered from her hesitation, Lilah disarmed Hobbs with Cliff's gun, shooting the weapon out of the Marshal's hand. Good marksmanship, thought Jamie. Hobbs stared at both of them uncertainly, the recent gunfire still reverberating off the rock walls.

After binding the stoic marshal in the cavern and burying Cliff, they resumed their investigation of the crevice. While Lilah dealt with the death of Cliff in heroic fashion, Jamie marveled at her indifference to the situation or, he thought, was it just her greed overpowering those other emotions?

"What have you got there?" asked Lilah.

Jamie forgot what he had found in the statue with all the excitement. Instead of answering her, he asked a question of his own. "What's today's date?"

"It's the third of June. Why?" She watched his eyes.

Jamie held out what he had in his hand. "I found it in the cavern. It's a newspaper. Check the date."

"May 7, 1868." Lilah seemed surprised.

"Somebody's been here within the last month and it wasn't Indians. Now why do you think anyone would venture into hostile Indian country like this?" He had his own guess.

"Somebody's after the gold," she declared with a sudden insight.

"That's what I think," Jamie agreed.

"You don't think it was me, do you?" She shrank back into herself.

"Don't be so defensive."

"Maybe Cliff or Ry?" she suggested.

"No, they wouldn't have gone to such trouble to follow us here if they already knew the location. It must be someone else. Someone who knows about the gold."

Jamie walked back to Ry and removed the gag. "All right, I can't remember but I'd like to. If you help me fill in some of the blanks, you and Lilah can split the gold."

"Why should I believe that?" asked the marshal sarcastically. "How do I know you won't kill me?"

"Because I could kill you right now if I wanted to," Jamie pointed out.

"What do you want to know?" Ry Hobbs' gaze was shrewd.

"First, how do you know me?"

"We rode together as bounty hunters--that is, until you stole hundreds of pounds of gold from the Confederates. I still haven't figured out how you did it."

"Do you know for sure that I did take the gold?" Jamie paced before his immobile prisoner.

"When the gold disappeared, you disappeared. The theft seemed obvious to me."

"All right, then let's assume that I did take it. Does it necessarily have to be here?"

"I don't know. I followed you not realizing you had truly lost your memory." Ry's speech seemed honest enough.

"You're a much more eloquent fellow than Cliff. How did you two team up?" Jamie stood still at last, facing the marshal.

"You and I only used Cliff when we needed an additional gun. He was good to have around in a fight but wasn't long on common sense. I figured I could use his tracking skills to find you." Hobbs half-smiled in self-satisfaction.

Lilah took a turn interrogating the bound man. "Did Jamie shoot Cliff in the leg?"

"Yes, Cliff was trying to steal his bounty."

Lilah appeared relieved at the answer, now that she felt her companion had just cause to use his firearm.

Jamie resumed the questioning. "What do you know about the Confederates chasing me?"

"Confederates? There are no more Confederates. The war is over. Don't you remember that?" Ry actually laughed.

"I do remember that," Jamie countered impatiently. "Apparently, Cliff didn't tell you he was hired by them to track me down. They want to bring me to justice, recover their lost gold, and rebuild their war machine."

"And you believed him? McCord, you've lost more than your memory. Why would he be after the bullion if he had to give it up to the Confederates?" The marshal smiled, an unpleasant expression.

"For the reward, he said. I think he was too afraid of them to steal the gold if he found it. I can't afford not to believe him. I have to assume the worst. Now who else did I know that I might have told where this gold is?"

"If I knew I would have asked them already."

"Well you think about it a little longer while I eat lunch." Jamie replaced the gag and left Ry alone in the cavern. Lilah walked out with Jamie, a concerned look crossing her face.

"I'm sure you were kidding in there. Because if we do find the gold and you let me split it with him, he'll probably kill me to get the rest."

"Probably," acknowledged Jamie.

"Probably! You would let him kill me? Cliff was right about you. You bastard! I can't believe I risked my life to bring you out here. I'll never trust another man again." Hot tears flooded her eyes, matching her hot words.

"As well you shouldn't. But calm down a minute. I have no intention of honoring my agreement with him." Jamie caught her hand in reassurance. "I'm just using him to get more information."

"Then why didn't you tell me?" she pouted, cooling off "Having me go on like that. Can't say as I appreciate your humor. But I'll go along with your plan."

After lunch, they explored the base of the mesa, finding no evidence of gold or any other thing that might jog Jamie's memory. The shadows lengthened as sunset approached, prompting Lilah to reluctantly offer some of their food supplies to the marshal. Jamie continued his painstaking exploration and within fifteen minutes of sundown, he discovered a clue that had eluded his inspection twice. There in the rock, evenly spaced holes, finger-sized and big enough for pitons, ascended the western face. Jamie knew instantly he would not find anything of personal value at ground level. He had to go up. Lilah prepared supper as he came over.

"I've found piton holes in the rock."

She looked over from the fire and started to speak when Jamie cut her off. "Should you be building a fire out in the open like that? It'll soon be dark."

"The Indians are afraid to come near here. We'll be safe. What about these holes? What do you mean?"

"Holes for wedges that someone used to climb the rock. It might have been me, for all I remember."

"Well, let's start climbing then."

He shook his head. "We don't have the equipment. I'll have

to go back to town."

In the night, Jamie dreamed of another world. There, he recognized a striking woman, a woman with long, flowing red hair, dark skin and blue eyes. He knew that he'd loved her and made love to her with volcanic passion. They were not quite man and wife but were as close as the concept would come in this strange society. Their relationship allowed casual love interests and their individual pursuits separated them by impossible distances, yet all this served only to strengthen their bond.

Then, one day, he visited her at her tropical estate and she seemed troubled, staring blankly toward the sparkling sea at the bottom of the hill. He asked her what was wrong and her reply, though unintelligible, conveyed a sense of dreadful foreboding.

Next, a blinding white light enveloped Jamie, followed by a floating sensation in a peaceful darkness. When the light returned, Jamie lay in a cave surrounded by unimaginable machinery and yet the devices were familiar. Knowingly, he groped for hand-held tools and tunneled his way out of the rock.

Eventually, Jamie peered down from his newly formed cave onto an alien valley. This land, barren and dry with sparse vegetation, greatly differed from the girl's estate. Animal life was also rare or well-hidden, indicating that his new existence would be Spartan in this new world.

While he contemplated this, a crazily pitched sound startled him. Growing louder, it chased the images from his mind entirely. Jamie woke to the sound of someone screaming.

The scream stopped abruptly and Jamie noted Lilah, already standing, looking for the source of the sound. With his head clearing, he followed her stare into the cavern. The scream had to be from Hobbs. Jamie ran into the cave and caught his breath at what he saw. Ry Hobbs had nearly freed himself using the sharp edges of the broken statue on the binding ropes, but his escape had gone awry in the end, due to his having a caved-in skull.

Lilah, now behind Jamie, carried a lantern, but he ushered her back, sparing her the gruesome sight. Too late, though, she saw the violated brain matter and ran out to be sick. Jamie followed her.

"The statue killed him just like it tried to kill me. I thought it was just falling but it was moving for me," cried Lilah hysterically.

"No, it wasn't." Jamie grabbed the woman's shoulder.

"How can you know?"

"Ry was killed by a falling rock. It's lying behind the statue."

"Really?" She sounded hopeful.

"I can show you if you're up to it."

She hesitated, but then answered yes. They walked back to the scene where Lilah tried to stare not at the corpse, but beyond it. Brain tissue, blood and bone fragments covered a rock behind the statue as Jamie stated. Surrounding it, lesser debris had also fallen from above.

"We mustn't let our imaginations get the better of us," he said.

"I'm all right."

"We can clean this mess up in the morning. Right now, I'd like to get back to sleep. That's when I seem to recall the most." His mind drifted toward some difficult to remember image he had just experienced.

"I'd like to bury him now if that's all right with you. Call me silly, if you like, but knowing there's a man with a crushed skull not twenty feet from me and I won't be able to sleep."

"I'll take care of it then." He waved her away.

The earth moved easily with loose shale completing the grave's covering. After his morbid task, he found Lilah fast asleep in spite of her trepidation. With several hours till sunrise, he lay beside her, gathering strength for the trip back to town in the morning. Trying to rest, Jamie glanced out over the moon-washed plain and his blood ran cold. Could it be? *Slow down Jamie. Check some points of reference to be sure. The scrub, the rocks, even the lay of the land. It's true. This landscape was in my dream. I saw it from above.*

Finally, assimilating the information, he jerked his head

around, making sure the mesa hadn't disappeared in some new reality. The flat-topped formation was still in place and it anchored his thoughts in the here and now.

He also knew that up there on its face was an opening. An opening he'd made to observe the very land that he was presently camped on. Now the climb was imperative and the sooner the better.

In the morning, as Jamie hurriedly stowed their gear, Lilah read the newspaper he had found in the crevice. She commented out loud on an interesting article. "I can't believe a military man is running for president. We're still burying the dead from the war."

"You'd be burying more from Indian attacks if not for the military."

"I'm not so sure of that. I think the army provokes them. And our protectors are no more civilized with their treatment of the captured than the Indians are. Anyway, people won't take kindly to one of those butchers in the White House. General Grant must be mad for even considering it," she scorned.

"To the Union, he's quite the hero. It will carry him to the White House."

"Is that your gut feeling?"

"No, I just seem to know that he will become president." Once again, a strange feeling shot through him. He *knew* things.

"Oh great! Now I've got a soothsayer on my hands." She laughed and returned to her reading, leaving Jamie to ponder his spoken certainty. To him it seemed a matter of record that Grant would indeed become president.

Later, Lilah packed the provisions in a quick and efficient manner albeit with some complaints. "Why does it always seem as though you have more to pack on the return trip?"

"You sound like me whenever I came back on the . . . ."

"Stage coach?"

Jamie looked up with his mouth agape. "No, I was thinking of something else."

"Probably the train, but at least there's always plenty of room on them. I remember when I was a little girl . . . ."

Her words were lost to Jamie as he stared skyward. He remembered the metallic dragonfly from his dream and knew it was a certain type of flying vehicle. He also remembered riding on a metallic bird, an airplane. His dream had not been a fantasy, the vision was real. Now, he reasoned out why he was so sure of Grant's presidency and Red Cloud's downfall. All these events, he had seen from a different perspective, a perspective possibly from the future. For a moment he felt that he would go mad, then he set the thoughts aside for a later examination.

Upon their return to Ute, Jamie half-expected trouble from the Marshal's deputies. A new marshal and his men, however, allowed them free reign. Ry apparently quit before following them, not telling anyone his business.

Without the law on his back, Jamie proceeded with his quest for his old identity. He sketched certain mountain climbing equipment and commissioned the blacksmith to make these articles.

Jamie finished his shave and tried to sort out all the facts he'd discovered so far, especially his place in time. With deliberate self-observation, he poured more water into the basin and rinsed his face off. Wiping his skin dry, he walked over to the lace-curtain framed window. Outside, people casually conducted their business. The wooden sidewalk outside the general store held female window shoppers and the more he looked at it the more incongruous the entire vista seemed. Looking away, he noted the sunlight on the worn but clean rug and found Lilah standing there.

"Good morning, Jamie." She had spent the night in her own house, again, for reputation's sake.

"Lilah, we have to talk."

She perched herself on the side of the brass bed and patiently waited for the conversation. He glanced at the furnishings, the wooden floor, the high chest of drawers with the pitcher and basin, the bed with the decorative brass head and foot boards. The setting all seemed out of place--or was it him? He sat beside her.

"Lilah, you know I've been remembering bits and pieces of my former life, right?"

"Yes, that's what we've been working for. It shouldn't upset you."

"Well hear me out. It seems the more I remember, the more I realize I don't belong here."

"Yes, we both realized that you're not from around here." Though she listened, she didn't seem to hear.

"No, it's more than just that. Let me see if I can explain. You see I now know that I was familiar with a much greater technology."

She stared at him, not understanding his point.

"All right let me give you an example. Take the general store. Sometime, you may want to know what kind of dress material is available. How would you do that?"

"I'd go over and find out, of course."

"Right! Where I come from I would talk to the manager without ever leaving my room. I'd use a calling device."

"You mean like a telegraph?"

"Yes, only he would hear my actual words and I his."

Lilah regarded him with a look of concern. He went on anyway. "Please keep an open mind about what I'm going to say."

"I'll try," she pledged.

"All right, I think I've figured out where I'm from. This possibility occurred to me quite a while ago, but I dismissed it as too fantastic to be true. Based on my returning memories I believe I'm from . . . ."

"From where?"

"I'm from a different time. A time that hasn't yet occurred."

"What?" she exclaimed in disbelief.

"Yes, you heard me right."

"How can that be? Time isn't a place. And even if it was, the future doesn't exist yet for you to come from it."

"I know that but apparently it's possible to travel to different time periods. I'm convinced that I'm literally from the future. And somehow I've been displaced back in time at least one hundred years." With his bold declaration filling the space between the two of them, he wondered if he was right, at last-- or, rather, finally, mad.

Part II

The Pawn

Chapter 9

General Troy Magnuson entered the surveillance room and leaned over the shoulder of the console operator. Both pairs of eyes focused on the CRT displaying their subject's movements.

"How's he doing? Have we learned anything yet?" asked Magnuson.

"No, not yet, and I'm beginning to worry," answered Dr. Balcone, the project coordinator. "We didn't think he'd remember as much of the present as he has. He must have an unnatural resistance to drugs."

The general straightened. "I thought you said your mind altering narcotic was completely successful in previous tests."

"It was. But his system is fighting it somehow." The scientist's voice sounded more than a bit defensive. "Like I said before, it's still experimental and we don't know how long the effect will last, even on an ordinary person. The trick will be to allow him to rediscover your so-called phenomena slowly, before he realizes his identity."

"Please don't make me remind you that time is critical here," Magnuson retorted sharply. "The longer it takes, the more vulnerable this operation becomes. When will he start to regain his full memory?" He looked down at his watch, which showed the date as well as the time.

"Not before we can give him another booster in his sleep. We can keep that up for several more weeks before it starts to compromise his health," suggested Balcone.

Magnuson stared across the windowless room, thinking. "What if we erase the memory of the phenomena, along with his identity?"

"General, that's a risk your people have already agreed to take. Do you want me to stop now?"

"No, no of course not. The pressure's just getting to me." Magnuson shook his head slightly and sketched a smile over his tired face.

"I understand, General. We'll do everything we can."

Balcone had dropped his edgy tone. "Incredible that his ancestor discovered the phenomena way back then," he added.

"Yeah! Even better that the family kept it quiet until now. Not one slip of the tongue in all the generations it was passed down from," the military man concurred.

"Were they ever going to reveal it, General?"

"According to him, when total world peace is achieved they'd go public with it. If you can believe them? Anyway, we assumed that was the real reason and tried to convince him that an end to the Cold War meant world peace. He chose not believe it. He cited several trouble spots around the world, i.e. such as the Philippines, China and Iraq. Arguing with him was futile." The general snorted and began to study the screen once again. "That's why I reluctantly resorted to this. But if the threat to the earth were any less grave, I'd still be trying diplomacy." He shook his head and glanced at Balcone, perhaps to see if his statement was believed. "As it is we have to know his secret to save the lives of millions, maybe billions, of people. Your experimental drug for selective memory loss seems to be our best bet." The general let out a slow sigh of worry and discouragement.

"You mean after you tried your own drug-induced brain washing techniques?" countered Balcone. He jabbed at the console turning off the monitor, then got busy on some other task.

"Believe me when I tell you I'm not proud of any of this," admitted the general, pacing away from the screen and Balcone. " but, as they say, desperate times require desperate measures. How's his physical condition at the moment?" The general turned to face the project coordinator.

"His condition? I'd say it's remarkable considering what he's been through. And strange that he seems perfectly healthy with that low body temperature." Balcone blinked rapidly, as if keeping an emotional reaction from bursting forth. "If I hadn't seen him myself, I'd think that he was suffering from extreme exposure."

"What is his temperature?" asked the general. He began again to pace throughout the room.

"It's eighty-nine degrees."

"Eighty-nine degree?" exclaimed the general, stopping dead in his tracks. "Did you test your equipment?"

"Sure did." Balcone laughed, but not as an expression of humor. "Tested it on myself and there's nothing wrong with it. People's body temperatures do fluctuate. But that's the lowest I've ever seen. I still can't get over that he's walking around. Anyone else would be in ventricular fibrillation." He smiled.

"You mean he should be dying?"

"That's what the textbooks say," acknowledged the biologist.

"I'll tell you one thing, though, I'd bet you won't find him on many skiing trips," declared Magnuson. "Can't have a very high tolerance to cold with a body temperature like that. Any record of him visiting any cold climates?"

Balcone considered the question for a while. "Not so far as we know, now that you mention it."

"I'd love to conduct a few lab tests on him," mused Balcone busily typing at the console.

"Not before we get the information we want," rebuked the General.

"Of course sir." Balcone flushed a bit.

"Have we found out what killed Mister Hobbs yet?" asked the General.

"Apparently it's exactly as Jamie explained it. A falling rock crushed his skull. Bizarre coincidence, huh?"

The general shook his head in apparent amazement. "I don't like to lose men like that."

"There was nothing we could have done without giving away our presence."

"No, I suppose not," agreed Magnuson.

Neither Balcone nor Magnuson said another word. Then, with a slight touch on the controls, the door slid open and the general left the other man to his work.

Chapter 10

Jamie negotiated the slope leading to the mesa's shear wall, still mindful of Lilah's reaction to his time travel theory. Obviously, she doubted his sanity and he wondered if it was wise to voice his suspicions on the subject. Banishing her from his thoughts, he concentrated on his upcoming climb.

Soft earth, heavy equipment and provisions hampered Jamie's progress up the slope. In some places he labored on all fours, but eventually passed the graves of Cliff and Ry. At the base of the vertical wall, he unloaded his equipment and located the piton holes.

Starting his long ascent, he sought the destination from his dream, a cave high up on the rock wall. Relentlessly, he climbed, eventually climbing beyond the piton holes, where increasingly scarce finger and toe holds slowed his progress. The activity demanded his full concentration and his world shrank to become the stone only inches from his face.

Several hours passed, as the shadows grew long. The oncoming moonless night threatened even his keen night vision, the darkness making the mono-colored rock spitefully hide its hand and footholds. A chill wind rustled Jamie's clothes as he rested on a rare narrow ledge and lit his lantern. Gauging his progress, he turned his head to spy a nearby mesa and the scrub brush below that appeared as sparse patches of stubbly beard. Some instinct told him he had another hour of his trek to go. He continued his climb, allowing the light to hang from his back.

Carefully inching his way up, Jamie occasionally startled bats as he swung the lantern around to illuminate the slight finger grips. Without sunlight, the wind seemed colder, reminding him of his dislike for lower temperatures. He endured, however, and from the ground probably appeared to be a firefly steadily ascending against a black background. A perfect target.

Jamie withdrew his hand from its purchase with a repulsive spasm, at the sound of a rifle shot. A bullet pierced the rock where his index finger had been a split second before. What the.

. .? *Unfriendly bastard is real close or has got a gun with one hell of a muzzle velocity.* Immediately, he hammered a piton into the wall, hung the lantern and rappelled twenty feet down the rope. *Got to stay away from the light!*

The next shot destroyed the lantern and Jamie looked down to protect his eyes from the shower of glass. Around the former location of the light, the gunman methodically placed shots in a spiral pattern. Using half-seen finger and toe holds, Jamie scurried laterally across the cliff. *That'll give me some time to think.* As the sounds of the bullets neared again, he dropped his satchel and screamed as if he'd fallen.

The barrage stopped, but now he was stranded on the rock with no safety equipment, no food and no defense. Once his trick is discovered, Jamie realized the shooting would restart. With no time to waste, he recklessly climbed the steep wall by feel. As expected, the shooting started again, but this time Jamie was protected.

He had discovered a large hole in the rock and as the bullets ricocheted off the cliff he hastily pulled himself up and into the space. The perfectly circular opening had smooth walls that gave off a dim light Jamie could see by. This must be the cave in my dream, he thought. He walked back into the interior until the sound of gunfire behind him lost itself in the circuitous cavern. Out of danger, he didn't stop to wonder who was shooting at him, but instead marveled at the internal structure. The construction of the place was obviously unnatural, yet he couldn't determine the method used to bore through the granite. Still, the cave was familiar to him. Jamie had been here before.

Eventually, he came upon a chamber with the same smooth, dim-lit walls. Within, he sensed a recent presence, a feeling that someone had been here in the last few weeks. Liberally scattered fingerprints that showed up in the odd luminescence confirmed his feeling, and he speculated at who may have been in this spot before, perhaps the one who'd owned the newspaper, or perhaps even himself.

Anyway, his conjecture ceased when he noticed three dusty consoles also containing the fingerprints. They were all made of a transparent material that encased symmetrical patterns of gold flakes. The flakes reflected light in various colored spectra, depending on the angle Jamie's eye made with them.

He sat in one of the ordinary looking chairs to examine the consoles and at the same time scrutinized the artificial light source. A luminescent material coated the walls and ceiling and its density, he realized, increased the deeper one went into the cave. Looking around from the console seat it felt familiar. It felt right! He spied another chamber off the one he was in and got up to explore it. There, he stopped short as several hundred pounds of gold bars glistened in the artificial light. *Am I the thief they accuse me of being?* he wondered? *Could wealth be that important to me?* Further inspection answered his questions. Pointing at the pile, several nozzle-shaped devices had apparently decomposed the gold directly beneath them. Indeed, he'd stolen it, as Cliff suspected, but not for monetary gain. The gold powered the technology these consoles used.

Jamie returned to the anterior chamber, where he picked up a device that he originally thought was part of a console. It was the size of a gun and had a similar handle, though made of the transparent material.

Taking off his jacket, he threw it from him and aimed the device at it. As expected--though why he expected it, he wasn't sure--, it changed color, and, when Jamie picked it up, it was heavy and retained its shape, unlike a yielding cloth material. The jacket had been transformed to lead. Aiming the device again, Jamie was, amazingly, able to restore it to its original cloth composition.

The information came to him then that the nozzle devices supplied the gun with atomic particles extracted from the gold. The process that transmitted the particles to the gun was well beyond any science even the early twenty-first century knew. The gun added protons, neutrons and electrons to the appropriate energy levels of the existing atoms in the jacket's cloth. This benign fusion reaction had changed the compositional matrix of the cloth to lead. Similarly, non- violent fission in conjunction with the gun's memory of the cloth matrix had reversed the process. Considering the available technology, the accomplishment was staggering. At one time, however, Jamie had taken this level of science for granted. He had a lot to re-familiarize himself with.

Striving to accelerate the return of his knowledge, Jamie continued his tour of the cavern, the familiar surroundings prompting him to lose himself in thought. With his guard down, Jamie didn't notice a man aiming a gun at his back, until he jolted to awareness at the sight of a shadow on the wall.

"Here for the gold?" Jamie asked coolly, his heart thudding, all the same.

He turned slowly, cautiously, his hands up to show the intruder he was unarmed.

"Caleb!" exclaimed Jamie, recognizing the gunman at once.

"Howdy, Jamie. I thought you were never going to show."

"Why'd you take so long to come after me?"

"Why? he asks. Because I was in prison, that's why. And if I had the gold now, you'd be dying a slow death by my gun. Two years of hell because I took off after you and the stolen gold. Thief and deserter, they called me." He shook his head in disbelief. "Put me on trial. Their kind of trial. Nice and quick! Wouldn't listen when I tried to tell them I was after the real thief. My thanks for being a loyal Confederate. After the South fell, it only took two years before the Union Army got around to pardoning Confederate deserters. By that time your trail was cold. I had a devil of a time picking it up again. Took months before I found enough people, Indians and all, who told me about the tall, green-eyed white man. So now here I am." Caleb's gaze never wavered from Jamie's face.

"Cliff and Ry were here, too. Did you see their graves?"

"Don't threaten me, McCord. I'm the one with the gun, you know."

A slow smile spread across Jamie's face, as if he found the situation more amusing than frightening. But he was trying to figure a way out of this. "No threat intended. I didn't kill them. Gold's been a lot of men's undoing."

"That's a strange statement coming from a man who stole hundreds of pounds of it. If not for greed what did you want with it?" Caleb's eyes flickered momentarily with genuine interest.

"Are you here on behalf of the glorious South?"

"Haven't you been listening? The South can go to the devil, for all I care. I'm here on my own behalf. Now show me the gold or I'll put a bullet in your stomach." His hand drew Jamie's attention to his six-shooter.

"The gold?" Jamie repeated, playing for time.

"Yes the gold, damn it. Where is it?"

"Can't you see it?"

"No stalling!" shouted the interloper as he cocked the hammer of his gun and aimed it straight at Jamie's head.

"It's over there." Jamie gestured with his shoulder.

Caleb had Jamie walk in front of him as they entered the chamber. But Jamie turned and noted the surprised expression on Caleb's face when he saw the gold for the first time.

"You hadn't been in this chamber before?" Jamie asked.

"I never noticed the entrance to it before. What are those things pointing at the bars?"

"Why they're obviously devices to extract atomic particles for use in the transmutation process." What else could such a setup be, after all?

"Never mind the double talk. Pick up some bars and carry them toward the cave entrance!"

"I can't." Jamie just about laughed at Caleb's ignorance.

"I said pick up the fucking bars!"

"A gravitometric field surrounds them," Jamie explained quietly. "It keeps the gold at absolute zero temperatures to power my equipment."

Jamie leaned his full weight on the invisible barrier and seemed to be standing relaxed at a thirty degree angle, supported by nothing but air. Caleb walked over, open-mouthed, kicked out with his foot and seemed more than astonished to feel something solid there.

With the speed of thought, Jamie took full advantage of Caleb's confusion. He disarmed him and now pointed the gun at his assailant's face.

"What do you say we leave the gold bars right where they are?" asked Jamie with a grin.

"Okay! Okay! I didn't mean any harm, you know. Just wanted a few bars to live off of. I told you, I'm no friend of the South and the Union doesn't care for me much, either. Let me go and no one will ever find out about this. I swear it."

"Don't you still want to kill me slowly?" mocked Jaime.

"That was just talk. I didn't mean nothing by it." Caleb talked rapidly, in apparent fear for his life, which made Jamie wonder what kind of man he'd been to provoke this reaction. Putting aside the thought, Jamie considered the implications of Caleb's find. Since Caleb now knew the location of Jamie's stash, others would come.

Chapter 11

In an invitation that wreaked of accusation, Senator Talmadge had demanded a meeting with Troy Magnuson. The general pressed Talmadge for the meeting's agenda, but this yielded nothing aside from the repeated insistence on the meeting's time and place. Poor timing, thought Magnuson, considering the recent breakthroughs in "Operation Timescale," but, confident of his project's progress, he had consented. At Dulles Airport, a chauffeur picked up the general and drove him to the senator's Virginia residence. Magnuson decided to dispense with the senator quickly.

On the way, he speculated about the senator's concerns. He knew the senior politician chaired a committee investigating high tech materials illegally funneled to hostile countries. Senator Talmadge had adopted this project when American equipment, in Iraqi hands, caused the loss of his son in the Gulf War. The senator probably wanted corroboration on the wrongdoing of some of Magnuson's colleagues. Lord knew Magnuson was privy to some incriminating secrets. He wondered who could be the senator's target, who was at risk. But he looked forward to matching wits with Talmadge.

A butler showed Magnuson into the senator's private study, instructed him to wait and closed the double doors behind him. Eventually, the senior senator from Nevada entered and again closed the doors as he entered. In person, Talmadge was a distinguished looking, gray-haired man, impeccably dressed and obviously quite fit.

"Please sit down, General" were the first words the senator spoke, not `good afternoon' or `nice to see you,' but just `please sit down.' Troy sensed he was in for some kind of a lecture.

"Can you tell me about this?" asked the senior statesman as he pushed a sheet of paper across the desk to Troy.

"Looks like a shopping list." Magnuson shook his head.

"Do you recognize any of it?"

"High tech surveillance, computers and some other things I don't recognize."

"That's all you have to say?"

"What do you expect me to say?" asked Magnuson, striving for a neutral, relaxed tone.

"All this material was received at Camp David under your name and now it's gone."

Troy Magnuson's stomach constricted as he realized his deep cover operation might not be deep enough.

"Senator, I'm involved in a lot of projects in pursuit of which I receive equipment. Not being a technician, I don't always remember what I'm signing for."

"Then you admit you have this." Talmadge's words came out with steely force.

"I admit it's possible," conceded Magnuson.

"All right, then let us speak plainly, shall we? Tell me about Operation Timescale."

Not nearly deep enough, thought Troy, as he took a deep breath and struggled with how he could minimize the damage.

"All right, senator. Operation Timescale is an exercise in high tech surveillance in underdeveloped theaters of operation. The president himself has sanctioned it. Our field agents complain that they can't very well hide a camera in an adobe hut without attracting some attention. Terrorists avoid scrutiny by conducting covert operations out of these areas. Hopefully, this experiment will yield techniques and equipment to eliminate the problem. It's really quite harmless." Magnuson felt the sweat begin to pour down his face. He licked his lips. Talmadge hadn't so much as offered him a glass of water.

"Very well said. But I don't buy your cover story and I don't appreciate my intelligence being insulted. You say it's harmless, hmm? I wonder if Mr. McCord would agree with you?" Talmadge's eyes, fierce with indignation, remained riveted on Magnuson.

"All right, senator I'm not going to play any more games with you." Troy reached into his pocket, causing the senior statesman to react with an explosive start. Leaping halfway across the desk, the senator reached for the general's arm, before realizing it was only a stone in the general's hand. *What did he think I was getting out--a gun?*

"Sorry to startle you, sir. Nothing to be afraid of here. I'm just preparing a demonstration."

The senator's face had gone white with anxiety.

"Are you all right, senator?"

"I'm never comfortable seeing men reach into their pockets when they've just told me they're not playing games." After a moment, Talmadge seemed to calm down.

"Look, general I'm sorry about that. I guess it was just a reaction left over from my days at Langley. No one ever really divorces themselves from the Company. Go ahead with your demonstration and make it the truth this time."

The Company as in the CIA, thought Magnuson. That explained how Talmadge had found out about the operation.

"Senator, have you ever heard of alchemy?" asked Magnuson. He put the stone-like object on the senator's desk.

"Isn't it some kind of sorcery?" responded Talmadge, ignoring the object.

"Yes, but more specifically, medieval, so-called chemists believed it was possible to turn lead to gold. Foolishly, they spent long hours trying to make themselves rich through this alchemy. Today, the idea is being discussed again, but this time with a more noble cause in mind."

"I'm assuming this is leading somewhere, General."

"Please bear with me, sir. This was how Operation Timescale was explained to me."

Troy Magnuson got up and walked over to the large globe in the senator's study and spun it around before continuing.

"You see, nowadays, the greatest threat to mankind isn't nuclear war. It's something much more insidious. Something that doesn't need any more human interaction to be a threat. It's genetic destruction via radioactive pollution."

"Really?" Talmadge continued to look at Magnuson warily.

"Yes, countless tons of radioactive waste is produced by

nuclear generators. We bury it in canisters that are sure to degrade after only a fraction of the half-life of the contents is over. And we keep adding to this mess year after year. As we speak, leaking radioactivity is creating mutations in plants and animals around the world. In Scotland, for example, they had a nuclear power plant accident in the fifties. The results were kept from the public, but, thereafter, local wildlife were born severely deformed. We, mankind, are at the same risk, unless . . . ."

"Go on." Talmadge's attitude had changed from indignation and censure to eager interest.

"Unless we can get Mr. McCord to help us," Magnuson concluded. He remained by the globe, examining it without really seeing.

"Come again with that, General? Future generations are at risk unless McCord helps us?" The senator's temper seemed ready to ignite again.

"Yes, that's right and I'll explain how. You see the stone I put on your desk. What do you make of it?"

The senator picked up the object in question and looked at it carefully. The stone had two distinct colors at opposite ends. One side was dark brown and the other was an off-white. In the middle, the colors blended.

"The brown side feels like wood," Talmadge observed.

"What do you think the other side is, Senator?"

"It looks like ivory."

"That's exactly correct. One side is indeed wood and the other is ivory. The section in the middle is a transition zone where one material melds into the other." Magnuson was pleased with his student's response.

"I didn't know our science could do that, but, like yourself, I'm not technically oriented." But the senator didn't seem happy with his thoughts and shifted in his seat.

Magnuson came around the desk and sat opposite Talmadge once again. "I'm told that a transition zone between two unlike substances can be the result of diffusion," he said. "This happens when one element tries to migrate to where it's least in abundance. For instance, carbon and iron can diffuse into each other under certain conditions to form a transition zone called pearlite, a form of steel. In our sample, it appeared that the wood diffused into the ivory and vice versa. Be that as it may…" Magnuson smiled. "You're right when you suggest that our science isn't capable of producing such an object. That transition zone was not produced by any methods we ourselves know of. It's much too extensive a blend. The bonding seems to be done on an atomic particle level." He picked up the stone and rolled it in his fingers for a moment.

"You're telling me then that somehow our Mr. McCord has done this and he can turn the nuclear waste to something harmless." A star pupil, indeed.

"We believe that McCord can neutralize the waste, but he didn't make that sample." Magnuson stated flatly. "It was made by one of his ancestors over one hundred years ago. His great, great, grandfather, Ian McCord, discovered the process in the mid-1800s. The secret was passed down to his son, Jamie, and then from one generation to the next. The McCords were, and are, genuine alchemists."

"I see. This technique is a hundred and fifty years old and we still don't understand it?" Talmadge looked skeptical.

"I'm afraid not, sir, but at least we know who to ask about it. At least we were able to prove the technology existed when samples like this one found its way to us. Then it was just a matter of finding those who mastered the art. Through Indian legends and other pieces of evidence, we identified the McCords as the owners of this very process. Eventually, we found Hunter McCord. The last of his line. When he dies, the secret dies with him. A secret that could save humanity." Magnuson only hoped that Talmadge could understand the urgency of the project.

"Surely you explained to him what you wanted before you spirited him away to God knows where?"

"Yes, we did," Magnuson declared to the senator. "He wasn't the slightest bit interested in helping. His answer was that he wouldn't reveal the secret until mankind had achieved world peace. Very noble, and our arguments fell on deaf ears. So we had to resort to this, I'm afraid, but I think the stakes warranted it."

"Thus Operation Timescale and the need for the ultra-sophisticated equipment?"

"Yes! With the help of some recent technological breakthroughs, we were able to set it up" the general said with enthusiasm. "When I left we'd just reached a milestone and I'd like to get back there as soon as possible."

The senator stared through the general for several moments before speaking.

"Super technology, huh? It reminds me of a story that was hot a few years ago when some scientists thought they'd discovered cold fusion. Do you remember it?" Talmadge reached out again for the stone and took it into his hands, measuring its heft.

Magnuson just shook his head.

"If you'll indulge me I'll attempt to explain it," Talmadge went on. "As you know, all modern nuclear plants use fission, which is the splitting of atoms. When the atoms are split, the released energy heats water in the containment vessel, which makes steam that drives a turbine, which, in turn, produces electricity." The senator paused and caught Magnuson's eyes. Then he stared down at the bizarre little rock again.

"You might have heard of another program researching fusion reactors," he went on. "The opposite of fission, the process fused the nuclei of atoms to *release* energy. Fusion is desirable because, unlike with fission, we could provide all the energy we'd ever need with minimal dangerous waste. Our sun itself is a natural fusion reactor. But since present science can't duplicate conditions on the sun, experts don't anticipate practical fusion reactors before the middle of the century. Anyway, a few years ago some scientists believed they'd found a short cut. They claimed they'd induced a fusion reaction in a beaker of water at room temperature. Their work was touted as the greatest scientific discovery of the last five hundred years. When other universities couldn't duplicate it, however, their claim was exposed as being a fraud. The incident left me with a sense of how fallible science and scientists could be, so I'm not convinced of the threat, or of the story you just told me." He set the ivory/wood piece on his desk. "I am convinced that you believe in this so called greater good, however, and are trampling someone's human rights in the name of it."

"Senator, I believe in this case . . . ." Magnuson straightened himself in his chair.

"I don't care what you believe, General. Kidnapping a citizen and running mind control experiments on him to yield some half-baked fictional technology is unpardonable. I'm ordering you to stop it right now." Talmadge gave him a look of absolute, unbendable steel.

"With all due respect, sir, I don't have to follow any orders from you. You'll have to take this up with the president first." This was the trump on which Magnuson had been depending.

"Don't fuck with me, general. I'll conduct a congressional investigation on you and the president if you don't stop now," Talmadge hissed at him. "Watergate will seem like nothing compared to this. The public will demand your heads."

"I'm willing to gamble that if the people knew of the circumstances they would back our project all the way."

"Then tell them now, if you're so sure," suggested Talmadge.

Magnuson shook his head in the negative. "I take issue with that, sir, because of the military ramifications of this discovery. If unfriendly nations got wind of this, they would stop at nothing to possess it. This knowledge is better kept under wraps by those with clearly defined, peaceable goals."

"I'm going to fight you on this, general. You and the president." Talmadge sizzled with his strength of intention.

"Don't do anything foolish, sir. Something you might regret."

Now the senator was the one who seemed intimidated. He said no more as Troy Magnuson arrogantly rose and walked to the door.

Chapter 12

"You look different than I remember you, Caleb."

"Prison does that to a man. I'm tired of holding my hands up. Do you mind if I put them down?" Caleb flexed his fingers, ready to put down his arms.

But Jamie stopped him with a word. "Yes, I do mind. But it won't be for much longer."

Jamie moved to the stack of gold bars and passed his hand over a circular object embedded in the rock wall.

"OK you can put your hands down now," said Jamie as he threw down the gun.

In bewilderment, Caleb looked at the gun and back at Jamie several times. Seemingly without a care, Jamie turned his back and resumed his exploration. He knew that his opponent was thinking him a fool. He turned his head and watched Caleb lunge for the gun on the ground. Only twelve more inches and he'd . . . Jamie observed the moment of impact. Abruptly, his forward momentum stopped as he encountered a barrier. The rest of his body caught up with his outstretched hand, crumpling him to the floor. Jamie crossed his arms and smiled at the results of his handiwork. He'd set the same sort of barrier that shielded the gold. That was exactly why he'd dropped the gun. He wasn't the fool Caleb took him for.

In his search for other exotic devices, Jamie discovered the mesa contained a complex network of corridors whose various sizes suggested that they weren't simply made for human occupation. Moreover, he realized that the only discernible machinery was in the upper compartment where he left Caleb. If any machinery ever had been down here, it had long ago turned to stony remnants.

It seemed perfectly clear to him now that the statue had been an artificially intelligent machine called a robot. The word sprung out of his thoughts as if he'd used it for a lifetime. The robot guarded this ancient relic of some technical race, but

Jamie knew that, as advanced as they were, they were not the makers of the transmutation equipment. That equipment had been put there much later, after the petrification of the mesa machine.

Eventually, he came upon a portal that was sealed with a thin coating of limestone. Compared to the other portals, this one was atypical. Curious about the man-sized entrance, Jamie tested the strength of the barrier by trying to kick through it. The material crumbled easily and air rushed in to fill the vacuum of the inner chamber. An airtight seal, thought Jamie.

"Shit!" He suddenly realized something, with a dread shock.

Almost getting lost on the way, Jamie ran back to the upper chamber with as much speed as he could muster. Finally, reaching the original cavern, he found Caleb within his airtight cell, dead of suffocation. *How could I have been so stupid? What a waste of another opportunity to regain my full memory.* Nothing to do now, but hope for more information from the equipment. Everything he'd seen so far held some meaning for him, so perhaps he could recover all his memories here.

Indeed, the exotic machinery swelled his mind with rediscovered knowledge and he remembered much more than just the equipment. For the first time, he felt comfortable with his identity, Jamie McCord. Of course, he knew he still had a lot more to learn, but he also knew that his rate of learning was increasing. The next discoveries would not come as painfully.

Jamie made a satchel out of rematerialized rock and packed the equipment he could easily carry back to town. Rounding the last corner, he was grateful to see rays of sunlight, and they indicated he'd been in the cavern longer than he'd realized. At the opening, he looked down and was again startled by the sound of gunfire. Damn, they were patient. Again, he flattened himself on the cave floor. Beneath him, he could see his antagonists defiantly wearing their Confederate uniforms, while firing their guns at a deafening rate. He had to act before a ricochet caught him. Taking out the transmuter, he willed a shot at the ground under the Confederates' feet, turning the slope at once to ice. The former soldiers slid down the side of the cliff, screaming, not realizing what had happened, until their guns were safely out of range.

Jamie, now oblivious to them, envisioned the transmuter, the gold and something new in connection with them. . . a pen. He remembered this very special pen in his possession and that he had foolishly given it to the doctor as a souvenir. But its important components would be undamaged by the fire and with its booby trap sprung, its remains would sit exposed like an open book. The technology was at grave risk of being discovered by someone. Although not a transmuter, its secrets could level the very planet on which he stood. This pen now needed to be recovered with all due haste. Even though his ability to understand didn't yet exist, Jamie felt other forces present, forces possibly from the future.

Quickly, he ran back into the cave and worked his way down to the lower compartments. Using the transmuter as a tunneling device, he created a small hole, approximately one-half inch in diameter, by turning the rock to air. When he had bored the hole through to the outside, he started a tunnel big enough for a man. The converted heavy rock created massive volumes of lighter air molecules, increasing the compartment pressure dramatically but then quickly exhausting the pressure through the original small hole. With the tunnel completed, Jamie exited the mesa with it between him and his pursuers. Turning the device back toward the tunnel, Jamie covered the telltale cave with a veneer of similar rock material.

Now, without the aid of any natural cover, his goal was to steal a horse and provisions in the full light of day. Silently, he rounded the mesa to the hostile side and spied his adversaries in a state of disarray. They avoided the icy patch that was quickly melting and tried to climb the mesa's sloping base once more. Using the distraction of their difficult climb, Jamie cautiously moved around to their flank, hurriedly mounted a horse and headed for town.

Jeremiah came to the dinner table and folded his hands for grace, per the family tradition. After the prayer was over, his mother noticed something in his hand.

"What have you got there, Jerry?" she asked.

"Just something I found." The child shrugged.

"May I see it, please?"

The boy of nine handed over his prize. Mrs. Tyler examined the smooth white object.

She was puzzled. "Where did you get this thing?"

The boy became nervous and started to fidget.

"Where, Jerry?" his father asked sternly.

"In the doctor's office."

"The doctor's office! Didn't we tell you not to go near there?" demanded Mrs. Tyler angrily. She didn't wait for the answer but turned to her husband. "Don't you think this has gone far enough? I don't even care about the money any more. It's just becoming much too dangerous. Right up front, they admitted McCord was unpredictable and might do anything."

"Yes, but we were counting on that money to start over. We decided the risk was worth it, remember?" The father looked at her anxiously, then at the boy.

"That was before the deaths," she countered. "Do you still think it's worth it? Really?"

"I'll arrange for extraction," agreed Tyler in a defeated tone.

Jamie searched around in the rubble of the old doctor's office. He poked and prodded all the loose blackened material with no luck, until a voice made him wheel about with his gun drawn.

"What you looking for mister?" asked a kid, who cowered when he spotted the gun.

"Sorry, son," said Jamie as he quickly put the gun away. "I'm looking for my pen. It's been in my family for generations. Have you seen it? It was a pearly white color."

"Oh yeah, I've seen that."

Jamie went over and put his hand on the boy's shoulder.

"What's your name, son?"

"Matt."

"Well, Matt, how would you like a nice shiny silver piece?" Jamie took one from his pocket and displayed it.

The boy grinned. "What do I have to do?"

"That's easy. Just tell me where the pen is."

"I don't know though. Jeremiah has it, but it's all broken up. Are you sure you still want it?"

"Where's Jeremiah?"

"He lives over there in the gray house." The boy pointed. "But you better hurry if you want to see him. He's moving away."

"Thank you, Matt. Here's your reward."

Without a word, Matt took the coin and ran off. Jamie walked over to the gray house, the general store with an apartment above. Outside, an old man swept the sidewalk.

"Howdy," shouted Jamie.

Startled, the old man looked up.

"Howdy," he replied suspiciously.

"Jeremiah around?"

"The Tyler boy? He's over at the livery stable helping his parents pack a wagon. If you want to catch them, you better hurry."

Jamie ran to the stable as the old man looked after him with a concerned expression on his face.

The Tylers loaded their supplies. The sunny day promised good things to come, as Mrs. Tyler reveled at their imminent departure. Her relief quickly turned to dread, however, seeing Jamie McCord walking toward them. Her husband noted her expression and turned to see Jamie, also.

"Okay," Tyler said quietly. "Everybody stay calm and keep loading the wagon."

"Mr. Tyler?" asked Jamie as he got to within comfortable talking distance.

"Yes."

"Howdy, my name is Jamie McCord." He offered his hand.

Len Tyler shook it.

"What can I do for you?"

"Maybe I can do something for you. I'd like to offer you a reward for recovering a personal possession of mine. Today, I discovered I'd lost a family heirloom. I searched in all the places I'd been since coming to town, including the remains of the doctor's office."

"Terrible tragedy that," said Tyler.

"Yes, it was. I grew to like the doc in the short while I knew him. Anyway, when I was searching the office a boy told me your son Jeremiah had my memento. If you still have the white pen, I'm prepared to pay handsomely for it." Jamie looked at the boy who wouldn't even glance in his direction.

"We found Jeremiah with something in his hand earlier. It didn't look much like any pen I ever saw. It was white but it wasn't whole. Wait a minute and I'll get it," the father told him.

The man walked over to the wagon buried his hand in a sack and withdrew half a pen.

"Is this it?"

Jamie looked at it from a distance of about ten feet, but didn't find the need for closer scrutiny. The white plastic that could not be duplicated by any known technique was unmistakable in the sunlight. He took a greenback from his billfold and displayed it for Mr. Tyler.

"Would ten dollars be sufficient?" he offered.

"You really don't have to." Tyler came forward.

"No please. I insist."

Tyler took the bill.

Jamie helped them load and saw them off, before leaving to examine his alleged heirloom. Mindful of the devastated building, he was pleased that his pen had weathered the flames so well, even considering the heat-resistant plastic case. Looking at it now, he flashed back to when he had been in Boston.

"Thank you, Mr. McCord. Please come again," said the restaurant's hostess.

His statuesque companion appreciated the courteous respect lavished on her escort.

"They certainly prize your patronage."

"They should. I've thrown a lot of business their way. Although they'd prosper anyway. Do you know of another restaurant south of Boston with a better atmosphere?"

Located on a small inlet, the Cohasset restaurant offered a large viewing window overlooking a typical New England scene. Several sleek yachts anchored outside were powered not by wind, but by combustion engines. Others docked at the restaurant's own facilities allowed the boating customers to walk up the pier's ramp to the entrance. A nautical flavor pervaded the interior, not surprising since this was the site of an old lighthouse. Jamie always enjoyed the ambiance, even through the ownership changes that had affected the food and service quality. Tonight's dinner had been an excellent experience, however, and he prepared to take his date home.

Outside, Jamie and his dinner guest waited for the valet as a cool ocean mist ruddied their complexions. After several minutes of receiving no attention, Jamie went inside, took the keys from the hostess and looked for his car. He found it hemmed in, so calmly he removed a pen from his suit pocket and rectified the situation. As he drove out, a man walked in the direction Jamie had just come from. Now at the entrance, Jamie opened the passenger door just as a loud commotion hailed from the parking area.

"What the hell happened to my car?" a man shouted.

Out of curiosity, Jamie's companion started to walk over to see what the fuss was about, until Jamie gently aimed her into the car. The valets, reappearing in a flurry, ran over to find an angry man whose car lay on its side. . . just as Jamie left it.

An impish smile curled up the corners of his mouth at the memory, but this was now and that was. . . whenever.

Back to business, he found a private spot where he trained his gravity suspension device on a bail of hay. The hay didn't move. Perhaps the pen had sustained some damage after all, he thought, or then again the strain of levitating several hundred pounds of gold nearly two thousand miles could have drained it. Carefully, he disassembled the partial pen and saw that all the internal parts seemed to be in good condition. In fact, they seemed to be in excellent condition, considering they'd been in an inferno.

Jamie pocketed the parts, purchased a looking glass at the general store and rebooked his room at the saloon. Now in private quarters, he dumped the parts out on the bed and examined the subassembly under magnification. The transparent encasement was neither burned nor discolored, its white plastic exterior providing excellent protection. Next, Jamie painstakingly scrutinized the other parts and found no apparent damage.

Frustrated by the exercise, he reassembled the device and attempted to use it again, but the device was ineffective. There must be something he'd missed. Jamie reexamined the parts repeatedly, each time finding nothing--and yet there had to be something. What was it? He had to look closer. His eyes focused on the heart of the device, even though the encased shiny metal flakes couldn't possibly have been upset by the fire. An impossibility perhaps but it was the only possibility left. Oh shit! This couldn't be. But it must be, it was the only explanation. Subtle and yet so damned obvious. All the flakes were green on one side and silver on the other, that was all except one, whose colors were reversed. Somebody had made a small mistake with this clever copy. A copy that could not have been made in the present--which was, after all, the past.

Chapter 13

Back at the livery stable, in the recent rain-moistened earth, Jamie noted the Tylers' wagon wheel tracks. Relieved that their trail was so obvious, he pursued the family that might or might not have been party to the counterfeiting of the pen. Within an hour, the dried ground made the tracking more difficult. Determined to continue, Jamie relied on his scant tracking skills, losing the trail completely and then regaining it again.

Intent on inspecting the ground, Jamie eventually succumbed to a sensation to look behind him. His instincts proved sure. A dust cloud indicated a band of men hastily following him.

He had to try to outrun them and follow the trail at the same time. When his lead diminished, he gambled on losing the trail in favor of more speed. Damn them! They were still gaining and there was no place to hide.

Jamie knew he would have to make a stand and he had only one way: use the transmutation device in the open. A moot concern now, he thought, since the counterfeited pen proved that his technology was no longer a secret.

He dismounted with the transmuter in hand and waited for the riders to arrive. As they approached, he considered that they meant him no harm and that their similar path might be coincidental. With closer inspection, however, Jamie recognized their defiant Confederate banner. These were the men who had attacked him on the mesa.

Captain Richards halted his troops as they reached Jamie's untended animal. The horsemen milled around, searching for their quarry.

"Where the hell did he go?" wondered the lieutenant.

They looked for tracks, but didn't see any.

"Fan out!" ordered the captain, shouting loudly. "We've got to find the bastard."

After a good twenty minutes of searching, the troop came up empty.

"Damned if I can find a trace of him, Captain," said the lieutenant. "It's like he never even existed."

"Well, someone rode his horse here. And without it, he can't intend to get very far. He's probably hiding nearby, waiting to recover the beast. We'll camp here and wait for him. Lieutenant, you take the first watch at twilight."

Jamie burrowed beneath the ground using his transmuter to change the earth to air. As soon as he had cleared an opening, he got in, sealed the entrance and waited for the troop to arrive above him. Then reconsidering their weight, he feared the ceiling would cave in and burrowed deeper. With ten feet of packed soil above him, he stopped and changed the walls to phosphorous for light.

Sitting down to deliberate, he sensed slight vibrations transmitted through the ground from above. His quarry neared and more vibrations set up a natural frequency, causing the earth to rumble, violently feeding off its own energy. What the hell was. . .? Jamie grabbed at the compartment walls in vain as the floor started to collapse into a hole. Unbeknownst to him, an underground cavern lay only a few inches below his compartment and he fell into it, amid sand and rock.

Got to break my fall somehow. Facing upward, he viewed the cavern's ceiling from a rapidly increasing depth. Upon hitting bottom, an immediate pain shot through his landing leg from multiple fractures. The only light shone from the hole he had fallen through and he realized the drop was about twenty-five feet. Jamie lay crippled atop the rubble that had accompanied him down, but he still clutched the transmuter. He swore at the pain, but recalling how quickly he had healed previously, he decided that with a little bit of time, and by using his directed internal force, the leg would be whole again soon.

A damp musty smell suggested water. He transformed a nearby wall to energized phosphorous to locate the much-needed fluid. The lit chamber revealed stalactites and stalagmites--some growing to meet each other--as well as a meandering stream. The water trickled through the cavern, disappearing into lower depths of darkness.

Painfully immobile, Jamie bit down hard, straightened out his leg and lay back invoking his will to heal the broken leg. His mind activated, repairing the injury, while the rest of him went dormant, allowing Jamie a respite in unconsciousness.

A square with lights on the front approached Jamie with a sign on top that read Penn Station. The square became a long rectangular prism with lights on the side as it neared the elevated platform on which he stood. The lights became windows, windows that revealed Asian, black, white and Hispanic riders, windows that showed them all living in the same community. *Where do I know this from? I remember! It's an underground train. A New York subway train complete with the customary graffiti and slogans.*

Turning away from the train, Jamie saw people standing, waiting for transportation to arrive. He turned front again as the sound of the screeching rails trumpeted the train's arrival--but that wasn't all they portended. A sharp object pressed hard against his back.

"All your money, man, or the point goes home!" whispered an unseen assailant.

In the blink of an eye, Jamie pivoted, knocking down a teenage black wielding a sharpened screwdriver. The youth got up just as the train doors opened, allowing the crowd to hastily board the train. Unwilling to continue the confrontation, the ruffian backed away, eventually breaking into a run. He'd hardly worked up a sweat, thought Jamie.

With the threat over, he turned in time to see the train doors close and start to pull out. Sensing a half-remembered intention to board the train, he cursed under his breath and looked back into the tunnel for the next arrival.

As he waited, he heard the sound of running footsteps behind him on the empty platform. *Looks like I'll get a workout after all.* His assailant returned with reinforcements. Now the attack was personal.

The sound of the next train echoed out of the tunnel as the three youths surrounded Jamie. *Hmm, they're going to try and push me under the train.* Immediately, Jamie jumped into the middle of them with a flurry of punches and kicks. A roundhouse kick to the screwdriver wielder either broke his neck or rendered him unconscious. Surprised by their victim's ferocity, the others hesitated. Taking advantage of this lull, Jamie broke the tallest gang member's jaw, causing him to fall back in pain.

Now, one on one, the remaining man rammed Jamie from behind, trying to force him onto the tracks. But much to the punk's surprise, his victim was not as off-balance as he'd hoped for. Spinning his torso, Jamie neatly avoided the headlong charge and hip-tossed the street tough to the platform. The train rushed by, inches from his prone body, and, sitting up, painfully alive, the kid received a vicious knockout punch from Jamie. Tomorrow's papers would tell a grim story, but not of an innocent victim, thought Jamie.

The dream dissipated and Jamie opened his eyes again to find his leg practically healed. He still had a dull ache, but at least he was functional. With his mobility back, he splashed water in his face and washed off as much dirt as possible. Reflecting on the positive side of the experience, he had remembered a very sophisticated talent for self-defense. He would engage the Confederates.

Night fell on the small troop of men. Most of the soldiers slept in their tents, trusting their security to a lone sentry. Greatly complicating the guard's task, a moonless night enclosed the camp in blackness. With only his sense of hearing to guide him, the soldier plumbed the depths beyond the campfire's influence. Remaining motionless, he heard nothing other than an eerie silence that even the insects respected. Continuing halfway around the camp, he stopped again to listen and this time heard a definite sound, earth giving way in a mini landslide. Possibly McCord, he thought as he pointed his gun into the blackness, but then realized the sound was coming from within the camp. . . behind him. In an instant, he imagined the hunted man concealing himself underground, waiting for an opportunity to strike. Realizing this, the soldier turned, but he was already too late. He was disabled without a sound.

The horses whinnied as Jamie approached, but then fell

silent, while he led one away on foot. He didn't worry about pursuit, since the horse he rode was the only one that didn't have its horseshoes dissolved to sand.

At dawn, Jamie picked up the Tylers' wagon tracks yet again. The older, fainter trail slowed his progress, but, considering their tremendous lead, he'd been lucky to find the tracks at all. Jamie could not be satisfied with the minor miracle of finding the cold trail, though, since each passing second increased the odds of propagating the pen's dangerous secrets. He quickened his pace at the risk of losing the Tylers completely.

In the distance, a dark blot grew into the remnants of a campfire. Holding his enthusiasm in check, Jamie dismounted, hoping that this camp had been the Tylers'. The depth of the wheel tracks indicated the wagon had remained stationary overnight. Also, the tracks of two children and two adults dotted the site. The campsite had to be theirs. What other family of four would venture this far from town? His spirits lifted at the confirmation and he poked around the fire for more clues.

Jamie liberated a burnt piece of green paper, an undamaged corner of a ten dollar greenback. The one he'd given to Len Tyler, thought Jamie, with interest. The man knew the pen was worth far more than a mere ten dollar note and apparently played a knowing part in the counterfeiting con.

Approximately a mile after the Tylers' camp, Jamie found scattered traces of their possessions on the ground. Trouble had occurred here, he realized. Eventually, he found the wagon bristling with arrows on its side with all provisions picked clean. Several sets of hoof prints marred the soil to such a degree that Jamie couldn't judge the size of the attacking force, but he was relieved to find no bodies or blood. A mixed blessing since the Indian's trail would be easier to follow, but now he would have to vie with a large war party for his prize. Still, for the children's sake, he was glad the family was alive.

From a Confederate saddle bag, left by the horse's owner, Jamie extracted a small telescope and grimly sought the Indians' direction. Their trail led south, but Jamie's attention was diverted west where a curious lone house stood miles from any visible settlements. The strangeness of it demanded an investigation, so more by instinct than anything else, he rode toward it, confident that he could pick up the Indians' trail again.

Jamie McCord spun his smoking six shooter around his finger and parked it in its holster. The belligerent man lay dead a few yards away. Why did he draw? thought Jamie. What was so important about a dusty shack whose roof needed mending from gable to gable?

Jamie's uncooperative spurs chinked as he climbed the two steps to the dilapidated verandah. The weather-beaten boards protested with creaks as they gave under his weight. Jamie realized stealth was irrelevant now that anyone inside had been alerted by the gunfire and was indifferent to the noise.

The shooting incident had reinforced Jamie's curiosity about the interior of the building. He cautiously pushed open the door barely hanging by its makeshift wooden hinges. With guns drawn, he entered the dusty chamber, glimpsing sunlight shining through several holes in the horizontal wall boards. Dust particles streamed through the sunbeams and wind eerily whistled through the apertures, creating an atmosphere that made Jamie tighten the grip on his gun.

His eyes quickly adjusted to the light, revealing a roughly assembled rectangular table in the center of the sparsely furnished room. This and two chairs were the only furniture, other than an unlit oil lamp and some shabby window drapes. Jamie flung aside the drapery and discovered a door on the left of the stone fireplace. Behind it, he found an old brass bed, a night table with another oil lamp and a rug floor covering. Two open windows, appointed with lacy curtains, blew in the light breeze, making for a better kept room, although still not worth dying over. Satisfied he was alone, Jamie put away his guns for a closer look at the other side of the room. Walking across the floor, he felt an irregular shape under his boot and he stepped back and turned the rug over to spy a trap door with a metal ring handle. Maybe now he was getting somewhere, he thought.

Opening the door, he descended via a long wooden ladder into darkness. Twenty feet down, he stood on the floor of a natural cavern like the one he'd occupied under the Confederate soldiers. Stalactites again reached down to meet the stalagmites as the sound of dripping water reverberated off the stone walls.

Panels of light illuminated the chamber enough for him to see a walkway with handrails leading to an unusual looking door. The metal door was oval and had a large wheel in its center, presumably for opening. Jamie took the wheel in both hands and rotated it until he heard the release of a locking mechanism. Inside, a large room featured metal walls--not the crude metal from the blacksmith shop, but something much more refined.

The exotic alloy paled, however, next to the other, plentiful oddities in the room, including boxes with glass fronts. Each one displayed a different picture behind the glass and Jamie was awed by the definition of these lithographic marvels. He moved closer to admire the detail of one picture and recognized his room at the saloon. What sort of technique could have accomplished these perfect replicas? he wondered in surprise. Moving on to the next box, Jamie felt as if he walked through some fantastic art gallery. This one showed the crowded main street in Ute and something else that caused him to catch his breath. Not trusting his senses, he leaned closer to banish what he thought was a trick of the light or his own imagination but closer inspection did not refute his first impression. His blood ran cold when he realized that, unlike most pictures he'd ever seen, this one's subject was in motion. The people moved, grisly simulacrums feigning the everyday business that real people would engage in. Open-mouthed, he stared as a fresh flood of confused memories filled his brain.

Suddenly he felt a presence behind him. Wheeling about, gun drawn, he recognized Lilah. She was not staring at the alien devices, but at him. She knew! She had known all along. His nerve remained steady, but his mind and senses reeled.

Chapter 14

Uniformed men surrounded Jamie, leading him down a corridor in a vast underground complex. Eventually, they came to something that resembled the subway station in Jamie's dream, except this place was antiseptically clean and the train was nothing like Jamie imagined. Someone mentioned "maglev" and somehow he knew it to mean magnetic levitation. The train floated on a cushion of air, electromagnetic repulsion giving them a very fast and very quiet ride, yet he knew that the technology was inferior to that used by his pen.

Exiting the train, they led Jamie still farther into a compound that sloped upward and flared out to enclose a series of offices. Military personnel appeared at every turn, some of whom stared at Jamie with a mixture of sympathy and curiosity. Ignoring their interest, he looked beyond them as the modern environment prompted a flood of fresh memories. Stopping outside one of the few offices enclosed by walls, Jamie read the name `General Troy Magnuson' in the brass plate. One of his armed escorts courteously opened the door, saying nothing. But he understood that he should enter here.

Inside, an officer, presumably the general, sat at his desk, obviously awaiting him. The man was large, as tall as Jamie when he stood to shake hands, in his fifties and in good physical condition. His short red hair stood out in contrast to the drab green color of his uniform. After the handshake, the general motioned a dazed Jamie to sit down, while the escort closed the door behind himself, leaving them alone.

"Welcome to the twenty-first century, Mister McCord."

Jamie looked around, taking in the details of the office. The windows behind the general revealed the town of Ute as seen from the second floor of one of the structures there.

"From the outside, this building appears as the post office," offered the general.

"Have you discovered the secret of time travel then?" Jamie tried to find his emotional and mental bearings.

"Hmm, not exactly, This town was all a facade constructed

for your benefit. Everyone you've met has been an actor--some in the service of the government, some not. I don't know how much you remember yet, but rest assured your full memory will return now that we've discontinued the drug treatment."

"Drug treatment!" said Jamie angrily, as he stood.

"We had to use an experimental drug genetically engineered to cause partial loss of memory on you. Your true identity, along with other recent memories, were erased to ensure the success of this operation. You see, we had to discover the mechanism of . . ."

"Transmutation?"

"Yes. Are you remembering our first meeting?" Magnuson appeared extremely curious about his guest's mental state.

"Bits and pieces. You needed the technology for radioactive hazards, right?" That seemed right.

"Exactly, and you may also remember that you weren't convinced of our. . . humanity's… dilemma. We tried to coerce you and I'm truly sorry about that. However, I have arranged for the government to make amends. You'll want for nothing in your life from now on. I hope you can forgive us."

"I resisted and escaped but you caught up with me."

Jamie remembered the dream of the metallic dragonfly. A series of odd details began to fall into place.

"Yes. You're a very unusual man, Mr. McCord. When we realized that our methods were ineffective, we concocted Operation Timescale, a sting operation. We've used as much historic fact and legend as we could scrape together about your great grandfather."

Now Jamie was completely confused. This was just too much information for him to assimilate all at once.

The general appeared to recognize the fact. "Look, I can see you're having trouble with all this. Why don't you get cleaned up, take a nap and I'll give you a complete briefing later on."

Before Jamie could say otherwise, the general called someone into the room via his intercom. A stern-looking officer entered.

"See that Mr. McCord gets some fresh clothes and a place to shower and sleep."

Standing, the general walked around the desk and shook Jamie's hand again.

"I'll see you later when you're well rested. Everything is all right now, thanks to you."

All manner of vehicles surrounded the mesa. Helicopters patrolled a wide perimeter to discourage curious civilians, as a crude lift ferried technical specialists to the opening. Inside the hollowed out mesa, scientists and technicians swarmed all over the equipment.

"Now where the hell do you suppose this stuff actually came from?" asked a technician.

"Beats the hell out of me, but as the general said we're not anthropologists. All we have to do is figure out how to use it all."

"Well, if this guy's ancestor back in the Old West could figure it out, then it should be a snap for *us*."

"This McCord guy's ancestor must have been big into mountain climbing to just happen upon a cache like this." The technician shook his head as he looked around.

"Yeah, it does seem strange. You'd think they'd have better things to do back then than climb some mountain." He shrugged.

"Oh well, it's not for us to reason why. You got that oscilloscope hooked up yet?"

In one of the vans at the bottom, a videotape played over and over again.

"Okay, now, here's where he transformed the dirt to ice under our Confederates," explained a scientist to a panel of his colleagues.

The tape showed Jamie aiming the transmuter.

"Did you see how he manipulated the device to gain that

effect?"

Heads around the room nodded negatively until one individual spoke up. "Can we get a better angle of it? A close-up of his hand, maybe?"

"Sure. I can zoom in."

Dr. Rivera made the necessary adjustments and replayed the scene, although not with the same resolution as the wider angle.

"How about now? Anyone see how he manipulated the device?"

A man in the front answered. "I didn't see a damn thing. His hand looked perfectly still to me."

"That's exactly the point. Whatever he used has no buttons or levers or triggers of any kind, and yet he achieved an effect specifically designed for escape."

"Maybe the device is triggered just by aiming and only transforms materials into ice," said another.

"No, we thought of that. Other films clearly show him turning his jacket to a heavy material, probably lead. That film also showed no sign of manipulating the thing other than aiming. Gentlemen, we've got a mystery."

An officer escorted a cleaned and refreshed Jamie back to the general. This time, Jamie walked through the mocked-up old Western town noting incongruent automobiles and people in contemporary clothing. He was stunned. Apparently, they were all preparing to leave, as if their job was over now. He was their job and, yes, that phase of their toying with him seemed to have been completed with his capture.

Outside the church, rows of pews awaited disposal or transportation. General Magnuson sat inside the revamped structure at a huge table, where electrically energized lights shown down on him. People now gutted the building that Jamie recognized as a mere prop in their game.

"You're looking like your old self again," observed the general jovially. "Please sit down. Our meal will be ready in a few minutes."

Without a word, the place emptied of all except the military personnel serving the dinner.

"Perhaps in the meantime you'll fill me in on why the hell this was so damn necessary."

"A very fair question, Mr. McCord. One I will be pleased to answer. Our work has to do with genetic mutations."

"Due to radiation, I'll bet?" Jamie couldn't stop himself from sounding angry.

"Yes. The negative effects on genetic materials caused by man made radiation."

"Like nuclear weapons and power plants." He paused. "Now I'm remembering. You said you wanted the transmuter to render radioactive waste inert."

"I sense a little skepticism."

"I'm always skeptical of military interest in new tech. . . I've said exactly this before, haven't I?" Jamie felt an odd sensation streaming through his brain. Much more was coming back to him and what was returned was a little hard for him to grasp.

"I'm glad to see your memory is returning." The general smiled.

Whatever the Army had done with him was wrong, but obviously the general felt strongly about it. "I still don't understand my connection with the Old West and the transmuter. Why did you need to scrape together information on my great grandfather?"

"That's easy. Your great grandfather recovered the secret of transmutation after it'd been lost. We set up the circumstances for you to act out his rediscovery of the transmutation phenomena." The general's eyes remained probingly on Jamie.

"Rediscovery?"

"Your ancestors lost the ability for a brief period, before regaining it. Except for that, the secret was passed down from one generation to the next. Since we had more historic information on the time of the rediscovery, we decided to stage it instead of the original find. We gambled that your father had told you the story so you could, subconsciously at least, lend yourself to the play."

"What happened after I was shot from the helicopter?" demanded Jamie.

"Please, Mr. McCord, we didn't shoot you. It was only a tranquilizer dart. After you were out, we started our drug treatment for Operation Timescale. The only drug, I might add, that you weren't immediately resistant to. Anyway, we mapped out a plan to convince you that you were your own great grandfather. Thus the setting of 1868." The general seemed a bit pleased with his ingenuity. "Then we had to aim you toward the events leading up to the discovery. After all the preparations were completed, we set you up on the plains with a horse and some Indians to fend off."

Jamie foraged through his mind to see what was missing. "Tell me about the history. I can't remember any of it."

"As well you shouldn't. That was one of the top priorities of the drug treatments. I'll fill you in now, but in time you'll remember it all on your own. You see, in the early part of the nineteenth century, your great, great, grandfather, Ian McCord, supplied food to the Indians during the drought. According to legend, he converted inorganic materials to food. A godlike ability so the tribe offered him a sacrifice, an Indian maiden. Being a civilized man, he didn't kill her, but, instead, fathered a son by her. His name was Jamie, your great grandfather."

Jamie nodded as if that confirmed something he already knew. "Two Eagles showed me my great, great grandfather's grave site. He was trying to tell me something, but I couldn't understand him."

"He was very old and frail," the general sad sadly. "We didn't expect him to contact you. He was one of two accidental deaths that I deeply regret. The other was Ry Hobbs."

From the way Ry's death had occurred, Jamie had guessed at once that Hobbs was the other accidental death. He reserved judgment, however, on whether to believe the Indian chief's death was actually an accident. As he thought about it, Jamie realized that when the chief showed him the grave site of his great father, he meant great, great grandfather. Things are not what they seem, the chief had told Jamie. Jamie was being warned about the whole deception. So what a coincidence that someone who was about to give away the operation accidentally died. But the general continued as if the issue were trivial.

"After Ian, Jamie continued supplying the Indians with food, until one day he failed to deliver. Then, for whatever reason, he disappeared from the West and resurfaced as a mercenary back East during the Civil War." The general was well versed in the McCord family saga. "About that time, history records that a great stash of gold vanished from under the watchful eye of a group of Confederates. Coincidentally, your ancestor happened to be in the company of that group and he also vanished. Rumors continued to persist for years. Did he steal the gold and, if so, how did he do it? Well that brings us to today and I don't mind telling you that we never dreamed we'd find that very gold powering your transmutation equipment."

A sick feeling stole over Jamie as he realized that he'd given away this information.

The general noticed his expression. "We found the opening in the mesa and installed cameras as soon as you left to get pitons and rope," he said. "Our major breakthrough came when the Indian girl vaguely pointed to the north and you picked out the mesa. We had known something lay in that direction, but had no idea where. We took another calculated risk in letting you fill in the blanks. But a very good risk, as it turned out." General Magnuson allowed his face to show his satisfaction with the outcome.

"Anyway," he went on, "some time after the gold was stolen, Jamie started to supply the Indians again. At first, when we were quite skeptical, we thought that he was simply buying food with the gold. Skepticism aside, however, the charter of our organization dictates that we investigate even the feeblest of clues that may lead to beneficial technologies. With our investigation starved of corroborating evidence, we were on the verge of throwing in the towel, when something changed our minds. We found materials in mid-transformation being sold by the Indians as jewelry. Where did they get them? It had to be from the McCords. Alchemy was. . . is… real. But why did Jamie need gold? We conjectured that he used the gold to buy parts for the repair of some faulty supermachine. A little while ago, we discovered the real story." The general beckoned in some soldiers who had arrived with a heaping tray of food. The men began to put down two place settings on the table.

"So it was all a scam," commented Jaime. "Nothing was real."

"Part of it was all too real" disagreed the general. "The two deaths on our hands and the one on yours. Although we'll have to accept partial responsibility for that one, also."

"You mean Caleb?"

"Yes." The soldiers set the food down alongside the plates and Magnuson waved them away. He began to serve Jamie from the dishes, which smelled better than anything he had eaten in the last...however long he had been here.

"He seemed very familiar to me, Jamie said, thinking of Caleb. "Even now I feel that he belonged in that time period."

"A lot of your preparation included drug assisted hypnosis" explained the general. "Imprinted on your mind were certain scenarios of the day, so they would seem familiar to you. You were shown images, accurate lithographs whenever possible, of the time period we sent you to. I'm not surprised that the setting seemed authentic to you. Caleb, for instance--his name was David Andrews, by the way--was a marvel of our make up department." Magnuson took a sip of the wine he had poured them both.

"Why so complex a scheme?" Now that Jamie thought of it, how much must this all have cost the government?

"History is complex. Much of what you experienced were actual reenactments. Everything else was contrived circumstances to hasten you in the right direction. For instance, the attack by the Confederates while you were climbing the mesa, the finding of the newspaper and the meeting with Caleb. All were designed to promote a sense of urgency in you."

Jamie nodded, feeling savaged in his innermost being. "So the operation was a complete success?" he asked sarcastically.

"Not yet. We would have preferred to prolong it a bit longer, so that you might demonstrate how the equipment works. But no one anticipated that you would recognize the counterfeit pen as quickly as you did. And you weren't supposed to follow the Tylers when they left the compound. We tried to throw you off the track with the Confederates and the fake Indian attack, but you found our outer post. And if you'll pardon the expression, the rest is history." Magnuson tried his soup, a small puff of steam suggesting that it was still warm enough to be enjoyed.

"Why did you give me the pen to begin with? It only made me doubt my situation." Jamie felt a bit ill and wasn't sure he wanted to eat, but he couldn't recall the last time he'd done so.

"You've answered your own question," answered Magnuson. "If we had completely submersed you in the Old West, you might've been happy just to stay there. Your pen and some of your modern possessions were planted as seeds for you to doubt your ordinariness. I dare say the strategy worked quite well since it spurred you on to discover your hidden talents." He continued, somewhat noisily, with the soup, a yellow concoction that smelled of spices.

Jamie flushed at the general's smugness. He had been used for the convenience of the military and he was not quite as happy about everything as the general was.

Magnuson placed his spoon down with finality. "Now I must ask you, will you help me understand your transmutation devices? We almost have the information, anyway, and it's for an altruistic cause."

"General, first you tried to force the information from me. Then you attempted to trick me into giving it up! And now you ask me that? You've certainly got gall. More than ever, I'm convinced that you should not have it. You may try drugs on me again, but I'd venture to guess they didn't work before or you'd still have me drugged."

"We won't coerce you.," objected the general, earnestly. "You're free to refuse if you want. Will you at least sleep on it though? Maybe tomorrow I can convince you of our humanitarian motives."

"Good idea. I am feeling a little tired." Jamie looked at the plate of chicken, saffron rice, and baby vegetables with some regret, but he was suddenly too tired to even pick up his fork. "Oh, one more thing, General, Jamie was my great grandfather's name. What's *my* name?"

"Hunter. Hunter McCord. Oh and by the way, where did you learn to handle a six shooter like that?" Magnuson began cutting the dark meat away from the bone.

"Are you serious, General? Thanks to you, I couldn't even remember my name. Never mind how I learned anything." Hunter stood, glowered at the military man, turned and left the church freely walking back to his quarters. Out on the street, however, he decided he didn't want to sleep underground, in spite of the amenities and headed back up to the room above the saloon. He wondered idly if he'd be stopped.

"Well do you think you've earned his trust?" asked Colonel Matheson.

"No way! He'll need more convincing," responded the general, finishing up his plate with gusto. His opening gambit with McCord hadn't gone too badly though, he felt. Still, the man had been through a confusing ordeal, although that might be to the good in softening him up.

"I agree, General," said Matheson at once. "And I'm concerned he's on too long a leash."

Magnuson shook his head in irritation. "As far as he knows he's perfectly free, and I'd like to maintain that illusion for now."

"I don't know, General. He's an unusual subject. I'd feel more comfortable if he had a constant escort."

"I don't think that'll be necessary here, Colonel. Where can he go? Besides, he must be completely disoriented. That by itself should serve to pacify him, making it easier to extract more information. But let's understand, this operation isn't over until we can transmute matter the way he does. We may still need him, so let's not antagonize him." Magnuson pushed his plate aside and wiped his mouth.

"You'll at least want to check in on him?"

"You bet I do. Tune in his room."

The CRT came alive as the colonel manipulated the controls.

"He's not there," reported Matheson calmly. "I'll check the saloon."

As the officer had guessed, Jamie was just lying down in the first bed he'd occupied after his rebirth.

"Have someone monitor him till morning," ordered the general. "We don't want to get lax at this late stage."

"Yes, sir."

The sun rose over the old Western town as sunglass-clad workers continued to dismantle and ship equipment. Military jeeps drove up and down the street with almost as much regularity as the transport trucks. Despite the noise, the man over the saloon slept right through the morning fuss. At approximately ten hundred hours, General Magnuson started to worry.

"Colonel, will you check on our guest personally? I know he's been through a lot, but twelve hours sleep should be enough for any occasion. See that he's all right and please be discrete."

The Colonel entered Hunter's room when his knocking went unheeded. Something was wrong. He stood over the bed and manhandled the sound sleeper, turning him onto his back. The man was not sleeping. He was dead. And he wasn't McCord but a soldier that Hunter dressed in his clothes.

Chapter 15

"His neck was broken?" shouted the general.

"Yes sir. Apparently our Mr. McCord wasn't as disoriented as he seemed. As soon as I discovered our man dead with McCord's clothes on, I ordered beefed-up security at the mesa and launched an all-out search."

"Damn it! He's got a twelve hour lead on us."

"Yes. And he also stole a jeep after nearly killing a sentry on the west perimeter."

"This is just great. I want you to find me the asshole who set up the security perimeter. And get after McCord pronto!"

"Yes sir! I'll be speaking with the injured guard, a Sergeant Patterson, shortly. Maybe he can tell us something about McCord's destination and/or plans."

"Just do whatever it takes."

The head nurse at Taos hospital held the phone receiver away from her mouth to shout an order. "Lil, will you check the patient in 302, please? I've got a colonel on the phone who's pretty upset that Sergeant Patterson isn't picking up."

"All right. Be back in a minute."

Lil quickly made her way to the sergeant's room and found the bed empty. He was probably in the bathroom, she decided, and knocked on the door.

"Sergeant Patterson?"

No response. Panicking, she threw open the door to find no one. She ran to the closet. The soldier's belongings were gone as well.

"Gone?" yelled the general. "Where the hell could he go if he was that injured?"

"Apparently, he never was injured, General," said Matheson

sheepishly.

Troy Magnuson fell silent, anticipating the next statement.

"The nurses described Sergeant Patterson as a tall, well-built man with black hair and green eyes."

"McCord," grunted the general in resignation.

"We found the real Patterson bound but unharmed. And the Jeep well camouflaged."

"Ever flown before?"

The question startled Hunter. He absentmindedly turned away from the window to face the questioner, a fat businessman with short gray hair.

"Uh, yes, but not for a while."

"You seemed spellbound by the view, as if you were new to flying."

"No, just appreciating the healthy landscape."

"Oh, one of those tree huggers, eh? I appreciate the environment, too, as long as it doesn't hurt business."

"Fine." He turned away again to be lost in the panorama out the window.

The businessman prodded Hunter with more questions. "So what line of business are you in?"

"Metals. Metal treatments." Hunter's eyes remained on the landscape.

"Really? I might have something you'd be interested in. I've got a brochure right here in my briefcase." The man ransacked through a stack of papers. "Here it is. Our metal finishing division. Take a look. It's an excellent service."

"Thank you," said Hunter as he folded the flyer and put it in his pocket.

"Well aren't you going to read it?"

"Look, I'm not in the mood for business right now. Can't you understand that?" He turned and glared.

"All right, I'm sorry." The man backed away.

A military contingent awaited the arrivals at Los Angeles airport.

"We've got something," said a security man into his walkie-talkie.

From his security desk screen, he watched those who had just landed streaming off the plane.

"What is it?" came the reply.

"I noticed one of the passengers who disembarked from Gate 7 now seems to be waiting at Gate 8. Maybe we spooked him from coming out of the terminal. He's real nervous. Could be McCord."

"What does he look like?"

"Tall, dark hair, wearing a surgeon's shirt and khaki pants."

"That could be our man. Okay, thanks. We'll handle it from here."

The officer motioned his men to follow. "We're looking for a tall, possibly dangerous man, wearing a surgeon's shirt and khaki pants."

The men filtered into the crowded area, just as people stood to greet the arrivals. Under the soldiers' watchful eyes, all passengers disembarked and were met. No McCord.

"Possible target in the men's room," came a report over the walkie-talkie.

Quickly and silently, the men entered the rest room. Under a stall door, a khaki pair of pants draped around a man's ankles.

"This bastard is the coolest I've ever ran into," whispered an enlisted man as he took his position.

"When you gotta go, you gotta go," came the reply from his comrade.

They kicked in the stall door and leveled their guns at a man reading a newspaper. His expression was more of surprise than of fear. With his pants hastily pulled up, they quickly hustled him away to the security area. Now, the green eyes showed rage.

"I thought it was too easy," stated the general.

"He was very clever," opined Colonel Matheson. "He picked out an individual close to his own physical stature and outfitted him with the military clothes he'd stolen. The man was paid to get off the plane and wait for the other flight. As McCord had calculated, we pounced on the suspicious behavior. For all we know, he may have walked right past us out into the city."

"Well, looks like we can't rely on McCord's confusion anymore," reflected Magnuson. "He's as effective at eluding us as he was before the operation began. We've got our work cut out for us unless we can figure out the devices ourselves. How's our research coming?" The general's eyes were weary and the expression on his face was one of worry. They were far worse off than when they'd begun; McCord knew how far they would go to trap him and he would be even more careful than before.

"The research isn't going very well I'm afraid. We're are still unable to invoke any phenomena." The colonel's eyes were red from lack of sleep and his tie hung around his neck, undone.

"So even with the equipment found, we're no farther along than when we started. Damn it!" snarled Magnuson. "If only we hadn't switched pens. He'd be unraveling the mystery for us right now."

Matheson shrugged. "It was a calculated risk, Troy. We knew the pen was one of his devices and that he suddenly wanted it back for some particular reason. If he'd gotten his hands on the real one, the operation might've been compromised right then and there. It was a good gamble. The fake was damn near perfect and I still don't know what gave it away." He slumped into one of the chairs in front of the general's desk and rubbed his forehead with both hands.

"Yes, I suppose you're right," agreed Magnuson, still in a state of distraction. "What about that star chart of his? Any luck there?"

Matheson brightened. "We've found that the symbols on the

sides of the pages are some sort of alphanumeric characters. He told Lilah they were dates and calculations to locate cosmic bodies. We're proceeding now on that assumption."

"Good, at least we're making progress on some front." Magnuson nodded at Matheson and their eyes met to exchange a mix of doubt and fragile optimism.

Hunter walked in warm sunlight toward the professional building in Jupiter, Florida that housed the office of Doctor Spain, a noted psychiatrist. Although Hunter was engaged in serious contemplation of this visit, the ocean's roar demanded his attention, too. Its blue waters awakened pleasant sensations from some time in his life that beckoned and suggested a home. Too long since he'd frolicked in the surf, he decided. That would be his first order of business after his appointment.

Doctor Thomas Spain, formerly a New York practitioner, had moved to Florida three years before to finish up his career. His papers on the mind's physiological manifestations had won him considerable acknowledgment among his distinguished colleagues. Inspired by his public fame, the doctor had opened his own New York practice. As his reputation grew, he expanded the office, while still carrying his own patient load. His patients lauded his unpretentious attitude and gentle demeanor. His financial future assured, he indulged himself with a small practice in Florida, picking a location convenient to the deep sea sport fishing he enjoyed so much, but never had time for. After a year of settling in, he found himself caring for some of his old patients as they retired to the sunshine state. Life was again uncomplicated yet fulfilling.

"Your one o'clock is here, doctor," announced his secretary. "Mr. James Hunter."

"Send him in."

"So you fell off a horse and your doctor stitched you up. Did he suggest this treatment for your amnesia, Mr. Hunter?"

"No, it's my own idea to go under. I've been remembering more and more, but I'd like to force the issue even faster. Since most of my progress seems to come in dreams, I thought I could access my subconscious directly through hypnosis."

"Well, Jim, I hope that patients self-diagnosing doesn't become a trend. It could be very dangerous both to themselves and to my profession." But the doctor smiled to show he was teasing.

"Will you help me?"

"All right. You are correct about hypnosis accessing the subconscious. But I must warn you that whatever you reveal under hypnosis is what you believe to be true, not necessarily what is true."

"Yes, but since I know I'm not insane, what I believe to be true must be true."

"A fair statement," agreed Spain, "but truth is a subjective thing in all of us. Our perceptions greatly influence what we feel is the truth. Also, you seem like a very determined man. Experience with others of your makeup suggests that I may not be able to hypnotize you. Would you mind if I administer a mild sedative first?"

Hunter jumped out of his chair. "Don't even think it…" He caught himself and sat back down. "Sorry doctor. Lately I've developed a very anti-drug mindset."

"I understand," said the doctor as he noted the reaction on a pad in front of him.

"Look, I'll try to cooperate with your efforts to induce hypnosis. I don't think we'll have a problem," added Hunter.

"Okay, then we'll at least try it. Just relax while I draw the curtains."

Hunter down-shifted an ultra responsive automobile, driving along a road that wound around mountainous terrain. Enjoying the challenge, he looked beyond the red hood, anticipating the demanding route. On his left, wind-blown spume disallowed reflections of the high white clouds that lazily floated in their own azure sea. Typical of the lush island, the shadows of clouds constantly meandered across the landscape, occasionally sprinkling it with life-giving rain. This constant cycle of sun and rain produced an abundance of flora in riotous colors. Maui, still largely unspoiled, dodged the commercialism that threatened Oahu. Reminded of home, Hunter drank in the beauty around him and continued on the road to Kaanapali.

Parking in the garage of his estate, he entered the house and discovered his maid cleaning the kitchen countertop. Hunter took a tropical juice drink from the refrigerator and tried to gauge her mood. Although only in her mid-twenties, she wore an ever-present somber countenance. Exotically attractive, she possessed European, Chinese and Polynesian features. In addition, she was well paid, intelligent and possessed a charming social survival savvy, yet she never talked about a social life. In fact, throughout her employment, Hunter never remembered her leaving her room at night for any social activity. Since she was steadfastly responsible, Hunter trusted her with the run of the house while he was away sometimes for as long as several months. Tonight, he again assumed the role of father figure, planning to take her to the restaurant at the Royal Lahaina. He decided this while absentmindedly sipping his drink and gazing at the sparkling Pacific from his patio.

Hunter was once again in the psychiatrist's office. Dr. Spain pulled back the shades allowing the light to enter.

"Welcome back, Jim!"

Good, thought Hunter, his real name was still secret, thanks to an earlier self-hypnotic command.

"What did we learn?" Hunter asked eagerly.

"We learned a great deal, despite my trepidation. You were an excellent subject. First, you are apparently a very wealthy and somewhat reclusive man. A financier who dabbles in many disciplines, some of them rather intriguing. I'd never heard of underwater mining before, but you've taken this technology quite a way."

With each word, memories flooded back into Hunter's mind. Sometimes they came too fast, too quickly for him to assimilate, since every word opened up a new world to be re-explored.

"All right, so I started in precious metals and then got into other industrial investments." Hunter continued to allow a flow of oddly familiar images through his mind.

"Right, although I did have trouble with your earliest

memories. Memories, for instance, of how you built your fortune. Those facts were kind of fuzzy. Probably buried more deeply, although precious metals were definitely involved. Frankly, I'm amazed at the list of your accomplishments for such a young man. And, in spite of your prowess in industrial technology, you are also very active in ecological preservation. Your companies are touted for their sensitivity to the environment. I always guessed these things to be at odds, but you pull it off. Very commendable." The doctor gave him an encouraging and admiring look.

"Industry and the environment don't have to be at odds," Hunter declared. "If you respect the ecology and use some creative intelligence, they can actually enhance one another."

"I just wish others had your attitude, Mr. Hunter." The doctor looked pensive for a moment. "As for this treatment, you realize that we only scratched the surface of your whole psyche. A lot more questions still remain to be answered. Your friends, associates and family for instance. Now, I have no doubt that you will eventually remember without hypnosis, but it will take time. It's up to you whether you want to schedule another session to speed things up a bit."

"So you believe what I've told you is the truth?"

In answer to that, the doctor picked up a magazine and threw it on the desk. The headline of the feature article was spelled out in big letters:

"NAMELESS PHILANTHROPIST SAVES BARRIER REEF"

Hunter looked up at the doctor, expecting what the man was about to suggest.

"From everything you've told me, I believe you're that mysterious philanthropist. I've read the article. The story is about an industrialist, noted for his ecological sympathies, who outbid rivals for the mineral rights around the reef. Without going into too much detail, the particulars all fit too well to be a coincidence. James Hunter is not your real name either, is it?" Spain said that without any accusation or judgment.

Hunter flushed and fidgeted in his chair. "No, it isn't," he admitted. "Can I rely on your discretion?"

"I've never violated doctor-patient privilege," Spain assured him. "And I'm not about to start now."

"Thank you. You've been very helpful and I may want to talk again, but right now I have to digest all this information before I can go on."

"Wait. There's one more thing you should consider."

Hunter waited, his expression inviting the doctor's statement.

"Do you recognize the possibility that your housemaid on Maui loves you?" The doctor smiled, as if to take away from his forwardness.

"Kim? She's just a girl," Hunter denied.

"Hunter she's in her mid-twenties and she has a strong commitment to you already. Maybe you should call her. Let her know you're all right. She may be very anxious at your disappearance. It seems as though you've been too preoccupied to notice, although she did figure prominently in your thoughts. I dare say you have strong feelings about her as well." The doctor was no longer smiling, but delivering a serious message.

"You're right, of course. It all seems so obvious to me now. I will contact her."

"If we don't meet again, it's been a pleasure meeting you, Mr. Hunter. Good luck." The two men stood and shook hands amiably.

Hunter awoke as the morning sun illuminated the borders around the shabby but clean motel shades. Today was different, vastly different than any day since he'd come to so many weeks ago in the desert. A new Hunter peered from behind those green eyes. During sleep, he'd solidified memories recovered by the hypnosis and added new ones. Although still not mentally whole, he had shed the awkward uncertainty that had dogged him since his escape, regaining confidence in his place in the twenty-first century.

His jubilation, however, was quickly displaced by his sudden concern for Kim. She must be a prime target for interrogation on his whereabouts. The more he thought about her, the more he mistrusted the military's altruistic motives. Almost certainly, Troy Magnuson wanted the secret of transmutation for some destructive purpose and since it had eluded him, Hunter's recapture would be given top priority. They would seek out Kim, if they hadn't already, and, at best, keep her under surveillance. At worst, Hunter shuddered to think what a desperate military would do to her. He couldn't rest until he knew she was safe. The matter of uncovering his past would have to be postponed.

At the supermarket, Kim studied her assignment book, while waiting in the long checkout line. After taking the appropriate university courses, she intended to contribute to Hunter's financial empire. Although not intrigued by science and business studies, she pushed herself in those areas because having such knowledge would place her closer to her employer.

Since Hunter had gone missing, however, everyday life thoroughly bored her. She existed in a dreamlike reverie, everything seeming so trivial against McCord's disappearance.

Usually, she knew him to be a responsible and conscientious communicator who never neglected to reveal his schedule to her. He was in trouble, Kim had reflected, so she'd contacted the police and they the FBI, but Hunter's reclusive lifestyle did not help her to convince them that he was in danger. Now, several weeks later, she still had heard no news of his whereabouts.

The FBI had interviewed her early on, gleaning as much information about Hunter as possible. This then was followed by occasional follow-up questions, but then even these inquiries ceased and Kim suspected that the investigation had been terminated. The bureau denied this and declined to talk about the case with her at all. She knew that she was helpless without them to pursue that matter. All she could do was bide her time and pray for the best.

Exiting the market, she wheeled the full cart to her car in the busy parking lot. A tall woman in her late fifties was loading groceries into the hatchback of her economy car parked next to Kim's. Kim didn't notice her or realize the difficulty the woman seemed to be having.

"Miss?" the woman called to Kim.

Her voice jarred Kim back to reality. She looked over with

what must be an annoyed and confused look on her face.

"Would you mind helping me? My arthritis is flaring up and I can't get this heavy bag into the car."

Kim felt embarrassed about her reaction. "Sure, let me," she said, as she took the full load and deposited it in the car.

"Thank you very much. I could never have wrestled that big bag in by myself."

The woman fumbled in her pocket book, took out a five dollar bill and handed it to Kim.

"No, no. You don't have to do that. It was really nothing."

After some polite verbal sparring, the woman gave in and took back the money, thanking Kim again. Kim finished loading her own groceries and drove off, resuming her immersion in her own musings.

A van casually drove along the mountainous Hawaiian highway, the occupants intent on things other than the scenery. In back, among sophisticated electronics, a strange conversation took place.

"How'd we do? Is she registering?" one of the speakers asked in eager anticipation.

"Loud and clear, although I still don't see how Jean injected her with that air gun without her noticing."

"She's good, damn good, at what she does."

The other man just shook his head in admiration.

"Okay, she's on the highway to McCord's home. The cameras are all in place as of about ten minutes ago. Our guys have just that long to get out without a trace before she gets back. It's going to be close."

A black and silver helicopter flew low over the fields, going in the opposite direction to Kim. The hum of the blades was enough of an oddity to arouse her attention and she watched in her rear view mirror as the big flying machine disappeared behind the mountains. One of those noisy tour helicopters, she conjectured and devoted no more thought to it.

Kim soaked in the last of the twilight before going inside. A cool ocean breeze brought the scent of wild flowers up the hill, as well as a dark chill, making the lonely girl rub her folded arms for warmth. She closed the sliding doors behind her, shutting out the nightfall that threatened to engulf the hillside and her psyche. The transformation, from day to night, occurred with unusual rapidity, since moonlight wasn't available to keep it at bay. A morose Kim, ignorant of the night's actual threat, yawned more from boredom than fatigue and prepared to go to bed.

Escaping into sleep, she sometimes dreamed of McCord and herself sharing an unlikely intimate moment and, with this thought in mind, hoped to dream of him tonight. Climbing under the covers, she fell asleep after the usual fitful bout of tossing and turning.

After only a few moments, though, something woke her, forcing her to full consciousness. Her breathing was inhibited. Oh my god! What was going on? She sensed a figure standing over her and felt a hand clamped over her mouth. She tried to scream, but couldn't and eventually realized the phantasm was whispering to her. The intruder was a man, all in black, whose tone was almost soothing. What was he saying?

"It's me, Hunter. Do you understand?"

Wide-eyed, she nodded her head, yes, and Hunter removed his hand. He started to explain that he'd eluded several visual detectors to get inside, but she just clasped her arms around his neck, before he could finish.

"We're getting out of here," he said.

While Kim dressed, Hunter scanned the room for listening devices with an electronic unit. Apparently satisfied none had been installed, he exited the house the same way he'd entered, using the shadows to spirit both Kim and himself out of the surveillance area. She marveled at his surefootedness in near total blackness. However, when the house's flood lights lit up, Kim realized her admiration was premature. A voice from behind them halted them in their tracks.

"That's a fairly crude bug detector for someone of your

talents, Mr. McCord," said a man from behind.

Hunter and Kim turned around to see an Army colonel standing casually with his hands behind his back, appraising them. Kim took Hunter's hand and squeezed it in either fear or reassurance.

"Crude but effective, Matheson," said McCord as he peeled off his black ski mask. "How's your reclamation project going on the radioactive waste? Have you figured out the equipment yet?"

"You still don't believe us, do you? Have you considered the possibility that General Magnuson was telling you the truth?" He paused for dramatic effect. "No, I suppose you haven't, because then the deaths of future generations would be on your conscience and we couldn't have that, could we? It's best to believe what we want to believe."

"You know I can't help thinking how much more effective an army would be with a device like that," countered Hunter. "Can you imagine a scaled up version of the transmuter? Why you could wipe out whole populations of people who simply won't listen to common sense. Or at least your version of it. Matheson, I don't think it's volatile material you fear, I think it's volatile people you really want to render inert. Who are you planning to turn to stone?"

The colonel shook his head in disgust. "You're wrong, you know. Very wrong."

"Oh come on. Now that you have me, won't you let me in on your little plot like the bad guys on TV?"

Matheson sighed and stared at the ground. "I was hoping to convince you of our good intentions, McCord, but now I see that with a mind as poisoned as yours my effort would be useless."

He looked up at McCord again. "Get out of my sight!"

"You're letting us go?" queried Kim, astonished.

To answer, the Colonel merely stepped out of the way, motioning with his upturned palm at the road behind him. Hunter was stunned. He didn't expect this, but he recovered enough to make his own distaste known.

"No, Colonel! You get out of my sight. I want you, your men and your equipment off my property before dawn."

Matheson merely issued the appropriate orders to his men and walked toward a vehicle that had driven up on the asphalt.

General Magnuson looked away from the drama on the screen.

"Satisfied senator?"

"Temporarily, anyway. Now maybe we can discuss the matter of killing that native American before he could spill the beans about your sordid little plot."

The general sighed and prepared himself for a dress down.

Chapter 16

Raindrops on foliage twinkled like jewels in the morning sunlight. Hunter peered beyond the colorful vegetation as the last of the surveillance equipment was removed in trucks. He went over the house by eye and device meticulously, paying careful attention to likely hiding spots for privacy-invasion gear. Satisfied none remained, he checked on Kim who, due to the long night's activity, still slept. He would have a long talk with her when she awoke.

"What a bunch of jerks," commented Kim as she brought a pot of coffee over to the table. Hunter had brought out two cups and gestured for her to sit opposite him and enjoy the view from the deck.

Hunter looked at her, surprised at the statement she'd made. For the very first time she was loosening up around him.

"You're being too kind. I had stronger words in mind." He smiled, nearly winked at the girl. But was she a girl, or was she a woman?

"So what is this secret, this technology they went to such lengths to get?"

"I wish I could tell you, but the knowledge would put you at too much risk."

"Then you think they'll be back?" She was taken aback.

"I think they're desperate men, capable of doing anything to get what they want. They'll eventually want another crack at me. My freedom, I fear, is only temporary. I'll have to prepare for when they come again."

"Damn them!" She watched him drink and freshened his cup with more of the special Kona brew.

"Would it really be that bad if you gave them the secret?" she asked.

"Yes, I'm sure it would be disastrous. I've dealt with their kind before. Even if they have the purest motives in the world right now, I'm certain that having the potential of this technology would be too much for them not to exploit later on. If another Mid East came up, for instance, and things weren't going well, don't you think they'd resort to a weapon that would overwhelm the enemy?"

"But they have such a weapon now," Kim said, "nuclear missiles."

"Yes, but so do others. A balance exists. Nothing or no one could counter this technology. Eventually those who possessed it would get progressively bolder and would impose their will on others. An empire would be started that would set back social development hundreds if not thousands of years. No one on earth, and perhaps beyond, would be unaffected." His eyes asked her to understand the absolute position he must maintain.

"This technology could mean that much?"

Hunter nodded his head affirmatively. He could see by the look on Kim's face that she was intrigued by this awesome conjecture.

"It must be a hell of a discovery." She smiled shyly.

"I'd say the rest of mankind is still about two hundred years away from discovering the basic principles of it."

"Wow! Then how is it that your great, great grandfather founded this technique over one hundred eighty years ago."

"The discovery was accidental, or so I'm told." Indeed, he had often wondered the same thing himself.

She looked off into space with an expression of wonderment. "I suppose if I were the military, I would use it if it would save lives," she said finally.

"So you agree with them?" The bitter taste was not the coffee, but the feeling that he was so terribly alone in his resolve.

"I didn't say that," she denied immediately. "I believe it's best to keep absolute power out of their hands. But what if you gave it to both sides, then we would have balance."

"Please, we lived under the threat of balanced nuclear forces for long enough." He let his discouragement shine through in his look. "Let's not make it worse by this threat."

She spoke after considering the issue, "Yes, I guess you're right."

They sat in silence for several minutes, pondering these cosmic issues, unaware of the continuing transmissions from the device previously injected into Kim's body.

"Well that's interesting," stated Matheson, deliberating over Hunter's conversation with Kim. "McCord doesn't doubt our motives, he doubts our moral fiber."

"Sure sounds holier than thou, Colonel," responded the technician on duty. "He thinks we couldn't resist using it for tactical advantages."

"He's one to talk," added the colonel. "He made himself rich off it. I'm going to report to the general now. Let me know if anything interesting comes up, will you?"

"Sure thing, sir."

Hunter used the day to relax and plan his next move, but eventually fatigue caught up with him and he decided to turn in. He knew Kim was also tired, but he could see she was too anxious to sleep.

"When do you think they'll be back?" Kim asked timidly.

"No way I can know."

"Hunter, I'm afraid."

"I'll be right here," he murmured, soothing her.

"I know, but I was wondering if you wouldn't mind sleeping in the same room?" She flushed scarlet.

Hunter guessed that she had sensed a change in his attitude toward her. He wondered if she wasn't taking advantage of the situation, if she really was attracted to him.

"I hope I didn't traumatize you last night."

"No, no. It's just that I'd feel a bit more secure if you were close by."

"Why don't you sleep in my room, then, it's bigger and there are two beds."

After a long night with the senator, General Magnuson contacted Colonel Matheson.

"Did the senator buy it, sir?"

"I think so, but we'll have to be very careful. Is the implant still registering?"

"Loud and clear, but it's not telling us much. They're just sitting tight, enjoying each other's company."

"Well, stay on it. The transmuter is on his mind now. My gut feeling is he will use it soon and, when he does, we'll have to be there to learn the technique."

"I don't know how we could do that, general. We've already got him on film using the device and haven't learned anything. I respectfully recommend we hold the girl hostage as a bluff. I don't think he would sacrifice her to preserve his military prejudice."

"I sympathize, Colonel, but we can't step that far out of bounds with Talmadge breathing down our necks. He did what he set out to do, I'm afraid. He's cowed the president. And if I may say so, my conscience is beginning to balk, too, at the price in lives and suffering. We'll have to take our chances with this method."

Kim nestled up against Hunter in his bed. Afraid to sleep alone, she took full advantage of the intimacy offered by her very understanding employer. Whether by intention or not, she seduced him and he wasn't immune. Sweet perfume, he thought, as he submitted to the smooth feel of her skin sensuously rubbing up against his. He couldn't seem to ignore this. The prominent swelling in his loins broke him down and he kicked off the sheet that covered them. Like a man possessed, he lost all control and frenziedly covered Kim's supple body with kisses. Apparently, he wanted this too much and had for too long. Their writhing and orgasmic moans titillated an off-site pair of ears, as unbeknown to them their coupling was being broadcast.

"Jesus, I wish we still had a camera in there," said a listener to no one but himself. He closed his eyes and imagined the scene.

Kim slept on as a refreshed Hunter sneaked out of the bedroom and into his study. A high backed leather chair welcomed his form as it had countless times before. His books lined the walls, friendly old references that he had drawn strength from on numerous occasions in the past. When, he wondered, did he ever have a greater need of strength than now?

He knew it was only a matter of time until his pursuers would tire of their fruitless research into his transmutation equipment and take up the hunt again. Now, he thought of what he had to do to elude the government and ensure Kim's safety. Beyond his self-interest, he promised himself that he'd do everything in his power to keep her out of harm's way. After careful consideration, he decided on the best method to accomplish both objectives, short of giving any dangerous secrets to the military.

With his mind made up, he decided to relax by pouring himself a drink and flicking on his impressive entertainment system. The speakers hummed to life with the sound effects of an old Western. He smiled, noting the same visual effects that he had personally witnessed in the Army's sting operation. Sipping his drink, he stood with remote poised but not yet willing to turn from the Western shoot 'em up.

His mind took over the plot, neurons discharging electrical energy like superconductors. In a millisecond, the memory of his capture played out to its conclusion, although his brain remained active with other scripted material. *What the Hell am I remembering?* Hunter dropped his full glass on the floor as he viewed the mnemonically stored events with his mind's eye. More memories of the Old West! Much more than my recent experience in Ute. But how? It's crazy. I've got to stop it! He placed his hands on both temples as if to keep his head from exploding. Nonetheless, watching these kaleidoscopic images, he resigned himself to one thing. In one way or another he must have been in the Old West, the real Old West. He didn't think the Army knew.

Now his mind overloaded and blackness closed in. He

wanted to cry out, but his vocal cords wouldn't work. Hunter McCord passed out.

Part III

Reunited

Chapter 17

An ancient Inca city lay dreaming for centuries, unknown by modern man until now. Accessible only by aircraft, the site occupied a precarious peak; yet nestled against its ruins lay a contemporary ski resort frequented only by the super rich. Off-season, non-skiers enjoyed exploring the haunted Inca city. This time of year, however, the Pico da Neblina offered the high spirited thrill seeker another type of entertainment.

A trolley lumbered up the mountain, its passengers overlooking the beauty of the immense Amazonian rain forest. The guide, Jorge, droned on in two languages, indicating several points of interest. Frequently, he lectured on the worldwide implications of an Amazon devoid of the oxygen producing rain forest. Peering out the windows, though, the passengers had trouble believing that this never-ending vista could be threatened by man unless they considered the global climatic changes that had already occurred. Several ecology minded visitors privately mourned the loss of the natural asset, as others would soon actually take up the cause of saving it. The trolley swung to a halt, as the visitors reached their destination, from which they would glide and swoop like the native, fruit-eating bats.

"Are you nervous, senor?" asked the guide of his last charge.

The man turned around and smiled at him. "No, I've done this many times before."

"But you are shaking. Are you sure you're up to it?"

"Absolutely, I'm just bothered by the damn cold."

The guide saw that, indeed, the man was cold although, he himself did not think the cool temperature intolerable. As with the other guests, he helped the man on with his equipment, reminded him of the safety rules and pointed him off, down the ramp. The short, sloping ramp ended in a shear drop of hundreds of feet, before leveling off to the forest floor below. With his check list complete, the tourist ran to the end of the platform and catapulted over. The rugged mountainside fell away from beneath him, as he cleared the jagged side of the cliff. Picking up speed, he marveled at the aerial view of the forest thousands of feet below.

At the base of the mountain, a clearing awaited the hang-gliding tourists who then had the option of riding back to repeat the process. Several thermal air pockets provided a lengthy and pleasant descent. Soaring in lazy spirals, the gliders dropped while absorbing the maximum visual experience. The foreigner, sensitive to cold, enjoyed the natural spectacle best of the experience as he rode well into the evening.

"Senor, it will be getting dark soon. Very dangerous for this sport. I must suggest you take the trolley back down."

"I appreciate your concern, but I promise I won't stay for a lengthy ride this time. Do you mind? I'm not going to be back here for quite a while."

"I don't know. I could get in trouble."

"Would this help?"

The man passed him several bills, which Jorge looked at in awe. "Gracious, senor. Enjoy your ride and I'll meet you at the bottom, later."

"One more thing?"

"Si?"

"I want to send a photograph postcard of myself back home. Would you mind standing at the bottom of the steps and snapping my picture when I come off the ramp?"

"No problem, senor."

The tourist handed his camera to the guide, who scurried off to a vantage point about ten feet below the launching ramp. From this angle, the man in his glider would be framed against the darkening blue sky.

"I'm ready, senor."

He couldn't see the man from his position, but heard the visitor's equipment rattle.

"Okay, here I come." The man glided off the ramp as the cooperative guide snapped the picture.

"I got it," he shouted.

The tourist, already distant, waved his acknowledgment. Jorge prepared to ride the trolley down in anticipation of his last, high-tipping customer, but as he neared the tram a loud noise from above made him jerk his head around. Looking up at the summit, he witnessed an angry thunderhead boiling over the top of the mountain. He had seen this phenomena before. The other side of the mountain trapped migrating clouds and forced them to climb over the obstruction. Usually, as the elevation increased, they spent their moisture in gentle rain showers. This storm seemed different somehow, malevolent. It lashed the mountainside with sheets of wind-driven rain.

Mother of God, thought Jorge. *This is the devil's spawn.* The storm advanced as though driven by some colossal will, the tumult buffeting the tram. *Looks like I won't be descending in this.* Torrential rains hid the peak and turned the sky green.

Looking out over the forest, he held his breath to see if the guest was descending but the man had opted for a lengthy route well out over the forest. Stupid Americanos! He would get himself killed. As Jorge watched, the wind forced him to grab onto a support structure. With his eyes still locked on the man, he saw him experience the first effects of the wind. His glider rocked unsteadily and he fought for control. He tried to run away, flying even farther over the jungles, but the storm caught up with him, wetting the glider's wings and quelling the thermal updrafts. The guest began to plummet and then disappeared into the raging pandemonium. Jorge thought he heard a scream, but then wasn't sure if it was just his imagination.

General Magnuson rubbed his face in his hands at the news of Hunter McCord's death. He was banking heavily on McCord's cooperation, in view of the Army's failure to decipher the transmuter.

"Are we sure the man was really him?" He leaned back in his office chair with a heavy sigh.

"I'm afraid so, sir" replied Colonel Matheson. "We have a photograph taken just before his jump and we matched the remains to his dental records."

"We're still continuing the dragnet. . . in case you're wrong?"

"Yes, sir, but it can't go on indefinitely. Talmadge is keeping a close watch on us. Even now, we risk provoking him."

"We wouldn't have to deal with assholes like Talmadge if McCord could see the greater good. Damn him! He never even wanted to believe in what we were trying to do. "The general brooded on that for a moment. "I suppose his will didn't leave anything of his technology to the government?"

"He divided up his assets between Kim Beliconti and the organization Greenpeace. In the end, he put his money where his mouth was, I suppose. Knowing this now, I don't think we helped our cause by our less-than-humanitarian methods." Matheson settled himself unbidden on the general's couch.

Magnuson jerked his head up in anger but thought twice before speaking. "That's irrelevant now, isn't it?"

The colonel nodded. Neither man was happy about the situation.

Chapter 18

The Cayman Islands glinted like jewels in the azure Caribbean, the sea aggressively carving a shimmering bay in the land. Gazing at the sparkling water, a tourist killed time, as cool morning trade winds ruffled his prematurely graying hair. Some early-rising native girls noted the physically fit man playing with his mustache. With a thoughtful expression, he checked his watch and proceeded toward an impressive building at the end of the walkway.

"Mr. Lepointe, it's good to see you again," said the sycophantic bank executive.

"Thank you. Did you receive my instructions?"

"Yes and they've already been executed, although I don't understand why you feel you must spread your assets out like this. Have our services been sub-par?"

"No, actually I've been quite pleased with your responsiveness. It's only that I anticipate some heavy traveling and will need funds readily accessible in various spots. Now, do you have the liquid assets ready here?"

"Certainly, Mr. Lepointe. If you'll just wait in my office, I'll attend to it. I won't be long, but please make yourself comfortable. My secretary will bring you anything you want."

Lepointe nodded and went into the executive's large office, which was appointed with expensive and comfortable furnishings. Sitting at the desk, he used the intercom to order a double espresso made from the local coffee beans. A very pretty secretary soon brought in a tray with the steaming cup. She smiled and left the tray on a coffee table nested among some sitting room chairs.

Lepointe walked over, picked up his cup and slouched down in the mini-sofa. He stretched out his long legs, sipped his coffee and scanned the magazines on the table. One of the cover headlines caught his eye.

"BILLIONAIRE ECOLOGIST DIES IN HANG GLIDING ACCIDENT"

The article described the irony of a man who stood for the natural order being killed due to it. *Couldn't have stated it better myself*, thought Hunter as he scratched his new mustache.

Hunter had thoroughly prepared for the day when he could not function using his own identity. He had used the persona of Monsieur Lepointe in past dealings with the Cayman banks, the new identity coming in handy now, considering Hunter's recent, untimely death. Even world class intelligence agents might envy him his ability to quickly abandon a persona and adopt a new one.

Reading more of the magazine article, he wanted to see how they accounted for the freak storm. Using the transmuter, Hunter had easily transformed the air molecules into water vapor, creating a low-pressure area dense with moisture-laden clouds. The real difficulty lay in obtaining and animating a dead body.

Posing as an agent of a medical school, Hunter purchased the body of a street person and then transformed it into an inert material. At the mountain's trolley stop, when he was out of sight of the others, he reconstituted the material into his own likeness. He'd maneuvered his glider and waved the cadaver's arms with remote controls. So they could identify him, McCord counterfeited his dental records to reflect those of his dead volunteer. All in all, the deception was a most spectacular one.

Doctor Spain looked out onto the busy sidewalk, absentmindedly appraising the brightly clad tourists. He generally appreciated the respite given him by appointment cancellations, but this time was something of an exception. Doctor Spain found himself inexplicably brooding over a patient, now deceased, who had said his name was James Hunter.

The billionaire ecologist headline confirmed McCord's death. Spain recalled the man vividly, in spite of their single, unrepeated meeting, having invested an emotional interest in him. Doctor Thomas Spain cared and had correctly feared for this man's future. Now, he preferred the distractions of working to have to mull over the patient's demise, even though he knew he'd eventually have to deal with his own feelings.

His amnesiac financier was a special man, who could have made a global difference given a longer life. Spain regretted the lost opportunity for him to make more progress on the man's unusual problem. A problem that had not been fully divulged to him, yet he was confident in his ability to have gotten at the truth. With Hunter dead, Spain knew this line of thinking was futile, but he couldn't let it go. *If only I'd had more time with him*, he thought, *maybe I could've prevented his death*. Hang gliding thrills! Why, with such a troubled mind, did he feel the need to pursue a sport that dangerous?

With an effort, he put the circumstances of the accident aside and considered his next appointment, glancing quickly at the list of people he was to see that day. He looked back to his desk clock and shook his head, since more time had passed than he had realized. As if on cue, the door opened and a tall gray haired man poked his head in.

"Your secretary was not at her desk, so I took the liberty of seeing myself in."

"That's fine, Mr. Lepointe. Please come in."

The well-dressed gentleman entered the room and gracefully seated himself with movements indicating a lithe fitness.

"Now, how can I help you?"

Lepointe drew out his wallet, opened it and showed the contents to Spain. Spain read it out loud. "Craig Lepointe, National Security Agency. Hmm, am I to understand then that you're not a paying customer?"

"'Fraid not, doctor, but I'll try not to take up too much of your time. Recently you counseled a man named James Hunter, is that correct?"

"Yes, that's correct," said the doctor suspiciously. "Is he in some sort of trouble?"

"No. At least not anymore. He's dead."

Spain tried to look surprised at the information.

The NSA man continued. "In life, he was known by other names and used several aliases. We believe he possessed knowledge vital to the nation's interests. We're now interviewing his last known contacts for anything that could lead us to this information."

"I don't know if I'd be much help to you on that score. I just tried to draw out some troublesome memories buried deep in his subconscious." Spain was more puzzled than ever about his former patient and somewhat annoyed by Lepointe's ploy to get in to see him.

"Well that may be useful in itself, doctor" replied Lepointe. "Did he reveal any of his other identities or who his associates were?"

"I'm sorry, Lepointe, but I can't help you with any of that."

"Mr. Spain, I don't think doctor/patient confidentiality applies here," said Lepointe with arrogant sarcasm, not even giving Spain the courtesy of his proper title.

"Let me put it to you this way, agent Lepointe, I wasn't lying before when I told you that all I did was help him remember his personal past. Furthermore, I do put my country before the well being of enemy spies, so trust me when I tell you that if he was an enemy of the U.S. he didn't reveal it to me." A grim smile appeared across Spain's face.

Lepointe looked skeptical.

"Fine, doctor," said Lepointe as he got up to leave. "Oh, one more thing. You may be contacted by some of our sister agencies, if you haven't heard from them already."

"You're the first government agent I've ever met. If and when any others come, they'll get the same answers." Spain's blood had begun to simmer at Lepointe's attitude toward him.

"That's what I wanted to hear, doctor. You've passed the test."

Spain looked at the man with distaste. "So you were testing me? To see what I knew?"

Lepointe laughed, which irked the doctor further. "No. To see if I could plant doubts in your mind about Hunter."

Now, Spain looked confused and Lepointe started to explain. "The mustache is real. I've got blue contacts on and I've dyed . .

. ."

"You son of a bitch," interrupted Spain as he recognized his entrepreneur patient. "You had me going." But Spain wasn't angry. His temper had turned to an inner relief. He got up and warmly clasped McCord/Lepointe's hand in a vigorous handshake.

"It's good to see you again, doctor."

"Likewise, but why this charade? Certainly you didn't go to all this trouble as a joke. You're hiding from someone, aren't you?"

"Yes. That's why I was hoping my disguise would fool you. I had to pass a test, too. I can't allow myself to be recognized." Hunter again sat in the plush, comfortable chair.

"Is the government really after you?" inquired Spain.

"Yes!" Hunter grimaced.

The doctor's happy countenance rapidly melted away, as he began to suspect paranoia in his patient. He considered the lengths McCord had gone to, to disguise himself. "Why?" he asked bluntly.

"They want something from me that I don't want to give up to them, a technology that has devastating military applications."

The doctor decided to assume for now that this technology was real. And if McCord actually was under government surveillance, that should become obvious, or so he deduced.

"Devastating military applications, from an individual? Is your technology something that's outlawed like biological or chemical weapons? Something you don't trust them with?" After all, McCord was the head of a large international corporation that could do a great deal with its research and development.

"No. I'll tell you all about it later," Hunter shook his head to redirect the conversation. "Right now I need your help on another front. I've decided I must have a friend I can take into my confidence and you seem like someone that I can trust."

"I appreciate your confidence, thank you uh . . . I don't even know your real name. What should I call you now?" asked Spain.

"I'm glad you asked," Hunter sighed. "It's critical that you call me Craig Lepointe exclusively from now on. I've completely divorced myself from the old identity, so that I could disappear."

"Did you divorce yourself of all that wealth, too?" asked Spain gravely.

"Yes, I had to, so my death would be convincing. Hunter McCord's estate is now mostly in the hands of Greenpeace, although I still retain a few paltry million." He smiled wryly.

The doctor just shook his head, recognizing this truth. "Hunter McCord was your real name?"

"Yes."

"Did you tell the woman who was working for you what you're doing?" He couldn't recall the name, but he remembered his patient caring for her.

"No. To tell her would place her in great danger as well. As a precaution, the Feds will watch her for a while, but when they realize she knows nothing, they'll tire of the surveillance."

"You think they didn't buy the story of your death?" Spain had fallen into his professional mode, although he refrained from jotting down notes in his usual fashion.

"They'll still actively pursue me for a while, in case my death was a hoax," stated McCord...Craig Lepointe. "But interest will evaporate if they find nothing. That's why these next few months are very dangerous for me. I can't afford any slip ups." His eyes met Spain's.

"You can rely on me, Craig," Spain responded with great sincerity. For some reason, he liked and trusted this man. "I'll do everything in my power to help you through this."

Craig nodded as the doctor speculated on Craig's mental well being. He decided to probe for clues of mental instability.

"You seem to be in remarkably good spirits," he observed. "Wasn't giving up the rewards of a lifetime's efforts difficult?"

"That's the least of my worries." Craig laughed. "Wealth is

cheap, given my technical knowledge. I'm sure I could rebuild it all again in a matter of a few years. What's more important to me now is discovering who I am completely."

Spain was pleased. "Then we're on the same wavelength. I'm curious about the real man myself. You probably want to go under again, don't you?"

"That's right, but first I think I should prepare you for something that may shock you." Craig leaned forward in the chair.

"You say that as if everything you've told me so far hasn't been shocking."

"Oh come now. I think you're up to it."

Spain wasn't sure of that. Most of his patients lacked the delusions he suspected Lepointe suffered from. In fact, the bulk of his practice dealt with helping retirees cope with their new found inactivity. Conversely, his latest patient presented an exciting if not disquieting puzzle. He'd had a nasty start when he thought the government was monitoring his patient load. With his mouth already dry from that nervous ordeal, he wanted a respite before his next surprise. "All right, but do you mind if my secretary brings us some iced coffee? She's probably back at her desk by now and I'm devilishly thirsty."

"Good idea. I could use some refreshment myself." Craig relaxed.

Thomas Spain pressed a button on his intercom. "Lisa?"

"Yes, doctor."

"Would you bring me and my guest some of that iced coffee please?"

"I'll be in, in a minute."

"Thank you."

He turned back to Lepointe who had a question for him. "Sounds young. She's new isn't she?"

"That's right. I'm afraid my other secretary, the one who was here the last time you were in, had a fatal car accident. She'd only been with me a month when a drunk driver ran her off the road." That had been a painful event for Spain, but more especially for the woman's new husband, whom he had spent time consoling.

"What about the other driver?"

"The drunk left the scene of the accident and they haven't found him yet. Lisa's just filling in temporarily, but she's so good I've asked her to stay on."

With that statement, Craig tensed his muscles nervously and Spain watched him carefully. Had that set off his patient's paranoid streak? What might he suspect from such a mundane, but sad event?

The door opened as the young woman entered. She walked forward and put a tray with two tall glasses of iced coffee on the desk. Containers of cream and sugar were efficiently placed near the glasses. Craig looked up and Spain saw a shift in his eyes, as if he knew this woman, which was, of course, completely impossible.

"Thank you, Lisa," said Spain as he nonchalantly spooned the sugar into his coffee.

"Anything else, doctor?" inquired the receptionist.

"No, I'm all set. How about you Craig? Would you like a snack or something to go with that?"

Craig glanced at Spain then looked the secretary straight in the eye. Spain was glad to see he wasn't shrinking from her.

"I had something before I came over," answered Craig. "The iced coffee should do fine by itself, thanks."

She nodded and left the room. Perhaps Spain himself was seeing too much in Craig's behavior. No, something was odd here.

"All right so what did you want to tell me that's so shocking," he asked.

Hunter/Lepointe looked at his watch. "Looks as if I'll have to take a rain check on this, Tom. I'll call to set up another appointment."

As he said this, Craig hastily scribbled something on a piece of paper, folded it and pushed it across the desk to a bewildered Thomas Spain. With a wink, Lepointe exited, leaving the psychiatrist pondering Craig's dramatic behavioral swing. He unfolded the paper and noted the peril in its message. Spain felt deep concern over this man who saw government conspiracies and enemies in every facet of his life. *The woman works for the government*, Craig had written. *I knew her as Lilah. Meet me tonight at Sagat's Point--10 p.m*

Chapter 19

The reborn Hunter McCord waited for Doctor Spain at the beach area. The ocean water reflected blackness as it stretched off to the distant horizon. One recognized its boundary there only because of a star-dense night sky. Conversely, white break water defined the ocean's shoreline. Someone approached. With keen night vision, Lepointe penetrated the dark silhouette to identify his newfound friend.

Thomas Spain struggled as he plowed through the sand. He would have parked his car closer, if not for the cliff that separated the beach from the road. As it was, he trekked parallel to the shore for some distance to meet Lepointe and, although not a heavy man, each step taxed his aged legs. *For Christ's sakes, McCord,* he thought, *why this place for a meeting?* The note had been explicit, however, directing him to this location at this time, and he'd had no opportunity to argue.

Thinking of the mystery of McCord's behavior, though, Spain quickened his pace to satisfy his curiosity. Despite the dark, he made out the red and white flag pole that indicated the boundary of the public beach. Soon after, he saw the outline of a man against the occasional white of the surf.

"Glad you could make it, Tom," said Craig before Spain's eyes could adjust to the darkness.

"You better have a damn good reason for this, Lepointe. I think I'm having a heart attack," said Spain trying to regain his breath.

Craig just smiled.

"I've got a good reason all right. One that might just save your life."

The doctor became silent and listened.

"I know your secretary. She looks somewhat different and is using another name, but I do know her."

A conspiracy in every facet of this man's life, thought Spain. "You're afraid she recognized you?"

"It's a lot more than that. She works for military intelligence."

"What?"

"I strongly suspect that your previous secretary's accident was not so accidental."

"You mean Lisa murdered her?" That was quite a complex story this multi-named man had thought up.

"I don't know if I can say that. But she's capable of it."

The doctor stared seaward, trying to digest this information. Spain couldn't even imagine Lisa Peterson uttering a curse word, never mind killing someone. He certainly hadn't bargained for this intrigue. Paranoid delusion? he pondered. Lepointe seemed to be living quite a self-created fantasy.

Craig continued . "We met at a government complex, top secret. There, the military tried to convince me to cooperate with them. Lisa was there but under a different name, Lilah Petrov. She's dangerous, Tom, to me and you."

"So do you think she recognized you?" repeated Spain.

"I don't think so, but I don't want to risk dying to find out." Lepointe turned and looked out to sea.

"What do you suggest?" probed Spain.

"Find a good excuse to fire her, for one. Then I don't know. If the government knows I'm still alive, I'll have to disappear again."

Up on the cliff, a pair of futuristic goggles peered over the edge. Spain and Lepointe appeared in the ghostly blue-green hues of a night vision scope. The wearer also aimed a directional microphone at the pair, but couldn't pick up their voices over the ocean's roar.

Lisa Peterson entered the doctor's office as she did every morning to drop off the mail.

"Lisa, would you sit down please?" he asked.

Without a word, she sat and assumed an attentive posture. Thomas Spain knew his embarrassment showed.

"I may as well get right to the point. Lisa, have you ever met

Craig Lepointe before?"

She sat there with a quizzical look. "No, doctor. Why do you ask?"

"He thought he recognized you from somewhere else."

"I'd remember a handsome man like that," she said shyly.

Spain smiled. "You're sure you've never met him?"

"Well at least not that I can remember. I could be wrong, I suppose. Now you've got me curious. When he comes in again I could talk with him to try and find out. When's his next appointment?" A meek smile tried to cover over her sudden alertness.

"He doesn't have one."

"Maybe I can look him up and figure it out," she suggested. "Where does he live?"

Strange that she would become that interested. "I don't think that'll be necessary, Miss Peterson. Thank you for your help. I'm sure you want to get back to your routine."

She made no attempt to leave. Spain sensed a tense silence. "Is there something else?"

Lisa just shook her head negatively and reached behind her under her suit jacket. She produced a gun and aimed it him. "Why all this interest in Mr. Lepointe, Thomas? He was disturbed to see me, wasn't he, doctor?"

Craig must be right about her. I've screwed up badly.

Lisa speculated out loud. "Now why would someone who's never met me be upset to see me? No one would unless, of course, he had dealt with me before. May I infer doctor, that Craig Lepointe is really Hunter McCord?"

His blood ran cold but he tried not to give anything away by his facial expression. "You can infer whatever you like while I call the police." Spain reached for the telephone but it shattered within six inches of his grip. He recoiled so violently from the explosion that he fell off his chair.

"I'm not a patient woman, Doctor Spain. Answer my question, please."

"I've never heard of Hunter McCord."

"I'll take a finger for that, Thomas," she threatened as she aimed the gun at Spain's hand.

Something in her peripheral vision seemed to stop her. Doctor Spain was also surprised by the intrusion. McCord/Lepointe came out from behind a curtain with a device in his hand that wasn't a gun. Lisa turned, aimed again, and fired. Nothing happened. She threw down the gun on the floor, where it bounced several times as if it had been transformed into rubber. Resignedly, she dropped her hands by her sides. Craig/Hunter walked over to her, gestured her up and frisked her.

"Enjoying yourself, Hunter?"

"Sure am and the name is Craig, Madame."

"Oh come off it. More than a new look is required to make an effective disguise." She gave him a withering glance.

"You should know shouldn't you, Lilah," Craig said as he continued to probe down to the miniskirt part of her business suit.

"You won't find any other weapons on me," she told him sharply.

"Who said I'm looking for weapons?" asked Craig with an impish smile. "Actually, I'm more concerned about bugs. I went to a lot of trouble to throw you people off. I don't want to give myself away if I don't have to."

"You people? The military has no idea where you are. I found you myself."

"How did you do it, Lilah, if that really is your name?"

She smiled and removed her blond wig, revealing her natural brunette hair matted down. "Sometimes you talk in your sleep. And it's Lisa Peterson, really."

Was it possible? Had he betrayed himself in his sleep? He looked at Spain who was taking all this in.

"I said I'd go to Jupiter, Florida?"

"Not exactly. We knew about your Jupiter estate. What the

Army didn't know is that Jupiter is your favorite place for healing. Sunny days, East Coast, bits and pieces you'd mutter at night after your injections. I gambled that you meant Florida and would go there where a noted psychiatrist just happened to have a practice nearby."

Hunter didn't know he'd had a Jupiter estate, till this moment.

"Very good. Now if you're not here for the military, what do you want?"

She stared at him for a moment before answering. "I want to help you."

"You want to help me? You would have shot me a few moments ago." He was startled by her declaration.

"I would've shot what looked like the gun of someone who was sneaking up on me," she countered.

"And the doctor who was protecting the location of his friend?"

"Shooting him? That was a bluff." She shrugged and smiled prettily at Spain.

"All right, let's assume that you're telling the truth, why would you want to help me?" Craig dropped into the other visitor's chair beside her.

"Because now I know why you didn't cooperate. And I agree with you." Her face reflected deep conviction.

"And how do you know why I won't deal with the general?"

"Because I have videotapes of your incarceration."

Craig sat spellbound watching himself in a nightmarish drama on the VCR at his apartment. This tape provided by Lisa, who sat nearby, showed excerpts of his capture before the Old West sting operation. He saw himself sitting in a chair in a stark room, obviously drugged and under interrogation.

"How do you transmute objects, Mr. McCord?"

McCord didn't answer. He remained completely stoic, fighting the drug's influence.

"All right, let's try something easier. How did you learn to transmute?"

Still no reaction.

"What was your great grandfather's name?"

"Ian McCord."

The interrogator turned to the camera. "He will answer any question except those concerning the specifics of transmutation."

"Keep trying," said a voice off the screen.

"Ian McCord discovered the process of transmutation, correct?"

"Yes."

"How did he do that?"

No answer.

"Was the process a chemical one?"

No answer. Now the questioner asked something for the first time.

"Could you recreate the circumstances of the original discovery?"

"Yes."

That answer was the seed that had spawned the Old West re-creation, thought Craig. The voice of a fourth person came from off-screen.

"That's enough. This has gone on much too long and is getting us nowhere. We need a different angle. Take him to his quarters."

The interrogator gently took McCord by the elbow and started to guide him out of the room. In that instant, McCord snapped out of his trance and struck the man in the jaw with his elbow. The sickening thunk of bone against jaw dropped the questioner to the floor. Lastly, the camera showed Hunter running up to it before it went black.

Now, his dream about the helicopter chase made sense to him. Those events had happened immediately after this video was made and sometime before his awakening in the desert. He turned off the VCR and stared into space. He knew they'd manipulated him, but seeing it like this fanned his rage. McCord craved revenge, but exercised iron control to plan an escape without rash actions.

He turned to Lisa, who sat on the couch with her legs curled under her. Seeing her like that, he experienced deja vu and it broke his concentration. Something about her manner again suggested someone else in Craig's past, someone whom he'd been very close to. He shook his head to clear the thought.

"So how are you going to help me?" he asked.

"General Magnuson thinks you're dead, but he's still searching for you in case your death was a set up. He'll have to act quickly, though, because Senator Talmadge is making things hot for him with the president. I'm going to try and steer you out of harm's way, so to speak, until the dragnet lets up." His eyes searched her face for signs of deception.

"I still don't understand why you're helping me. Why are you willing to stick your neck out?"

She shrugged. "I guess your case has become personal with me now."

"Why?"

"My family has a gripe against the government." Her voice filled with feeling.

"What does that have to do with anything?"

"Shut up for a minute and I'll tell you."

She took a deep breath before starting. A memory seemed to be causing her some anguish. "At first, we thought that our family was cursed or we were the victims of some real bad luck. It was cancer. All kinds--leukemia, Hodgkin's disease, tumors everywhere. Cancer killed my cousins and my brothers. Almost killed me, but I survived it and the treatment. Then we realized a bizarre coincidence. Other families were stricken the way we were, but mostly those in Nevada. Something was wrong and we sought answers. We formed a support group and petitioned the government about suspected nuclear-weapons testing. After some hedging, they revealed documented cases of cancer as a result of such testing. They admitted their guilt and offered reparations. But suffice it to say that the money didn't ease the pain of our losses." She paused for a minute and looked at him, but he almost felt as if she didn't see him.

"So you see," she went on, "I had a personal interest in the mission. The idea of rendering radioactive waste inert and saving future generations helped me cope with my own losses in a positive way. And working toward that helped me reconcile with the government. But then I discovered I was lied to. Being around the decision makers, I was privy to certain information. They told you the reason they wanted the transmutation technology was to render radioactive waste inert, right?" This time her gaze connected with him directly.

Here it comes, thought McCord. "Right," he agreed.

"Well that's only part of the plan. They also want to use the technology to neutralize any military opposition in future conflicts. They've arranged a program to modify the shuttle to carry a large scale version of your transmuter."

"In other words an offensive weapon." Validation was sweet though the cause was so entirely sour.

"Exactly."

"You know I really wanted to believe them. That mankind had matured enough to handle this responsibility. Now it appears as if I was right in the first place." Craig looked thoughtful for a moment.

"Is it safe to go back to doctor Spain?" And could he trust her? Her story was certainly a convincing one. And if she was still with the government, why would she have confessed their terrible plan?

"Yes, it should be. I'm the only one who knew about him. You're using him to recover your memory, right?" Her look was one of sympathy.

"That's right," he concurred.

"What if they had an antidote for the drug treatments we gave you. I might be able to get it for you." She seemed to be thinking of the `how.'

"A nice idea, if I could get my system to accept it."

Lisa looked puzzled, so Craig explained. "My body has a peculiar resistance to drug compounds. It rejects them, sometimes violently. That's why the military's truth serums didn't work on me. When they tried the genetically engineered drug, they were apparently only partially successful, since I started to remember before I was supposed to. Now that I think about it, I count myself lucky that I didn't suffer some sort of brain damage." He shook his head in disgust at their careless treatment of him. "Anyway, I have no doubt that I'll eventually remember everything. But re-creating my oldest memories will take time."

"So you don't even want to explore the possibility?" She seemed disappointed--either because she truly wanted to help, or because another government scheme was in the works for her to carry through.

"For my particular body chemistry, the risk of an adverse reaction outweighs the advantage. I think I'll stick with non-substance-oriented remedies for now." He looked carefully to see her reaction.

"Of course it's up to you, but I'd at least like to find out if it exists." He wasn't sure what to make of her statement.

"I'd rather you didn't. If you were found out, they would discover me by manipulating you. It's just too dangerous for both of us." He'd trust her for now, but keep his eyes open. He needed Spain.

"Fine. So what the hell are you going to do?"

"I'm going to see my doctor." He could at least trust one person in this world, aside from Kim, whom he didn't want to endanger.

Chapter 20

"That bitch was going to shoot off my fingers. You don't actually trust her, do you?" said an indignant Thomas Spain.

"She said she was bluffing." Craig/Hunter gestured in dismissal of the question.

"And you believe her? You're not that naive."

"Speaking of trust, do you believe me now?"

"I suppose I deserve that, but put yourself in my position. Here comes a guy, who I hardly know, telling me the government is after him and my secretary is a spy." Spain smiled, thinking of his original reaction.

And Craig Lepointe laughed out loud. "I don't blame you one bit. I was just having some fun with it."

"You knew I didn't believe you?" Spain's jaw actually dropped.

"I was encouraged that you didn't. Any professional worth his salt would have been skeptical. That's why I covered my bets after I told you about Lisa Peterson, a.k.a. Lilah Petrov. I was always nearby." Lepointe crossed his legs and relaxed back in the doctor's guest chair.

"So now I'm predictable. Well, fine. Predictability may have saved my life."

"You don't buy her goodwill story, I know, but consider this. She hasn't brought the whole U.S. Army down on me, has she?" While Spain struggled to issue a biting retort, Lepointe continued. "Now don't get me wrong, I think we should certainly exercise caution. I'd just like to give her the benefit of the doubt. For now, anyway."

"What do you mean we should exercise caution? You don't expect me to keep her on as my secretary?" The older man looked as if he had bitten into something sour.

"You know, she's typing her resignation letter right now. She didn't want to threaten you. It's the only way she knows," Lepointe said soothingly.

"Oh and that's supposed to make everything all right? I just don't trust her. You shouldn't risk trusting her, either."

"What do you suggest I do? Kill off Lepointe? Disappear again?" Craig Lepointe sighed wearily.

"Why not?" asked Spain, as if switches of identity were an everyday occurrence.

"For one thing, it's a hell of a lot of work to set up a new persona with sufficient funds at my disposal. Two, I wouldn't have the luxury of returning here and dealing with you. Three, how do I know she'd be convinced of my next death? It's no good. I'll have to deal with her now." He understood full well that the government could have its spy cameras and spies in place, set in motion by Lisa.

"Okay, Okay. I see your point."

"Don't worry, I'll try to minimize my risks. Now with that aside may we continue my therapy?" The sense of need to find out about his past pressed in on him.

"I suppose." Then Spain leaned over his desk to emphasize his next point.

"But before we go any further, I want to know what this is all about. What've you got that military intelligence is willing to kill for?"

Craig pulled the transmuter out of his deep jacket pocket.

"A fancy dust buster? You've got to be kidding." Spain fell back into his chair in disbelief.

"Remember Lisa's gun? It didn't fire when she aimed it at me. This is why. Watch closely." Craig took a pencil off the desk, aimed the device at it and handed it to Spain. Thomas remarked in surprise at the weight. "You now have a pencil genuinely made of lead."

Spain dropped it on his glass topped desk. The pencil made a clanking noise before coming to rest. Craig aimed again as Spain came to the edge of his seat.

"Now it's platinum." The silvery color seemed to confirm his statement. Aiming one more time, the entire pencil turned to gold.

"Jesus!" stated Spain as he jerked back into his swivel chair.

He probably wanted to say more but couldn't seem to come up with the words. "Jesus!" escaped from his lips again.

Craig took advantage of Spain's stunned attentiveness and went on to explain the Army's sting operation.

"My god, this technology is a hundred and fifty years old?" Hunter watched Spain trying to process the bizarre news.

"Apparently my great, great grandfather was way ahead of his time. . . and ours." Hunter picked up the pencil and examined it himself. No surprises there. Gold. Pure gold.

"I'll bet some greedy bastard is trying right now to convert some crap to precious metals. You know the biggest threat here isn't military," declared Spain. "It's economic. I'm not sure I'd be so calm with the technology in their hands."

"Relax, they have the equipment not the technology." Hunter smiled at Spain's reaction.

"How long do you think it will take them to figure it out?"

"A lot longer than they have the research money for" said Hunter with assurance. "That's actually the least of my worries. But now I have to tell you something that might shock you."

"Shock me?" said the doctor with mock seriousness.

Craig grinned, acknowledging how silly his statement must sound. "I know. It sounds ridiculous after what you've already heard, but wait. The best is yet to come."

"I was afraid you were going to say something like that."

"Do you believe in reincarnation? I think I've remembered some things from previous lifetimes."

People clad in black arrived in one horse drawn carriage after the other. The sun beat through an overcast sky, still gray from an earlier rainstorm. With grim expressions, the women shuffled along over muddy grass while clutching their parasols. Their long dresses presented the tedious problem of keeping the hems from dipping in the puddles. Rims of some of the men's top hats dripped captured rain. Lately, rainy days abounded even for San Francisco. The entire globe had experienced unusually dank weather due to the recent cataclysmic explosion. Even the fastest steamships had struggled through rough seas, barely making it in time for the services.

As the mourners reached the grave site, bagpipes wailed their sad lament. Some onlookers shed tears.

After the ceremonies, many noticed a stranger among them who watched the proceedings with emotionless interest. The crowd shunned him. He, the estranged son, had made a special effort to attend his father's funeral. Accepting the adulations of the deceased gracefully, he continued to present a stout, unwavering expression. Like his father, he possessed a strong jaw. The undeniable family resemblance allayed the suspicions that had preceded his arrival. They had whispered that the so-called `long lost son' was only some charlatan, here to usurp an old man's fortune.

"With this business concluded, I must return to Phoenix," the young stranger repeated to the few who inquired. The will bequeathed the whole estate to him and since he apparently was the only child of a somewhat reclusive father, he found the disposition of the estate uncontested. *Must not gloat*, he thought. He hid his joy with great aplomb, an attitude that met with the approval of those attending the reading after the funeral. After dispersing the lingering well-wishers, the son proceeded to his waiting carriage. The driver, following instructions, whisked him off to the busy train station.

At sunset, he boarded the train for his journey home. *The sun still sets in that ruddy hue out here*, he noted. Damn catastrophe was halfway around the world and nearly two years ago. *If it's like that here, I wonder what the Indonesians see? Or do they care after the thousands of deaths. I wish it didn't have to be that way. No sense grieving, though.*

He proceeded to his private drawing room where his bed had been pulled down by the porter and a bottle of champagne chilled in anticipation. The corners of his mouth curled up slightly at the thought of the casket being lowered reverentially into the ground. The doting well wishers hadn't even guessed at his true nature. Smugly, he prepared for the arrival of a young lady whom he'd met earlier. His new life was going to be a good one, just as the last one had.

Hunter snapped out of his hypnotic state with a startling realization. He was the stranger in the scenario, the long lost son who felt smug over his father's funeral. What kind of man was he? How the hell could he remember such things? He went to a mirror on the opposite wall and studied his own reflection.

"Could I be imagining all this?" he asked aloud to no one in particular.

"Yes," responded Doctor Spain.

Craig had forgotten he wasn't alone and jumped at the sound of the familiar voice.

"Sorry to startle you."

"Forget it, doc. Did you hear what I saw?"

"I believe so and probably more than you recall."

"Well, what do you think?"

"I think you believe you've been reincarnated several times."

"And you don't think so?" asked Craig, seeking relief, reassurance.

"No," said Spain without hesitation.

"Why not?" Craig said, slightly agitated.

"I don't believe in reincarnation. No proof whatsoever in all of human history shows us reincarnation is real."

"Then how can I remember things that happened before I was born?" Craig demanded.

"Neither of us knows these things really happened. You could've been remembering TV shows for all we know. Craig, you are an amazing man who happens to be humanity's sole keeper of an astonishing secret. A secret that could devastate the entire planet. That's a lot of pressure for anyone to bear. How does the mind handle such a responsibility?"

This statement took the wind out of Craig's sails. Again, he felt as he had when he had been in the Old West, confused about who he really was. This time was worse, however, since he thought he'd been making progress rediscovering himself.

The doctor apparently recognized that his friend was crestfallen. "Believe it or not, this is still good news," the doctor lied. "You are remembering something."

Craig could almost read the doctor's thoughts. He was wondering about Craig's ability to differentiate between fantasy and reality. Government agents after a new technology? That might be one thing but reincarnation was stretching it.

"I'd like to check this out. Maybe we could confirm some of the details from my visions," Craig insisted. "I know you're not sanguine about this and I don't blame you. All I'm asking is that you take notes on any details I tell you when I'm under. I'll do the research to check them out."

"This seems to be important to you, so of course I'll help you," Spain agreed, "but I must warn you your research could be a dead end. I want you to be prepared for that disappointment."

"I understand."

"All right then, let's try to get some verifiable details, shall we? Your last submersion didn't give us much."

"True, but we do know my memory or vision took place in San Francisco circa 1890, if I can judge by the clothing styles. Maybe we can try to get some more out of that image."

The drawn shades darkened the room and Craig was again in a subconscious realm. Thomas Spain tried to re-invoke the time period from Lepointe's last session.

"What year is it?" asked the doctor of the unconscious Craig.

Craig hesitated, trying to pry the information from the depths of his memory.

"I don't know."

"Look around you, what do you see?"

Thomas Spain could tell that Craig was looking around the scene via his mind's eye.

"It's nighttime on a beach. A ship is anchored offshore. Steam is coming out of its stack. I think it just got here or is preparing to leave. The beach is lit up with torches on long bamboo rods stuck into the sand."

Craig raised his hand to run his fingers through his hair. "It's windy out. Coming off the sea, blowing inland. Kind of cold for the tropics actually. Could be a storm brewing."

He turned his head around, scanning the office--or, more precisely, his vision of an alleged other lifetime. He was really involved now in what he was seeing.

"I love the colorful foliage here. See how it rustles in the breeze, waving its rainbow blossoms in the torchlight? Sweet scent. The wind has blown some of flowers onto the sand. It's a shame I have to be back in Phoenix by August."

Thomas Spain perked up at the time reference.

"August of what year?"

"1883."

Excellent, thought the doctor. Now at least they had a frame of reference to verify any facts from. He continued to probe. "Is anybody with you?"

"Yes. A large group. They look like dark-skinned Orientals."

"Describe them. What are they doing?"

"They're just standing around looking up at the sky, afraid. Fear is in all their faces. I don't know why. Their clothes are scanty and ragged, but clean. Probably fishermen."

"What?"

"They're fisherman. It's so obvious to me now. They live off the sea. Some Polynesian-style pontoon boats with nets are sitting on the shore. Some are half in the water, bobbing in the surf. Looks as if the tide came in pretty quick. Even some of the torches are in the waves now. I can see their lights reflecting off the water. Somebody better get those boats to higher ground, if they want them for tomorrow." Craig hesitated as if continuing his surveillance of the beach. "Wow!" he said.

"What is it?"

"The wind has really picked up. Some of the torches have blown out. Women and children are scurrying back to their huts. Must be a typhoon or something. Maybe that's why everybody's looking at the sky."

Craig looked at the ceiling in the doctor's office. His mouth fell open, as if in shocked surprise. "Holy Christ!"

"What do you see, Craig?"

"It's not nighttime at all. We're in the shadow of some gigantic black cloud. It extends from the sea to halfway over the island. Behind me, I can see clear sky and it's in daylight. What the . . . ?"

He looked at his outstretched palm fingering it with his other hand. "Ash! White ash is falling from the sky. It's a volcano. Somewhere there's been a massive eruption."

He looked over his shoulder and spoke to someone.

"What is it?" he asked of no one in the room.

Spain noted that Craig was acting out some scene from inside his own head. He was impressed that the account was being told from Craig's point of view, as if he'd really been there. Could it be?

"Yes, I see it." Lepointe was staring at the doctor's office wall now and for the first time with an expression of fear. "Quickly, everyone off the beach!" he shouted. "Now," he reinforced, "if you want to save your lives."

Spain winced at the raised voice. Briefly, he wondered if the other tenants in the building had heard Craig yelling.

"What's the matter?" asked the doctor, but was cut short by Craig rising from his chair and trying to run.

"Craig, stop!" commanded Spain, as he also got out of his chair. "You're back in the present! We're not in danger."

Craig stopped and stood still.

"Sit down, please, Mr. Lepointe."

When Craig was seated again, the doctor also sat back down. "No harm will come to you. You are merely an observer. Do you understand?"

"Yes."

"Do you feel comfortable enough to go back?"

"Yes."

"OK, the sky is dark and the wind has picked up. You've looked up to discover the dark cloud and decided a volcano has erupted. Someone has directed your attention elsewhere. What do you see?"

Craig wrestled with his emotions, trying to answer but still wasn't quite able.

"You're in no danger," the doctor reinforced.

The statement affected Craig. Apparently, he trusted the doctor since he immediately calmed down.

"It's the shoreline."

"What about it?"

"It's receded."

"You mean like low tide?"

"No. The tide was never this low. The fisherman's traps are exposed and the steamship is almost on it's side."

Thomas was confused.

"This is the precursor of a tidal wave. Stupid people! Don't they realize? They're going down to the water. Hey! Get the hell away from there. Damn it! It's no use. They either can't hear or are ignoring me. Too late to get them, I've got to get out of here if I'm going to save myself."

He paused as if straining to hear something. "Do you hear that? Sounds like thunder but I don't see any lightning."

Then the doctor noticed Craig's eyes widening.

"By the great lost empire! Have you ever seen anything like that?" He arched his head as if looking at something tall in the distance.

"It's got to be at least a hundred feet high to be seen from here. Even here the roar is deafening. Got to start for the high ground. Hurry. "

"What is it, an eruption?"

"No, damn it! Can't you see? Look at the horizon. It's like a moving mountain of water. The lowlands aren't going to stand much of a chance when it hits. Come on with me. We'll try to climb to the top of that hill." Craig's breathing accelerated, as if he were running, though he sat in his chair. His legs jiggled, however, as his breathing increased.

Spain surmised that Lepointe now included him in the disaster being played out in his mind. He was talking to Spain as if the doctor were actually there with him.

"How you doing? Need any help?" His face was red with effort and he continued to huff as his eyes blinked, and sweat poured down his ruddy face.

"No, I'm fine," responded the doctor.

Craig climbed as fast as he could. The ground raced past his vision, until he encountered loose earth at a steep angle. He looked behind him and was surprised to find his elderly friend keeping up. *He must be in pretty good shape, but I think we can afford a moment's rest.* He slowed and, turning around completely, he saw the enormity of the wave nearly filling the horizon from left to right. He felt like an insect who had strayed too close to a dangerous surf.

The natives, exploring the temporarily exposed land, now realized their life-threatening mistake. They ran back from the shore, but they were already too late. Some knew this and just stared at the instrument of their impending deaths. Was their refusal to run stoic defiance, or Oriental fatalism? No time to consider that now.

"We've got another fifty feet of tough climbing. Let's get going," yelled Craig above the sound of the roaring surf.

The gravel gave way under his grasping hands and feet. The effort was like swimming against the tide. The old man tried the climb but was too spent from his previous exertions to keep up. He sat where they'd rested, leaving his fate to chance.

"I'll try to lower a vine when I get to the top," shouted Craig.

He estimated thirty feet to go. He had to reach the top in time to help the old man. He heard the wave approaching. *Can't waste time turning around.* Hands and legs pumped like a machine, until, finally, the top of the hill appeared.

As he pulled himself up and over, he noticed the dark mass swirling in the sky beginning to thin out and disperse. The sun penetrated the cloud cover, the light streaming through in several mini sunbursts. *I've been too busy to notice. The light should help me find some vines though.*

He glanced back at the rampaging mountain of water and then forced himself to look away. The sight of all that power threatened to mesmerize him. Its height almost rivaled that of the hill he stood upon but as the wave approached the shallows, the crest of the of the tsunami started to topple over. Soon, tons of angry white water would pound the island, leveling the native's huts. Those people not crushed would surely drown.

Christ, where's that vine? Miraculously, Craig spied a length of rope out of the corner of his eye. Quickly, he scooped it up, looped it around a palm tree for leverage and lowered the rest to his friend.

"Tie it around your waist!" he yelled.

Craig saw the island bisect the wave, which tried to engulf the land as it came on. Reaching the shore, the surge toppled over itself, losing the towering height it had gained in the ocean depths. The water smashed against the bottom of the cliff, sending shock waves through the ground, staggering Craig. He retained his balance, however, and hauled on the rope as fast as he could. *Damned thing is double crested.* The second wave rode the level of the water left behind by the first wave. Craig realized this one would challenge even the hilltop as his arms ached from pulling on the rope.

I've got to get the old man up. Looking over his shoulder and down, he saw the colossus bearing down on the man he was trying to save. He tried to force himself to look back at the tree and exert more pulling force, but was unable to look away. The next few seconds passed in slow motion, as he watched the cascading water fall with tons of force toward the helpless elder. The white water impacted the cliff up high again, rocking Craig where he stood. He held on, while still looking over his shoulder to see his friend engulfed in white churning foam. Where was he? Craig waited for the water to subside, whereupon he spotted a prostrate form at the end of the rope, not ten feet below the top of the hill. Was he dead or alive? Finally, a hint of motion--or was it just the rope swaying? The old man looked up, battered and bruised, but grinning at the same time.

Craig Lepointe emerged from his vision mentally exhausted, yet feeling strangely unburdened.

"How are you?" asked Spain.

"Pretty good, actually."

"That was quite an experience you just had. And I must admit that it seemed as if you were there. The event was all told through your point of view."

"Did you get any verifiable facts to check on?" Craig asked eagerly.

"Historical ones, nothing personal."

"So now you're saying I was imagining from a history book."

"I'm not saying anything, yet. I'll reserve judgment until I can check this out first." Thomas Spain held up a pad of paper covered with notes.

Chapter 21

Planning his library research, Spain thought the alleged calamity Craig described in Indonesia sounded noteworthy enough to have been well documented. He had a year and a general location to work with.

"Excuse me," he asked the librarian, "where do I find information on natural disasters in the 1880s?"

"Are you looking for something specific?" returned the middle-aged woman.

"Yes, but I don't know what. I'm counting on recognizing it if I see it."

"Can you give me any specifics I can work with?" She seemed eager to help.

"I know it happened in Indonesia in 1883. I think it involved a volcanic eruption and or a tidal wave." He looked around, as if his eyes could spot the right book on their own.

"Krakatoa," said the librarian, with a pleased smile.

"What?" He glanced back at her.

"It's Krakatoa you're looking for. You can find it in the . . . ."

She didn't have time to finish her answer, before the doctor was off to conduct his own search for the now-named disaster. *Krakatoa*, he thought, *why didn't I recognize it before? I've heard of it.* Finding the correct shelves, he picked the appropriate books and staked out a table where he could sit and read.

Krakatau (or Rakata in the native tongue) is a volcanic island between Sumatra and Java in the Sunda Strait. It was the site of the largest explosion in recorded history. On August 27, 1883 the third of four explosive eruptions could be heard at a distance of 3,000 miles.

The doctor skipped over the details of death and destruction, looking for the follow-up effects.

Tidal waves as high as 120 feet decimated the nearby islands as well as the adjacent coasts of Sumatra and Java. The material made airborne by the blasts is estimated to be 5 cubic miles. A gigantic dark cloud resulted from the eruption and rained ash on the local islands. After ten days the ash had encircled the earth, causing climactic changes. Twelve months after the fact, weather bureaus still reported red sunsets . . .

"Red sunsets!" said the doctor out loud, causing heads to turn.

He flipped back through his notebook to one of his earlier sessions with Craig. He found what he was looking for. Craig had said that the rays of the setting sun in San Francisco still had a ruddy hue from the recent catastrophe near Indonesia.

Several hours later, Thomas Spain put the book down with an awed expression. Craig had described every detail of the disaster with accuracy and great personal feeling. *Can one get that kind of perspective just by reading historical accounts? I've just read the story of Krakatoa. How do I feel? Certainly impressed but not moved as though I'd lived the experience.*

What he had found in the book still wasn't an incontrovertible demonstration, but the circumstantial evidence was mounting to support Craig's claims of reincarnation. Spain thought the best way to get proof absolute would be to bring Craig closer to the present in his visions. Then, he could interview him about personal interactions and possibly confirm the details with any individuals who might still be alive.

Thomas Spain, noticeably excited, greeted Craig Lepointe at the door. Armed with several hours of library research, Spain could show that Craig was at least an accomplished student of history.

"Craig, I've confirmed the details of your last session. I must admit you do have a very empathic feel for this period of history," Spain began cautiously.

Craig just nodded.

"I think I've figured a way for us to prove conclusively whether you've experienced past lifetimes, as you think. All we have to do is find a piece of personal history to confirm the theory. It has to be something that isn't written down.

Something that somebody knows who lived during one of your lifetimes and who is still alive today. So let's try to get you to a point in this session that is closer to our own time and . . . ."

"That won't be necessary, doctor," said Craig vacantly.

Spain felt a deep shock at Craig's sudden change of heart. "Why not?" he protested.

"Because I'm not reincarnated."

To Thomas Spain's surprise, he was actually disappointed at that admission. Throughout his research, he had become more comfortable with the possibility of reincarnation. "What have you remembered?"

"I remembered that those memories are legitimate but not because of reincarnation."

"Then what?" Spain brushed off his sense of having been let down and focused on Craig,

"What I'm about to tell you is even a bigger pill to swallow than reincarnation." Craig gave the doctor a grim look.

"You're never at a loss for surprises, are you? All right, then, what is it?" The doctor felt as if he'd ridden up and down on the crest of a tidal wave himself in the last week or so.

Craig struggled for words, but the doctor interrupted him first. "You're not going to tell me you lived then, are you?"

The look that Craig returned proved that this was exactly what he had been going to say.

Spain chuckled a bit. "Don't be ridiculous. Next, you'll be telling me you're immortal or something." The doctor had let his emotions run away with him. This wasn't the face to show a man possibly struggling with mental illness. He regained his sobriety.

"Tom, I have no doubt in my mind that I've lived at least since the days of the Western frontier," announced Craig.

"You realize that's not possible, don't you? You're confusing your incarceration with the real thing," Spain gently suggested.

"It's not possible for a normal human being, no."

"Oh? And you're not a normal human being, then?" Spain

approached this carefully, not allowing his voice to be judgmental or sarcastic.

"Well, obviously not, since I've lived this long." Craig leaned back in the well padded chair, as if he were weary beyond belief.

The doctor just looked at Craig, trying to evaluate him.

Craig sat up and went on. "I can prove that I'm not a normal human being."

"All right, prove it then," suggested Spain. But he worried that if he crushed Lepointe's delusion, the man's mental house of cards could come crashing down.

"Do you have a thermometer?" asked Craig.

Spain got up went into the bathroom off the office, searched in the medicine chest, and returned with the device.

"What's the normal body temperature of a human being?" Craig asked.

"Ninety-eight point six degrees Fahrenheit but it can vary by a degree or two from individual to individual. It wouldn't mean anything if that's what you're going to show me." Spain wanted to be direct and honest with Craig, yet respectful of his possible fragility.

Craig placed the thermometer in his mouth. After a minute, he took it out and handed it to the doctor. Spain looked at it and then at Lepointe.

"Would you open your mouth, please?" asked the doctor.

Craig complied, and Spain examined the interior.

"Let's go for another minute," said the doctor as he placed the thermometer back in his patient's mouth.

The time elapsed and Thomas Spain reexamined the device.

"Still eighty-nine degrees, Tom?"

Spain remained silent, staring at the digital device, as if trying to fathom a magic trick.

"I know you're a doctor of the mind, Tom, but I think you also know what condition I'd be in if I were a normal human being with that body temperature."

"You'd be dying," said Spain, without hesitation.

"Want some more proof?" Craig challenged.

Spain looked up. Craig went over to a bookshelf and randomly picked one out. He then turned off all the lights and closed the shades on the windows. "I will now read the text from this book in the dark," he told Spain.

He read part of a psychology journal aloud. After a couple of paragraphs, he opened up the shades, turned on the lights and handed the book to the doctor for verification. His reading had been accurate.

"I have better than average night vision," he said. Then he took a letter opener and inflicted a long cut on his forearm before Spain could jump up and stop him.

Spain went wide eyed. "What the hell are you trying to do, kill yourself?"

"Just more proof."

"I'll get a wrapping of some kind." Spain was upset, to say the least.

"Don't bother, doctor. Look." The blood flow was already stemmed." In a few hours the cut will be completely healed. You'd never know it was there."

Spain looked at him for the longest time in wonderment. "But you had a great, great grandfather who lived in the early 1800s."

"That was me," stated Craig. "The whole line of McCords since that time have been me. You might say I'm my own family tree." Only a shadow of a smile crossed his face.

"Then you were the one who discovered the secret of transmutation?" Spain felt dizzy, wondered if he could tolerate such knowledge as this. Why him? Why did he have to bear witness to such a thing?

"I am the one who discovered the secret of transmutation, but don't ask me how," answered Lepointe.

"Does the Army know?" asked Spain sharply. No matter

what, he still had grave concern for his patient.

"No. You're the only one I've ever told. I've been pretending to age and die each lifetime, leaving my fortune to my supposed heirs--myself."

"Are you from another world?" guessed Spain. His heart was thudding a bit harder and faster than normal for him.

Craig smiled. "No, I don't think I'm from another planet. I believe I'm a mutation of some sort."

Spain's mouth was dry, but he tried to retain his lifelong rational outlook. "A mutation. Could there be others like you then?"

"Maybe. Right now, I don't know."

"Code blue in ER 3," emphatically roared the hospital speaker.

The doctor rushed in as an intern was already inserting a long needle directly into the patient's heart. Confident in his intern, the doctor didn't question the need for the procedure. Looking down, however, he recognized the patient.

"What the hell is he doing here? Didn't we kick him out this morning?" he asked as he took the paddles in hand.

"He still must have had several drugs in the smock he'd stolen. Looks like he OD'd."

The thief lay like a cadaver, as the CPR team furiously worked over him.

"Okay, I've got two fifty," said the doctor as he rubbed together the paddles. "Clear!" he commanded.

Everyone jumped back and he rushed in to supply a jolt to re-start the dormant heart. The body jerked spasmodically and relaxed. They watched the cardiogram.

"Nothing!" shouted one of the aids. "His temperature is down to eighty nine degrees."

"Already? That's not possible," objected the doctor.

"I've double-checked it."

"All right, let's try it again. Give me 350 this time."

Preparing for another charge, an aide bounced on the patient's chest for a count of five beats.

"Breath!" he shouted.

The man at the patient's mouth then squeezed a bulb apparatus forcing air through a tube into the lungs. Now, the paddles were charged again.

"I've got three hundred fifty now. Clear!"

Again, the body jerked upward as the electrical energy contracted the muscles. They watched the monitor, intensely hoping for a positive sign.

"Come on you bastard, beat!" intoned the doctor. "All right, one more time with 400."

They beat the man's chest and forced air into his lungs until the doctor yelled clear. Again, the body spasmed and once again all eyes tuned to the cardiogram. A long three seconds passed before the crew finally admitted defeat. One by one, their heads bowed, their best efforts useless.

"That's it then. Let's call it at 3:58 and clean up," suggested the doctor. "We gave it our best shot."

The people left the room. No one waited outside for news about the deceased vagrant. His life had passed unnoticed in the world. Impersonally, they bagged him and wheeled him to the basement to be hauled off.

Yet again, the large black man entered the room, jaded to the presence of death. His white hospital uniform hung loosely about him due to his habit of never buttoning it. Why bother, he thought, since his fellow employees avoided this part of the building, anyway. His lonely role bored him and, eventually, familiarity begat apathy as well. Desensitized, he uncaringly ate and drank while witnessing the sometimes gruesome condition of his night charges. Tonight, he passed the vagrant drug thief, sat at his desk, propped his feet up and read the paper. Oblivious, he went through his usual ritual before filling out the tedious forms necessary for hospital bureaucracy.

The wan glow of the desk lamp sent artificial rays of light over the man's shoulder to the tables beyond. They illuminated the vagrant's body bag as it swelled from internal activity. A blade protruded from the material and began to cut a slit in the plastic. The noise drew the attention of the watchman. He swirled around to note the cutting of an opening in a dead man's wrapping.

"What the fuck?"

The newspaper fell from his nerveless fingers. A hand appeared out of the body bag and spread the slit wider. What the hell was in there? His muscles on autopilot, the watcher moved, though not conscious of his own progress, until he was halfway out of his chair. His vocal cords, on the other hand, were paralyzed.

The vagrant sat up through the opening in the bag and looked straight at the hospital worker. *Please let this be a dream*, prayed the morgue attendant. He flew the rest of the way from his chair and flattened himself against the wall, sliding along it to the door, not daring to take his eyes off the phantasm. Now, the dead man's lips moved and froze the orderly in his tracks. What was he saying?

The vagrant stood up and discarded the anal capsule he'd smuggled the blade in with. Then he removed his only piece of apparel, the toe tag. The corpse seemed vital, healthy and aware. He certainly didn't look like the living dead. Silently, he slid off the table and strode directly toward the hospital worker.

The live man finally found his voice for a blood curdling scream. With the dead man within arm's reach, he found a knife in his pocket and sank it deep into the corpse. Not waiting to see the result, he ran for the door and fumbled with the handle. Something caught him from behind and twisted his neck into an unlikely position. The large black man sank to the floor while the vagrant casually watched.

The only animate life-form in the room withdrew the blade from his abdomen and wiped off the blood. Naked, he considered the problem of getting around the hospital unnoticed. Out in the corridor, he heard some commotion and conjectured that someone had heard the last scream of his victim.

Two white-coated men ran toward the morgue. As they got there, the door burst open and another white-coated man staggered outside, bleeding from the stomach.

"What happened in there?" said one of the runners.

"Was attacked," said the wounded man, barely able to talk and grimacing in pain.

One of the runners comforted the wounded man as the other entered the darkened morgue. He fumbled along the wall to find the light switch, but, before he did, his feet found a pile on the floor--a man either dead or unconscious. Turning on the lights, he noted a naked black man on the floor. Quickly, he felt for a pulse, but the man was dead from a broken neck. Looking at the face, the runner recognized the dead man's features.

"Hey! This is Derek."

He glanced back into the corridor to see his companion dead of a cut throat. Looking over the other shoulder, he saw the wounded man standing over him and noted the picture of the dead black man on the stranger's hospital ID badge. That badge would be the last thing he'd ever see.

The killer'd had his fun and now got down to business. His wound healed and he was ready. He knew what he wanted and where to get it. Casually walking down a corridor, he met a night nurse coming in the opposite direction. The vagrant exchanged nods with her and proceeded toward his goal. He reached the pharmacy and deftly jimmied the door lock.

Gaining entry, he closed the door behind him when he heard another faint scream from the distance. The sounds of running feet indicated his handiwork had been discovered. Nonchalantly, he eyed a virtual treasure trove of hallucinogens, uppers and downers. Excited by his find, he filled the pockets of his overcoat with everything he recognized and even some things that he didn't. Out the small window, the corridor lay empty, inviting him to simply walk out of the building.

"Hey, you, hold it right there."

Turning around, he discovered a single hospital security guard pointing a gun at him. He obeyed and raised his hands while the man approached. When the guard was within arm's reach, he grabbed the semi-automatic. The hospital security man fired point blank into his chest before loosing control of the weapon. The vagrant quickly reversed the gun and shot the man straight in the head. He dropped the pistol and turned around to leave.

"Why go to all that trouble?" asked a voice from behind him.

The vagrant wheeled around, startled by the presence. A distinguished looking gray-haired man stepped from around a bend in the corridor.

"Joe," uttered the murderer nervously.

"Only my friends call me Joe."

"Don't get in my way!"

"Why the antics with the CPR team? You could have just disguised yourself as a doctor or hospital worker." The older man appeared repelled by the tactics of the younger.

"Not that it's any of your business, but they recognized me from trying that before, plus it wouldn't have been as much fun." He swiveled his head in all directions to see if any one had heard the shot and was coming their way.

"Blood thirst was never our trademark," the older man growled in a low voice.

Joe spied the full pockets of the overalls. The thief noticed his stare. "Don't give me that look. I've decided that I can take whatever I want and no one will stop me."

Joe grabbed the man's wrist with a steel grip, pulling up the sleeve of his garment.

"Fresh needle marks."

The addict pulled away his arm with just as much strength. "Don't make me hurt you, Joe."

"You're no better than them," Joe said with anger. He, too, was on the watch for anyone who might have heard the shot and who decided to check up.

"Why? Because I don't have your genetically designed soldier's constitution for resisting drugs. Well I'm glad I don't.

The ups and downs are a pleasure you'll never know."

"It's a false self-destructive inclination I can do without." Joe produced a device from his pocket. "I can't afford the risk you present. None of us can."

Before the vagrant could protest, Joe used the device. No projectile hit and no visible damage appeared, but the thief threw his hands in the air, where they abruptly shook and spasmed. Eventually, the spasm stopped and he crumpled to the floor. No CPR team was present and, even if they had been, no one could revive a heart made of stone.

Chapter 22

Hunter realized that his life span always presented problems for him in assimilating himself into society. For that reason, he also could not develop a relationship with Kim. Her aging and inevitable death would be too hard on both of them. Disappearing without her, he at least planned for her well being. He contemplated this while watching Lisa stretch out her long limbs on the plush sofa of his hotel suite.

"Are you making any progress with the doctor?" she asked.

"Uh huh. My memory is awakening, although not as fast as I'd like. Is there anything else you can tell me about myself? Something you may have seen in my file at military intelligence?"

Lisa looked thoughtful for a minute, before shaking her head in the negative.

"No. Nothing that I saw, anyway. But bear in mind, I wasn't privy to everything."

Craig looked away. He tried to think of some other possible way of getting information, before Lisa added another thought.

"Wait a minute. You talked in your sleep. Muttered things that I didn't understand and sometimes in some other language." She sat up, attentive now.

"Things like what?"

"Let's see. Control system?" she asked herself. "Yes! Control Systems. You talked about a control system."

"Control system?" That rang a faint, faint bell, but he wasn't certain what it might mean.

"Yes. And mapping from a satellite. Hey, where you going?"

That was a reminder to him. Craig jumped out of his chair and ran into the bedroom. He returned with the notebook Lisa recognized from their stay with the Hopis.

"So that's what this is all about," he said as he flipped through the pages. "I've been tracking this satellite. No wait, it's more than that. I've been controlling it, but why and from where?" Damn the military for disrupting his life, his memories, and his ability to do what he needed to.

"I think I know. You said something else: Satcon. Must be satellite control and its at Elephant Island, wherever that is."

"Elephant Island? Near Antarctica? That can't be." He was startled and stared at her to see if she was kidding, or trying to manipulate him for some project that the Army might have newly devised. He hadn't forgotten she might not be quite as loyal to him as she appeared to be.

"Why can't it be on Elephant Island?" she asked.

"I'd never go to that kind of climate."

"Then it would be a perfect place to hide something from someone who knows you well enough to know your preferences," she pointed out.

What she said actually made sense. Even though he seemed to have an aversion to such places, he half remembered going there.

"So when do we leave?" she asked cheerily.

The ice breaker made slow progress through the Antarctic ice pack. The white parts of the ship seemed to glow, as they reflected the winter formations bathed in frozen moonlight. Craig stood on deck, the wind stinging his face, while he tried to acclimate to the harsh environment. He hated this land with its six month nights and sub-zero temperatures. Beyond the ship's stern, Craig heard a tremendous rumbling. Thundering its freedom cry, a giant piece of glacier sheared off its parent and slid into the sea. The sight mesmerized Craig, but he found he couldn't stand more than five minutes in the polar air. His thin blood afforded him the least tolerance of anyone on board, yet he seemed to recall once taking this route in relative comfort. He had a strange feeling that he'd forgotten to take something with that would have made him impervious to the cold.

He retreated to his cabin, where he spent most of his time in the company of several electric heaters. Although not the perfect solution, they at least made his trip tolerable.

Every now and then, a heavy thud reverberated throughout the ship as a large ice floe collided with the icebreaker. The randomness of this frightening sound kept him from ignoring the constant droning of ice sliding off the hull. Craig still wondered why the hell he would choose this location for the satellite control. Lisa said no one would suspect him of hiding it here, but that logic now seemed woefully inadequate to justify his suffering on the trip. After several minutes of these ruminations, he reminded himself that his immediate purpose was to find any trace of his lost life. Nothing else mattered.

A knock on the door snapped him out of his musings. It was Lisa.

"Wow, it feels like a sauna in here," she commented.

Craig just returned a look that asked: Is that the most important thing you've come to say. She read his expression as if he'd spoken out loud.

"The captain says we're about ten hours away. He suggests we get some sleep before landfall, but I'm too excited. Do you mind if I spend some time with you? I have some questions I'd like to ask about this satellite."

"Come on in. I'm sure I won't be able to sleep, either."

She stepped in and peeled off all but her last layer of tight-fitting thermal underwear. She sat in the chair next to his bed. Her curvaceous body only teased Craig, since he couldn't bear the idea of removing any clothing layer of his own.

"So tell me about this satellite," she proposed. "I saw nothing in the files about it."

Of course she might be spying for the Army, but that didn't matter. He really didn't have very much to give her now. "I wish I could tell you about it," he answered, lying back, closer to the heaters. "Apparently, I thought it was important enough to track its position. Now, all I remember is that there is indeed a control room for it on Elephant Island. Why there of all places, I'll never fathom."

"What does it do?" Was her question casual, or was she pumping him for information?

"I don't know," he said in all honesty.

"How did you get it into orbit." She wrinkled her forehead in puzzlement.

Craig just shrugged. "I'm hoping that when I see the satellite uplink station these things will come back to me."

"Oh," said Lisa, disappointed.

"I do remember one thing about it, if you're that interested."

She perked up a little. "What?"

"The technology behind it is the same basic science that accounts for the transmuter."

"You mean it's a transmuter in orbit?" She recoiled, as if she realized the implications of a world subject to a transmutation ray.

"No, it's just based on the same technology," he corrected.

Lisa furrowed her brow.

"All right I'll try to explain. Simply put, the transmuter is like an ultra-sophisticated computer that can effect changes to its surroundings. For instance, if I want to change A to B, the transmuter analyzes the atomic particles in each of A's atomic energy levels. Then it compares them with an internal catalog to identify the substance and stores it in memory. All elements' atomic structures are stored in its memory. Now to actually change A to B it takes protons, neutrons and electrons from an atomic particle source and either adds to or takes away from the appropriate energy levels of each atom in A." Telling her this could do no harm, even if she passed the information on. The military would need to understand a great deal more. "The mechanism the transmuter employs to transfer the atomic mass is what's common to both the transmuter and the satellite. In effect, it uses fusion and fission, but without any catastrophic explosions or radiation release."

Her eyes were riveted on his face. "A benign fusion and fission process. If I hadn't seen the results of all this, I'd never believe it. Do you know how to make a transmuter?" The sweat had begun to pour out of her. Her T-shirt was already soaked.

"I used to be able to make transmuters. But right now I don't remember how." He smiled, because if that was what she wanted, she would never get the information, so long as he was in his present state.

"That's too bad. But let me ask you, if you change lead to gold, is it a permanent change?" She wiped the sweat from her hairline with her hands.

"Yes, and when I reverse the process the lead piece would be totally identical to the original, right down to the impurities on the subatomic level."

"Why would you want to reverse the process?" She put her hand on his thigh and he covered that hand with his own.

"Well, we wouldn't want to keep lead as gold because we don't want an economic collapse. You can't add cheap gold to the world market without serious consequences. You see that, don't you?"

"Of course I do. I'd just want to make a little gold and only for myself." Her lips curved into something of a little girl pout.

Craig took away his hand, while removing her own. The greed comes through no matter who she is, he thought with disgust.

"A girl can dream, can't she?" asked Lisa with a smile. "Besides, didn't you make some interesting gems with the device yourself? General Magnuson had some strange jewelry that he got from the local Indians. Part wood and part ivory, but blended into each other like no one had ever seen. Was that the transmuter's work?"

"Could be. If my atomic particle source is insufficient to complete the transformation I'm left with a sample that's wood on one side, ivory on the other and a microscopically interwoven transition zone in the middle." He shrugged. He no longer cared to tell her about the process, although talking helped to pass the time.

"But wood is an organic material."

"The transmuter can deal in organic chemistry as easily as inorganic. My ancestor fed the Indians by changing rock to fruits and vegetables," he pointed out. And no need to tell her everything, either.

"Do you think you'll ever remember how to make one?" she probed.

"It seems that I'm remembering the most recent events first. That must be one of my earliest memories." In fact, the more they discussed it, the more his brain began to clear.

"So your father taught you at a young age, huh? You must have been a very gifted boy to absorb this knowledge." She batted her eyelashes at him with the compliment.

Craig smiled inwardly at her ignorance of his life span. "Thank you. But right now, all I know is how to use the devices--not make them. Anyway, there're still more blanks for me to fill in. But you know, the more I think about it, the more I appreciate what a fantastic feat building them way back in those days was. Can you imagine trying to build a computer with the materials available in the early 1880s? It would take years to make the processor chip." He shook his head. How *had* he done that?

"Maybe the original one was a big, bulky rudimentary model. Your father's fathers could have refined it over the years to what it is now," Lisa suggested.

"That makes sense, except that I don't recall any difference in the performance of the transmutation process between then and now."

"Well. how could you? You weren't alive back then." She gave him a look as if he might be a little but dumb.

A careless slip of the tongue, thought Craig. He'd have to watch that. "I mean I don't recall hearing about any difference. Even the Army states that my ancestor converted common rock to fruits and vegetables. Fruits and vegetables, mind you, not some shapeless organic paste but apples and corn. That's pretty sophisticated for a rudimentary device."

"Yes, I see your point."

They both sat silent for a while, wrestling with the puzzle. Lisa finally spoke. "How do we know that the science was developed in a short time frame? Maybe it was in development long before the 1880s. Maybe that's just when the transmuter was first used. You said yourself building a processor chip would take years, and for this technology to spring up overnight doesn't make sense."

"So you're saying the development might go back to the 1700s or earlier?"

She shook her head affirmatively.

"Well, that's even more bizarre. Somebody built the equivalent of a microprocessor in the eighteenth century?" As they talked, he had the sense that her suggestion not only didn't make any sense, neither did the idea that he'd developed the technology a hundred years later.

But she seemed convinced her idea was right. "Why not?" she insisted. "The fact is the transmuter exists although it shouldn't, given even the present technology. The impossible has happened. Is it so hard to believe my theory?"

Craig smiled. "Suppose not," he reflected. "But we need more answers. Maybe this trip will provide us . . . ."

At that moment, the whole ship lurched. Even though the cabin lacked portholes, they knew the ship was pointed upward and at an angle. The impact threw Lisa on top of Craig who held her at arm's length while he listened with some trepidation. *Do I hear rushing water? No, it's just running feet.* His stomach began to unclench. After a white-faced Lisa regained her bearings and righted herself, he heard the engines roaring. *That's as loud as I've ever heard them,* he fretted. *As if they're in neutral at high RPM.* Slowly, the ship slipped back into a normal position.

Craig lunged out the door as the engines ceased blaring. He looked up and down the corridor. Where the hell was everyone? Now, from the upper decks, he heard angry shouts. He couldn't make out the words, but it sounded like orders, angry orders. Lisa had come up beside him and they climbed the stairs to the upper decks and went outside. Near the ship's bow, they heard another sound coming from below them, the sound of pumps. Racing to the bridge, Craig even forgot the subzero temperatures.

"What's going on, Captain?" he asked, trying to keep the worry out of his voice.

"'Fraid we hit a big one, mister. We had no business coming in this far. I should never have listened to her," he said as he pointed at Lisa.

Apparently, they'd had a conversation Craig was not aware of.

"We'll not be going any farther now. I guess we were lucky it wasn't a lot worse. Taking on a little water, but the pumps are handling it. I've radioed for help. A chopper will be here soon to take you two back."

"Back nothing!" exclaimed Lisa. "We're going ahead. You can launch the snow tractors from here, right?"

"Snow tractors! Are you nuts, lady?" The captain's jaw dropped and he shook his head in amazement. "We're still at sea, you know. This ice can change at any moment."

"I don't need a lecture, just do it, all right." Her eyes had grown intense and fiery and although Craig, too, wanted to make the trip to Elephant Island, he wondered exactly what Lisa's reasons were for such vehemence.

And as persistent as Lisa was, the captain was not so easy to convince. "I'm responsible for your safety and I'm already in enough trouble without adding to it. You're not going anywhere, but back to the Falklands," he ordered and turned his back to go.

"I think we're going to Elephant Island via snow tractor, don't you, Captain?" she said in a commanding tone.

He turned around to find her aiming a gun at his head. "Jesus, lady, you're not serious, are you? Mister, can't you talk some sense into her?" he appealed to Craig.

Craig was just as stunned as the captain. Was it his well being that motivated her to such extremes or what?

"It's out of my hands, Captain."

The tractor made tortuous progress as Lisa drove across the floating ice pack. She turned on the headlights, despite the ambient natural light, hoping they would help detect dangerous flaws in the ice. Even though the surface bore no major cracks,

Craig and Lisa held their breath at every creak. They saw the ship back away from the dense pack.

"They must have gotten the leak under control," said Lisa.

"Yeah. Looks like we're committed. Should I thank you, now?" Or should he accuse her of doing something very reckless?

"No need. I'm as curious about you, as you are. Maybe even more so."

"I was being sarcastic." A violent shiver passed through him as he spoke. The cold was difficult for him to bear.

"I know," said Lisa as she took the time to look over at him.

Something she saw in his face made her ask: "You don't regret this, do you?"

"How could I, after the diplomatic aplomb you used on the captain?"

"The gun? It was empty you know." She sounded surprised. Of course pulling a gun on people was her habit, so she must think it a legitimate means of negotiation.

"No, I didn't know and I wish in the future you'd let me in on these little pranks." He shivered and pulled his parka tighter around himself.

"You know it's quite obvious that your heart isn't in this trip, even though you say that finding your lost memory is your top priority," she chided him. "I felt you needed a good boot in the ass to get on with it. Also, while we're on the subject, for someone who's willing to take on hostile Indian tribes and gun slinging desperadoes you're being a big sissy about a little snow and ice." She took her eyes from the ice to observe him for a moment than quickly turned back to the danger of the "road."

"You know, I'm getting this uncanny feeling you're trying to tell me something," he quipped. But all joking aside, he had begun to shiver uncontrollably. Yet, looking at his discomfort rationally, it wasn't going to kill him. Nothing really was.

"What's your story, Craig? What are you not telling me?"

"You think I'd hide something from you? The woman who

played me along in a government sting operation?" He cast his eyes out at the endless span of ice. This was hell, a hell without fire.

"You still don't trust me?" she asked in annoyance.

"Only to a point." They had probably passed that point when she'd pulled the gun on the captain.

"How can I prove myself?" Those lovely lips pursed in contemplation.

"First by answering some questions--such as how is it you can order up an icebreaker like it was a cab?" Exactly which team was this woman playing on?

"That's simple. I used my old intelligence contacts." She slowed the snow tractor, carefully negotiating a rough patch in front of them. The ice creaked threateningly.

"Then you've left a trail to follow," he pointed out.

"A word-of-mouth trail only and I doubt my former compatriots know about all the personal connections I've made throughout my career. I'm sure we haven't been tracked," she stated definitively

"You sound like a veteran," he observed, relaxing slightly as they passed over the worst of the bad area.

"I started young because I had a knack for this sort of thing." She leaned forward to better see the track ahead.

He came on the alert, too, his keen eyes intently seeking out further risk. "How does anyone develop a knack for this sort of thing?"

"They do when their parents were both double agents in Copenhagen during the Cold War." Her arm came out to push him back in his seat.

He tried to quell his anxiety. Immortal though he might be, he wasn't impervious to all possibilities. "I see."

"That's where they met and married. I was born there, but grew up in the Southwest U.S." Maybe that was why the Army had chosen her for the job. She had known the land well and was a rider.

"How romantic." He saw nothing, but ice surrounding them. Even his brain was beginning to freeze.

"You have a sense of humor, now," she tossed back.

"Yes, and it looks as if I'll need it."

"No that's not what I mean. You didn't have one before, or maybe you did but you didn't use it that much. Maybe this means something." She peered into the bleakness ahead.

"I think it means I'm freezing my ass off in a tractor at the bottom of the world and I'd like a humorous escape so I don't have to dwell on it." Indeed, Craig hadn't felt the worst of the cold during their bantering. Now, however, he was painfully aware of it again.

Sweat soaked Lisa's thermal underwear, the only thing she wore due to the temperature that Craig had insisted on. He, on the other hand, wore his parka in spite of the interior heat.

"There it is," said Craig in sudden excitement.

"Where?" She appeared oblivious to the dot on the horizon.

"Over there," he pointed.

"I still don't see it."

"You don't see the dark spot in a field of white?"

She stared at the direction where he was pointing. "I think I see it now. It's so hard in this damn light, though."

"This means we're close to land now, so let's rev her up. The ice will be very dense here." Even he could hear the relief in his voice.

The dark spot on the horizon grew into an enormous hangar-shaped building. Recognizing the structure, Craig assimilated new memories. The structure was a biosphere, containing giant green leafy fronds spread out to create several overhead canopies. One could easily imagine themselves in the jungles of the Amazon inside. Geothermal energy carefully yoked provided the essential heat and power to support the various flora and fauna.

Craig and Lisa walked along a crushed-stone path, still wet from some hidden sprinkler system. Visibly impressed, Lisa enjoyed the tour Craig gave her. Rabbits darted in front of them and birds chirped overhead as they marched deeper into the shelter. Lisa spied some of the more colorful birds foraging for food in the trees and on the ground. In true biosphere fashion, every living thing depended on each other. The warm, moist environment suggested an ecological marvel maintained with simple existing technology. After their Antarctic ordeal, they welcomed its ambiance.

"It took years to build and fine tune the delicate environment," he recounted, recalling his efforts. "I had to use overhead lights to simulate the temperate latitude's day and night cycles." He took off his heavy outerwear. "It represents the most ideal ecological balance ever to be artificially constructed. The setting has practically no maintenance requirements. All byproducts of the life-forms are recycled naturally. My companies built this as a showpiece for the world, to hopefully inspire them to preserve the environment. I wanted to prove that with the resources available right now, it's possible to purify the air and water and not hurt any economic interests. In fact, in some cases my techniques would actually help the economy."

"Have you proven this?" she asked, her head turning this way and that to take in the details.

"This model right here successfully purified the air and water after we introduced industrial toxins into both supplies. Granted we only added small amounts of the chemicals due to the constraints of the model. However, I have plans for other biospheres a thousand times more efficient that can be built tomorrow. As a matter of fact, these ideas aren't unique. Plenty of other people have used similar proven techniques of natural recycling and purification, but they, like me, lack wide support."

"What kind of support?" She had taken off her boots and sought out the grass with her bare feet.

His memory found the answer to that question. "I wanted funding on an international level to build a larger scale aquatic model that could recycle wastewater for a city. Such a project would enhance the ecological health of the area for future generations, as well as provide jobs. Unfortunately, I found there to be little interest."

"That's an understatement. I never heard a thing about this," she declared. "Didn't you invite the press to see your model?"

"Yes and they came, but their perception of the public interest precludes reports on anything positive. I tried to make a case for the importance of making the public aware. No one took up the cause. The project was too costly and too risky, they said." The two of them found seats among a plot of wildflowers. He hoped the nearby plants weren't the province of a nearby hive of bees.

"Not one thought the plan was important enough to go public with?" She seemed outraged as her hands fondled the green ground cover as if it were a treasure trove of pleasure and healing.

"All right, one did. But the exposure was so limited, the story quickly faded. Negative reporting is the most lucrative." His superb eyesight found a nest of fledglings in a large oak a few feet away. A parent bird distributed nourishment to the little chicks. Robins, he decided.

"I don't agree with that," Lisa refuted. "People generally want to hear good news, but to care about it, it has to be the right good news. Something that hits close to home. Remember when the first Persian Gulf War ended? Sons and daughters came home and the threat of another energy crisis evaporated. That was great press and what a celebration." She smiled and turned over on her stomach, her eyes scanning the beauty of this sanctuary.

"Then the public is too short-sighted to see the benefits of a clean environment," grumbled Craig.

"That's why it's important to really lobby the issue," she asserted. "Hammer the message home." She stood and stretched her limbs as if she was coming to life. The air was, indeed, sweet and the ambient air balmy.

He got up alongside her and they continued to walk. That he had forgotten this place was simply unbelievable. What a miracle. "I wish I still had your enthusiasm," he said. He was nearly convinced now that she was, in fact, on his side. She seemed to want to champion the same causes that he did.

Now, the growth in front of them thinned enough for them to see a room-sized structure ahead.

"Yes, now it's all coming back," exclaimed Craig, upon entering the room. "This is the control room for the biosphere environment, as well as the satellite uplink station."

On a long table at the other end of the room rested a conventional personal computer, a printer and two monitors coupled to an unconventional looking control box. Craig sat and brought up a colorful chart on the screen indicating temperature, humidity and other environmental parameters.

"Can you access the satellite?" she questioned him.

"I think so. It'll take me a few minutes to re-familiarize myself with the program first."

Busily, he worked on the problem, while she toured the interior of the chamber, littered with computer printouts showing graphical representations. Lisa picked up a few to examine.

"These are all graphs showing the levels of toxins in the air," she called out to him.

Craig stopped what he was doing and looked, too. He was just as surprised as Lisa at her find. "That's right, they are."

"Do you remember why you were plotting this?"

"I don't know."

She looked back at the graphs. "Carbon monoxide and carbon dioxide concentrations in the outside atmosphere plotted against time. It looks like the level has gone steadily upward since the fifties and is now accelerating. Isn't that what they call the greenhouse effect?"

"I think it is. Those gases will trap the heat from escaping into space. We will definitely experience global warming if the trend isn't stopped." Although he had known this, really, his heart sank.

"Then, according to you, anyway, it's a reality, isn't it? The politicians don't need to have it studied any further." She shook the pages in her hand, showing the proof.

"It is a reality that trapping these gases in large amounts will overpower the earth's ability to deal with them naturally but . . . ." He thought a while, trying to figure out the science. He pulled her hand to him and examined the charts.

"But what?"

"But the earth isn't compensating as well as it should. According to these charts the rate of rise is far too rapid." His heart rate sped up. This was terrible news, actually.

"How do you know that?" She peered over his shoulder.

"I remember a mathematical model I made and applied to this problem a while ago. I think I have it on this computer." He began to rattle away again at his keyboard, searching for the calculations.

"A mathematical model of the earth's pollution levels? Is that possible?" She pulled up another chair and took a place right beside him.

"Sure it is. I proved it out. Look I'll show you."

Lisa watched as Craig brought up a picture of the planet on the monitor.

"The hardest part was getting accurate inputs for the sources of toxins. The formulas themselves weren't that difficult--just long." He tapped the keys.

A long equation appeared on the screen with several variables. The integral and differential symbols from calculus dotted the equation.

"It's really just fluid dynamics on a macroscopic level," Craig explained, engrossed. "The trick is the interaction of different pollutants with known anti-pollution devices and the natural counterbalances. I remember getting all the bugs out of it was a lengthy task. The way I tested it was by predicting a future condition and then waiting to see if I was right. After successfully predicting thirty years of atmospheric conditions, I'm completely confident that all the bugs are out of the program." He'd said 30 years. Had his work here started that long ago?

Another picture of the earth appeared. This time, certain areas were colored differently. A legend for the colors accompanied the image in the lower right corner.

"This is what the earth would be like today, if the pollution levels of the sixties had grown at the rate of that time." The United States appeared mostly brown with some yellow. Craig moved the pointer to the brown areas, causing a second monitor to come to life. Lisa read some of the narrative on this monitor as it was simultaneously printing out below. The text said: Mass deaths, mostly asthmatics, mean temperature increase of .2°F, sea levels up 5 to 10 feet.

"Obviously, that's not the case now," Lisa commented.

"That's right. The improvement is because of the public outcry. Laws were passed and controls were imposed. They worked to a great degree." He smiled but continued to focus on the monitor as he input other possibilities, for his own information.

"Well I don't know if I'd say a great degree," she objected.

"I would. Have you seen the Rumanian countryside lately? It's a perfect example of industrialization without controls. The people didn't have much say and the government valued manufacturing technology above the people's lives. The trees are barren there now and certain of the heavy industrial towns are rife with black lung disease and stillborns, among other health disasters." He glanced up at her.

"I get the point but that still doesn't prove this is accurate."

"There's more." He typed in further information and a different earth came to life with different color codes.

"Here's the earth of today with the current levels of toxins. Note Rumania in gray. Now see the United States. Mostly yellow with pockets of white and some of brown."

"Can you zoom in on specific areas?" She rolled her chair closer.

"Yes." After he gave her a brief lesson on the program, Lisa tried to confirm that the algorithm did all Craig said it did. She zoomed in on England, since she happened to know some of its recent natural history. In the fifties, London had been a dirty city due to massive coal burning. With coal burning long since abolished, it should now be different, she said.

Lisa pressed a function key to show present day London. The model's colors indicated a clean environment and the text was accurate, down to the salmon returning to the Thames. The recovery of the city was a triumph for environmentalists and totally unexpected by the general public and Craig's program accurately depicted the situation. But she was confused.

"This formula couldn't have predicted human intervention. How did your model of London show changes wrought by the English public."

"The formula can't predict human intervention, but the satellite senses reduced toxins. I then research the cause and maintain a catalog of them in the computer. Here's a list."

He leaned over, pressed another key on the console and a list longer than the screen scrolled down. Lisa read one of the items. K112: Pittsburgh, USA; scrubbers installed on steel plant stacks, 1970; reduction 1×10^4 lbs./°F- year.

"You must have included thousands of these. You went to a hell of a lot of trouble with this."

"Much too much trouble for me to be satisfied with anything less than the best accuracy possible. Believe me, my program has predicted every major environmental change for the last thirty years with 98 percent accuracy. And, by the way, that includes the effects of the nuclear disasters at Three Mile Island and Chernobyl." He gave her a triumphant look.

"I believe you."

Craig let out a breath with that statement. He realized that proving himself to Lisa had become important to him. Was that need just ego?

"If the rate of rise of pollutants took you by surprise, though, was your present earth model really accurate?" she queried.

"The increased rate happened too recently for the results to be that obvious. See how the slope of the curve changed in the late eighties? We won't see the effects of it until a few more years down the road. But the thing that bothers me is that neither the satellite nor I picked up on some new source of pollution that must exist for this curve to be justified." He *was* puzzled and quite concerned.

"Are you sure the charts are right?"

"Now that I'm here and seeing these things again, I do remember triple checking it. I must have missed an input someplace." He scrolled through the list of satellite inputs.

"What about the Kuwaiti oil well fires?" A good thought, but here they were on the list.

"No, the satellite got that," he answered her. "And the fires still wouldn't account for the size of this surge. It's something major, very major that's doing this," said Craig as he indicated the graph. "It's as if someone spread the tectonic plates apart, allowing thousands of tons of toxins into the air."

"Sounds like those geothermal vents they've found recently at the bottom of the ocean," offered Lisa. She was quite up on these things, he noted.

"The ones with the strange life-forms around them?" He had been interested by the news as well.

"Yes, tubeworms and the like."

"Those have been a constant for a long time, though," rebutted Craig.

"Do we know that for a fact?" she challenged.

"I'm sure those tubeworms didn't spring up overnight."

"No, I suppose not."

They puzzled over the phenomena for a time before Lisa broke the silence with a request. "Can we see what would happen to the earth if this rate isn't stopped."

"Sure."

Craig manipulated the keyboard and conjured up the image of the earth again. "This is fifty years into the future."

Most of the planet was brown with large pockets of gray. Only the poles were white, but even they had started to show some yellow.

"Doesn't look good, does it?" said Lisa. She made a face.

"No, it sure doesn't but eventually the curve has to level off. We'll get equilibrium at some point. Let's look ahead one hundred years."

The poles looked completely yellow. Gray covered most of the planet, but that wasn't the major transformation. Looking at the USA, Craig noted both coastlines were changed. Quickly, he nullified the color coding to see the changes in the landscape itself. The oceans had reclaimed a lot of land. The St. Lawrence River had widened threefold and the Great Lakes, fed by it, were now one gigantic inland sea. This sea stretched farther north and south than did its component lakes.

On the West Coast, Southern California had ceased to exist. Baja, California had become an island cut off from the mainland by the northern expansion of the Sea of Cortez. The East Coast showed a greatly reduced state of Florida. Chesapeake Bay had marched inland almost to the Appalachians.

When they looked outside the States, Lisa noted the lack of permanent ice at both poles. The Mediterranean had absorbed the Black Sea to the north and the Red Sea to the south. Turkey was almost nonexistent, as well as Italy and Greece. In the South Pacific, Australia had become a giant atoll. The British Isles were now a myriad of smaller islands. North and South America no longer joined, since Central America was gone.

"That's what it will be like in a hundred years?" asked a horrified Lisa.

"Yes, unless this toxic production is stopped."

"Most of the worlds' population lives within a hundred miles of the coast. What will happen to all the people?"

"My guess is that since these massive changes will occur in a mere century, the planet will see cataclysmic upheavals. A lot of it won't be gradual enough for people to prepare for. Many will be caught by surprise." He looked grave.

Lisa sat back in her chair, stunned. "Somebody once speculated that the coasts as we know them would be underwater in our lifetime. Looks like they could be right," she said.

"They were, judging by these charts. This is the result of the greenhouse effect, all right. Notice how the surface area of the water has increased all over the world?" He faced this information calmly. He had seen many changes in his long life.

"These changes will mean the end of society," Lisa said, shock showing on her face. "A new world order but not the one Bush Sr. intended."

"Man will have some new coastlines to inhabit, although with a greatly reduced population that will most likely fear the oceans. The coastland will be unspoiled for quite a while." He returned to his calculations, then glanced up, when she said nothing.

Lisa looked at him strangely. "Sounds like you're all for the new geography."

"Well, maybe such a disaster would be good for humanity. Think of it, though. A new beginning with a people very conscious of the environment. It could be worse."

"You're crazy. Hundreds of millions would die. Don't you realize that?" The tone of her voice rose.

"Yes, much would be sacrificed, but maybe that's what's required for world leadership to take the ecology seriously." He saw she wasn't taking his response very well.

"You can't be serious."

"Don't get me wrong, I don't want to see hundreds of millions of dead."

Lisa nodded, but he felt a new tension in their relationship. She probably believed that he wouldn't want to see wholesale death and destruction, but might wonder if the desire for an environment conscious world would overpower his humanitarian ideals. Yet if she was uncertain about his motives, he surely still was concerning hers.

"Can you stop the trend with the transmuter?" she asked.

He shook his head. "I'd have to build several large scale versions of it, but that wouldn't be a long term solution." Did he sound as if he was hedging? How badly did he want to stop the toxins? He even doubted himself somewhat, although he knew he really wanted a clean world for all of mankind. Still, a catastrophe would be the best guarantee that the pollution would slow. A new society might be based on nontoxic technologies.

"Well is their anything wrong with implementing a short term solution until the long term one is found?" she demanded, as if he were personally trying to force the end of civilization.

"The time and energy wasted on a short term one would be better spent on the real cause," he answered bluntly.

"I must remind you that lives are at stake." She rose to her feet and looked around, desperately, seemingly searching for the answer.

"I'm well aware of that but let me make one thing clear. If this is a natural phenomena, I'm not so sure I should interfere." Either her thinking was slow or his was worked extraordinarily quickly.

"Why not?" She paced. "If something threatens humanity's survival, natural or unnatural, we have to stop it if we can." White hot anger came through in her voice. Then he recalled what had happened to her family as a result of the atomic testing in Nevada. Of course, she would be angry at him for not trying to help.

"Yes, but our survival as a race wouldn't actually be threatened, and I'm not so sure my interference wouldn't bring down a worse catastrophe on us." That was the fact she wasn't seeing in all this.

"How do you mean?" She stopped in her tracks and looked at him, waiting for his answer.

"I mean, if this trend stops by itself, but I'm still manipulating the environment to combat it, it would leave certain natural forces unchecked. The natural rhythms of the planet cannot be interfered with. Those checks and balances have to be maintained. There must be equilibrium that comes on its own. Besides, assuming I even remembered how to build these giant transmuters, I'm not sure I'd have the resources on a grand enough scale to do it." He no longer had money or staff at his disposal. After all, he was no longer the multimillionaire environmentalist he'd been.

"So what do we do then?"

"First try to figure out if this is natural or unnatural. If it's natural, mankind will have to deal with it via its own devices.

What's the matter?"

Lisa was shaking her head in disbelief. "So if the oceans rise, you won't lift a finger to help? You speak as though you're not a member of mankind. You're a man, aren't you? You owe the rest of humanity any techniques you have that can help them survive." He didn't disagree with her but saw the matter with a greater distance and discipline than she did.

"That's the key, isn't it?' he interrupted. "Help them survive. I think that includes not giving them anything that they could destroy themselves with out of ignorance. Would you give a gun to your son who was being bullied at school?"

"There's that detachment again. You're so fucking much better than everybody else, aren't you?"

Craig could see that she was on the verge of a tantrum. He had to defuse the situation. "That's right, well maybe except for you. Now shall we get started on trying to find out what's going on?"

"You bet we should and don't think this argument is over. I, for one, can't sit idly by and let humanity go down the drain. I'll take any risk to save the species. And, now, I'm going to get some gear out of the snow tractor."

So much for defusing the situation, he thought. She was a very determined woman, determined and dangerous. He worked at the keyboard.

Lisa came back in and practically threw their supplies on the floor. "Where shall I put these?" she asked.

"Look, you're still mad, so I'm going to lay my cards on the table and hopefully then we can start to work together again. I don't think this phenomena is natural. On a large scale, these types of changes are unprecedented. Furthermore, the longer we argue the longer before any possible solutions can be implemented." He half watched her, half calculated his next move.

Lisa just stared at him biting back her anger. Eventually, as his words sank in, the tension drained out of her. "Fine," was all she said.

"I think I know why the satellite didn't register this upsurge in atmospheric toxins. The satellite only picks up anomalies or spikes. For instance, when Chernobyl blew, the radioactive gases measured far above the ambient background radiation. That's what triggers the satellite to take a reading." He went back to the data and studied what the satellite had reported.

"I think I see what you're saying. If this trend was so gradual and so widespread the satellite wouldn't recognize it as a spike." Hmmm, good, she did understand.

"Exactly and it looks as though this rise in rate is worldwide." He scrolled on and on, devouring the information and putting it all together in his head.

"As if all the geothermal vents increased their outpourings?" she asked.

"There you go with the vents again," he sighed. "I thought we ruled that out."

"Maybe *you* did, but not me. Just listen and you'll see it actually makes a lot of sense. Have you asked yourself why they are such a recent discovery? There's a whole world down there, complete with its own specialized life forms and yet we've only discovered them within, what, the last couple of decades?" She took the seat she'd had before.

"It's not like they were advertised, Lisa. Look at the technology needed to find them. I'm not surprised they were hidden for that long. Are you trying to tell me that a self-contained ecology sprang up overnight?" He laughed.

"I'm not suggesting they evolved overnight, but what if they grew overnight? The technology to find them has been around a lot longer than a twenty years or so. What if the only reason we found them is that recently they've had rapid expansion? That would answer the question of the tubeworms existence. They were always there, but they used to be confined to a much smaller area. Now, with the heat from these things increasing exponentially, they can exist farther from the fissure's heat source. Make sense?"

Indeed, he had to admit she did make sense. "I suppose. If this has, in fact, happened, then we should find a zone of dead animals around the fissures."

"That's right," agree Lisa, making the same leap in logic. "Those that were close to these vents would be killed by the increased heat and discharge."

"My thoughts, exactly." He ventured a smile. At least her anger seemed to have faded.

"Now that we have this theory, how are we going to prove it?" she asked.

Craig looked up at her with an expression of amazement. "I don't believe this. First you drag my frozen ass down to the bottom of the world and now you want me to dive a couple of miles to some underwater hell? What else have you got planned for us? A barbecue in Death Valley?"

As Lisa slept, Craig returned to the computer. Something gnawed at his subconscious, something about the last scene of earth he had brought up, showing one hundred years into the future. He had seen it before, or at least thought he had. Craig summoned up this image again. Silently, he stared at it for several minutes, trying to force some remnant of memory. In his mind, he moved land masses around like a puzzle. *What the hell is it?* he thought. *Why am I trying to make something out of this obscure piece of a possible future?* His mental topography wouldn't fit the computer model and, although he wasn't exactly sure why, he knew the image didn't feel right.

Having tried all the permutations his mind could conjure up, he attempted something else on the computer. Responding to his instructions, the program provided a view of the planet in two hundred years. North America was split by a shallow sea that extended from the Gulf of Mexico to the Arctic circle. Western Canada and its corresponding latitudes possessed a climate like present day Florida. No permanent ice could be found at either pole. He looked at the map open-mouthed. This is right, he thought. It's what I remember. Now, more neurons fired as electrical activity increased in his brain stem.

Quickly, he banged out a command on the keyboard and waited as the computer responded. At the top of the screen it read *Natural History: Cretaceous Period*. The map looked nearly identical to his planetary model of the very late twenty-second century. Europe and the Americas were closer together, since the continental drift was that much younger. Alaska and Kamchatka were connected by a strip of land that didn't exist in either the present or future earth, but, other than that, the differences were negligible. *Why is this important to me?* he thought. *Something about the planet again looking as it did one hundred million years ago. Is there some significance? Every time I think I'm close to finding out who I am, another discovery puts me that much farther away.*

Part IV

Infinite Destiny

Chapter 23

The temperature dropped. Lisa's clothes, warm enough up top, sadly lacked the heat retention for a deep dive. She considered generating her own heat by doing some exercises, but the small submarine allowed little movement. The discomfort made it difficult to concentrate on her task.

Looking at her watch, she blanched to find how little time had passed since boarding this steel trap. To break the monotony, she'd admonished Craig over the radio for wimp-ing out on the ride. The banter amused her and also reassured her that a familiar world still waited for her up top.

She peered out the porthole into an inky blackness. To conserve power, the exterior lights remained dark until their destination was reached. Without them, this night was perpetual, since the sun's rays never plumbed these depths. The surface of the ocean lay as far above them as the clouds were above their heads at sea level, yet the bottom was still miles away. Incredible that any living thing could survive the immense pressures, she thought.

With nothing outside to see, Lisa looked to the interior for interesting stimuli. Her driver, Jimmy, was cheerful enough, but not a good source of company right now as he intently plied the controls. For someone working for intelligence, he didn't carry himself like a spy, thought Lisa. Probably untrained in the finer arts of subterfuge. Only in the service on the strength of his technical assets, she conjectured. Just as well that he took his job seriously.

After appraising him, she continued to take in visual details. The ghostly glow of Jimmy's display lay a crazy grid of colored light and shadow across his face. Other than that, the submarine's interior light was extremely low.

She also noticed the sounds, especially the hull popping noises indicating increasing pressure outside, and that made her uneasy. The sonar gave off its own peculiar pinging noise as it caromed sound waves off the bottom. The pinging became more frequent as the wave-flight times shortened with the decreasing distance to the ocean floor. Suddenly, the pings got very close together.

"What's happening, Jimmy?" asked Lisa, leaning over his shoulder for reassurance.

"Either one of two things. We're either descending much faster than I thought or there's an underwater mountain beneath us." He flicked a switch to change the scale of the ultrasonic depth finder. The frequency of the pings slowed.

"Let's see what it looks like, shall we?" suggested Jimmy.

He punched a button and a previously blank monitor lit up with the contoured grid of an approaching mountain.

"Looks like a whole range down there. I guess no one has ever approached the fissure from this angle before."

"We'll call it the Jimmy Range for its discoverer."

"Well, since we don't want the naming ceremony to be a memorial service, I think I'll give them a wide berth," he joked.

The propellers angled to drive the bathyscaph parallel to the ocean floor. Lisa watched the electronic image of the mountains shift with the sub's relative position. Now, directly over the undersea gorge, they descended again.

"Better put on another layer," advised Jimmy. "It's going to get colder still before we reach the vent."

Jimmy had underestimated the vent's thermal output. Instead of putting on more clothing, Lisa peeled off another layer as the temperature rose rapidly. *Hard to believe it could be this warm this far south in the Tasman sea*, she thought.

Jimmy turned off the sonar alarm when it began to ping continuously. It imaged a valley with an ill-defined center on the display.

"The sonar is confused with all the semi-solid material spewing out of the crevice. Better use our eyeballs," he said.

The sub's powerful lamps illuminated the outside. However, even with thousands of watts, the visibility was barely twenty feet. That twenty feet, though, exposed an alien world that Lisa would never forget as long as she lived. The incredible variety of colors, took her breath away, with bright reds, greens and yellows littering the landscape. Hundreds of otherworldly life-forms inhabited this lightless vista. Crabs, the likes of which few people had ever seen, walked sideways through a jungle of bright red tubeworms. Plant life, no less colorful, waved in the currents from the nearby geyser. These creatures thrived on chemicals lethal to the surface animals. Considering these wonders, Lisa momentarily forgot her reason for coming. Jimmy quickly reminded her.

"Only so much power and air, miss. Sorry to tear you away, but there's the camera."

Lisa prepared the specially designed camera built into the sub. She focused and snapped a dozen pictures.

"Now I need to get closer to the geyser."

"I'll try and get closer, but I won't jeopardize our safety whether you get what you want or not."

"I wouldn't have it any other way."

Jimmy maneuvered the sub in closer. He didn't have to go very far.

"Stop there. This is all I need," instructed Lisa.

She viewed a barren, charred world, replete with fossils of all the animals she'd seen, but none were so noticeable as the dead worm colony. Their calcified remains reminded her of a petrified forest. She snapped pictures in rapid succession eager, to prove her theory to Craig. As she scanned the area exposed by the searchlights, she spied a dark shape at the perimeter.

"Jimmy, can you bring her around to my right."

"That's starboard you, landlubber," he said with a smile. "Right full rudder."

The dark shape came into view--some rusted part of a ship, now overgrown and teeming with life. No big deal, thought Lisa. After she completed her picture taking, Jimmy angled the propellers for ascent.

"Shit!" declared Jimmy over the radio.

"I don't like that word, Jimmy. What's the matter?" asked the surface commander.

"It's our oxygen. Must've sprung a leak."

"It's dropping?" queried the captain, hoping he'd drew the wrong conclusion.

"It'll be gone before we reach the surface." His tone was calm, but the words he spoke spelled their death. Hearing him, Lisa was terrified.

"What about your backup system?"

"Even with it, I estimate we'll be without air for twenty minutes. Better make that a half-hour folks. The leak in the main tank is increasing."

"Stand by Explorer One. We'll analyze the situation up here," he said as he flicked off the radio.

Up above, Captain Richards strode about the shelter in the biosphere, visibly disturbed. "Damn it! We don' have a lot of options."

"Can we get to them with another oxygen supply while they're on the way up?" suggested Craig.

He stopped and grimaced at Craig. "Our other sub can't couple to their hatch."

"How about this," said Craig, "the leak must be obvious, maybe we can repair it with the other sub."

Quickly the captain got on the radio to the bathyscaph. "Jimmy, if we can repair the leak from the outside will you make it?"

"Fraid not, captain. Just passed zero pressure in the main tank. We're now on auxiliary."

Craig got on the line.

"Jimmy try to conserve the air in the sub. Do you have anything on board that can knock the both of you out?"

"Yeah, a monkey wrench--but no drugs, if that's what you mean."

Nobody smiled. Now Lisa got on to talk to Craig. "Craig there's another way," she said.

He listened.

"I have the transmuter," she announced.

"You what, how, why?" he sputtered. Furious as he was at her deception, he wanted the technology to save the lives of Lisa and the submariner.

"Gold fever, I'm afraid. I couldn't resist. I found it in the false bottom of your case. I'm sorry."

Craig noticed the captain had a puzzled look on his face. He obviously wondered what a transmuter was.

Lisa pleaded with Craig over the radio. "Tell me how to use it, Craig. Tell me so I can save two lives."

Craig just stared at the handset, in hesitation.

"God damn it, McCord, tell me."

Craig's eyes widened as she used his real name. She would spill all, if he didn't cooperate. In a way, he was glad. Now he'd have to save them, something he truly wanted to do.

"We've only got about eight minutes, so hurry it up," she insisted, "or you'll have no secrets left in five."

"All right, now listen carefully. The first thing you've got to do is assimilate the device to your own personal signature."

"How the hell do I do that?"

"If you shut up a minute, I'll tell you."

After eight minutes, all communication with the sub ceased. Attempts to raise them were ignored.

"I was hoping that whatever you told Lisa would work, but I'm afraid it doesn't look good," stated Captain Richards.

"Why? Just because they're not answering? Look at the sonar, they're still coming up. Somebody has to be piloting it, right?"

"I wish that were true. The sub has an auto pilot."

Craig fell silent, going over the instructions he had given Lisa in his mind. Had he given her the right directions?

"We'll know for sure in another minute," said the captain, as if reading his mind. "They're almost here."

This is a hell of a long minute, thought Craig. But finally, the bathyscaph broke the surface, where all eyes trained on it, anticipating movement. There was none. *C'mon, Lisa, pop the hatch.* Divers connected the winch cable to the submarine. Water poured off its white hull as it was pulled from the sea and swung over the main deck. A crewman climbed up to open the hatch.

"Hey, it's opening by itself!"

A loud cheer went up. Jimmy popped his head out first but his expression didn't denote someone glad to survive a life threatening situation. The captain leaned over to Craig.

"There's no rip in the air tank."

Rip? thought Craig. *I don't even see a scratch. What the hell is going on here? Did she trick me?* As he walked around the sub, a clang made him look up. With a lot of effort, Jimmy deposited a gold block on the side of the sub . In the cold air, his breathing was visible and rapid. Slowly, he climbed out, immediately followed by Lisa with a gun in one hand and the transmuter in the other.

"Hold it right there," she commanded the submariner. "Captain, if you don't want any bloodshed, you and your men get in the hold."

The captain hesitated.

"What the hell is this?" he asked, outraged.

"Now, god damn it!" as she jammed the barrel into the back of Jimmy's head.

The look on Jimmy's face made Richards acquiesce. The captain nodded to his men, who slowly marched to the hold's opening in the deck. As they walked by, just under Lisa, the gold block slid down the curved surface to crash on the deck. Taking advantage of the diversion, Richards jumped up to take the gun away from the crazed woman. It went off with a loud report.

For one frozen moment, both Lisa and the captain remained motionless. Then, the captain slowly slid back down the sub, his knees buckling when they hit the deck. Craig saw a neat hole in the center of the man's forehead. Like a professional assassin, Lisa had never taken her eye off the captain.

"Anyone else?" she yelled.

The horrified looks on the crew's faces indicated no more heroics would occur. Craig, still watching all this, tried to make some sense of Lisa's violent outburst. *Why is she doing this?* he wondered. *Can't just be for gold, can it?* She disregarded his scrutiny as she watched the crew file into the hold. And she had said the gun wasn't loaded. So much for her veracity.

Craig addressed her as calmly as he could. "I've noticed that ocean voyages really bring out the trigger happiness in you, Lisa."

Again, she disregarded him. Can't mistake her seeming to ignore me for carelessness, he thought. She's an expert at this and I'm sure she's got a bead on me even in her peripheral vision. She's got the situation well in hand. Surprisingly, though, she allowed the last crewman to stay up top and lock the hold. The man turned around to remove a hat and false mustache.

"Colonel Matheson!" confirmed Craig. Well, he had suspected her, but not to the extent he should have. Damn her!

"Hello, Mr. McCord or is it Lepointe?"

"It doesn't matter now, does it?"

"Well, don't get down on yourself, McCord. We never found the evidence to prove your death was staged. It was only out of desperation that we continued the mission with Lisa. In fact, if it wasn't for her, we wouldn't be standing here right now. You were really suckered by her, weren't you?"

A tightlipped Craig just stared at Lisa. *Something was wrong with her,* he thought. She was acting oddly, even for her. Matheson continued.

"You couldn't have been thinking clearly. Although she is lovely. You know my father used to say don't let your dick do your thinking for you."

"Yes, but even with my dick I could come up with a better disguise than you did. You didn't really think it fooled anybody, did you?" Craig/Hunter was angry--very angry. And he was especially enraged that an innocent man had been killed. But he wasn't going to let his emotion get the better of him. He intended to stay calm and handle the situation as opportunity allowed.

Matheson just smiled, walked over to Lisa and took the gun and transmuter from her. She remained where she was, as if in a trance. Damn her again and damn his own stupidity for thinking he had the situation under control.

"Consider your position, McCord. Are you sure you weren't fooled?"

"Your friends on the ship, don't you trust them?" Hunter asked, in turn.

"Friends?" Matheson said and laughed. "We have no friends in the spy business, just temporary allies."

Then almost as a gesture to prove this, he pushed Lisa alongside Craig.

"Now you can die along with our brainwashed plant, but you'll be happy to know that I'll be doing her a favor by shooting her."

Craig was confused. What was Matheson talking about?

"You see, the way we tracked you was by an ingenious satellite location device. We knew you'd sweep her for electronic tracers, so the boys in the lab whipped up something special. Her hair pieces are passive location devices for a satellite. They're energized by microwaves. Broad range, low amplitude to find her, then tight range high amplitude once her exact location is known. She's dying."

Craig looked at Lisa who was still in a trance-like state. He plucked the hair piece from her head and threw it into the sea. His head throbbed with absolute fury, but he made no move.

"It's better for her to die this way," Matheson explained. "The bullet will be quick and painless, now that she's oblivious."

"You bastards!"

"Please don't mistake my gloating for disrespect. I enjoyed our little chess game and I'll try to make it quick for you, too." He gave Craig a friendly nod of acknowledgment.

"So now, we're expendable, right?" So this was what the

Army had planned for him all along.

"Not just expendable. Your neutralization is mandatory, based on your compromising knowledge." Matheson looked him straight in the eye, as if entirely unashamed by his part in this.

"How do you know you have the secret?" challenged Craig.

"I recorded what you told Lisa in the bathyscaph. Now you disappoint me, McCord. That lame attempt to save your life isn't worthy of you. Face it, you've been conned."

Craig was repulsed by the man's coldness. "Then by all means use the device, if you can."

"As soon as the general arrives, I will."

At that exact instant, everyone seemed to simultaneously hear helicopter blades beating the air. The sound had been there for a while, but they had been preoccupied with the conversation. Now, the chopper landed on the pad on the ship. Several armed men preceded the general as he exited the vehicle while protecting his hat from the resultant breeze. The helicopter idled, but the noise of the blades was still very loud.

"Good work, Matheson," shouted Magnuson.

"Thank you, sir."

Magnuson then turned to McCord and Lisa.

"I'm sorry about this, McCord, but believe me it's for the best."

"The ends justify the means, huh, general?"

"I've always believed that, mister, yes. I've decided that the world will be better off under our rule and that includes the United States."

That was a bit of an added shock, but Craig digested it as best he could. "So you've turned renegade and proven my views on human morality. You're not responsible to any law." Magnuson was the enemy of all mankind, by his own statement, and though he might rule, that was not an enviable position for a human being to be in, Craig believed.

"There's just our law now. It didn't start off that way, but, as

I said a moment ago, I think it's for the best. Now, before we neutralize you, I'd like to see a demonstration."

"Certainly, sir," returned Colonel Matheson. He took the transmuter and proceeded with the exact steps outlined for Lisa. "I'm ready, general."

"All right let's do something simple. Change that railing support to jade. I've always liked jade." Magnuson smiled.

The colonel pointed the device at the post. All eyes turned to it but after several moments it became obvious that nothing was happening. Magnuson went over to inspect the target.

"It's not jade." A note of anger crept into his voice.

"I don't know what happened, General," stuttered Matheson.

"Nothing happened! Except that you've wasted my time and maybe blown any opportunity we had to get the technology for good."

"I don't understand, general. I did exactly what worked before."

Craig laughed out loud. "I guess this means no world dominion, General."

Magnuson pulled a gun out of his jacket and pointed it at Craig.

"I'm through dicking around with you, mister. Either you tell me how to use this thing in the next five minutes or die."

"I guess I'll have to die." He shrugged. In fact, he wondered what would happen if Magnuson were to shoot him. He was immortal, but did that include protection from a speeding bullet? Probably not.

Then Magnuson pointed the gun at Lisa. "Her, too? I've heard you're sensitive to cold. Let's see how sensitive, shall we? Take off your jacket."

Craig ignored Magnuson.

"Take it off if you want her to live?"

"She's going to die, anyway."

"Yes, but how she dies is up to you. We could make her

linger. Draw out the pain for maximum discomfort."

Craig removed his jacket.

"That's better. Colonel, attach Mr. McCord to the sub winch, please."

Craig, held over the frigid waters, shivered from the long exposure, but exercised inhuman willpower not allowing his extreme misery to show. *I should be dead already. Must be way past my maximum tolerance of this temperature.* His heartbeat had become irregular. *In a few moments I'll go into shock and then it won't matter what the bastards do.*

"All right, dip him in," commanded Magnuson.

The water stung every part of his body. *Jesus, feels like a thousand needles jabbing me.* They pulled him out and again held him above the water. Now wet, the wind chill broke his willpower. He shivered uncontrollably and then went numb. *Have I lost circulation from the tight ropes or am I already in shock? Getting harder to think.*

"Bring him back on deck."

As he was lowered back to the deck, he saw his reflection in the bulbous porthole of the bathyscaph. *I'm completely white. Near death.*

"Nothing like a refreshing swim eh, McCord?"

A commotion from behind made Craig strain to look up. Lisa, broken out of her trance, had made a charge at the general but was subdued by one of the armed men. Craig tried to speak but gave up the attempt.

"I compliment you on your fortitude but it's obvious the cold is seeping into your marrow. Wouldn't you like a hot bath, McCord?"

Only partially aware of his surroundings, Craig feebly gave Magnuson the finger. He'd had a long run and had done his best for humanity and the planet.

Appearing frustrated, the general ordered McCord into the water again. The winch lifted him a foot off the deck, when, suddenly, without warning, a thunderous concussion rocked the ship; all of Magnuson's men dropped to the deck.

Metal and glass rained down, as the remains of the helicopter belched a fireball into the air. Flying shrapnel cut McCord's face but only the warmth from the explosion registered with him. Before Magnuson could react, Navy Seals came off a submarine that arose from nowhere and subdued the general's men.

A thermally outfitted frogman cut down McCord and covered him with a blanket. The Seals mopped up the rest of Magnuson's men, but Craig was only vaguely aware of a flurry of activity around him. Then, he was whisked inside, warmed by some heaters and handed a hot cup of coffee. He needed help to hold the cup steady.

"Turn up the temperature," commanded a man who had just entered the room.

McCord took in his features as he came to stand right in front of him, smiling.

"Senator Joseph Talmadge," croaked McCord in amazement.

"My friends call me Joe," said the distinguished looking gray-haired man.

"Am I one of your friends?"

The senator nodded.

"We have a lot in common, Hunter. Probably a lot more than you know at the moment."

Craig dropped his coffee, as he suddenly got a chill.

"Looks like you're in no condition for conversation right now. We'll talk again later after I get you out of here." The senator signaled one of the Seals into action.

"The girl, too?"

"If you want."

"I want."

"Then so be it." The senator smiled.

Chapter 24

Still chilled to his bones, Hunter awoke in a strange bed. He looked around the richly furnished room with the aid of daylight. When first shown the room, he hadn't noticed or cared about the appointments. Wing-back chairs and a coffee table adorned a spacious corner, obviously set up as a sitting area. His comfortable bed sported a canopy not to McCord's tastes. Strangely, a scent of flowers filled the room, a room noticeably absent of any such flora. Plush red drapes outlined a large open window, allowing in the noises of the busy outer world.

After his just having awoken, his limbs resisted movement, but curiosity drove him to see what was outside. Swinging his legs out of bed, Hunter noted that they were as white as he'd ever remembered, no doubt the consequences of spending a couple of weeks in a frigid climate. At the window, he squinted in the bright light but eventually his eyes adjusted to peer out onto a large expanse of beautiful green lawn. The long driveway surrounded an island of very colorful flowers. In fact, someone impeccably manicured the entire landscape surrounding this mansion. Shaking off his sleepiness, he acknowledged the distant voices of some Hispanic gardeners who must see to the whole estate's exterior upkeep. From the south wing, he also noted servants' quarters where room air conditioners noisily hummed. Feels cool enough, he thought. What was the temperature?

He looked for the wall thermostat he had seen earlier. It read eighty-seven degrees. Another 5 to 10 degrees more and it would be perfect, he thought.

Quickly, he dressed and went downstairs, hoping to interview his host.

"Is the senator available?" he asked the butler.

"He's expecting you in the study, sir," replied the servant, who showed Hunter to a double-doored room.

The doors were open and, inside, the senator pored over some official looking documents. Talmadge appeared genuinely happy to see Hunter and motioned him to sit.

"You're looking a lot better, Hunter. I hope this little episode hasn't turned you off swimming."

Craig didn't expect to, but he smiled. "I'm sure I'll be swimming laps in your pool in no time, but right now I'm more concerned about the girl. Where is she?"

"In the room next to yours."

"Is she comfortable?" The senator caught the implication of Hunter's question. "Not only comfortable, but should live to be a hundred."

"I wish that were true. Those bastards in military intelligence purposely zapped her with microwaves so they could track me." He shook his head in complete revulsion.

"Yes, we know."

"You do? Then why are you are telling me she'll live to a hundred?" So the senator was simply trying to be soothing.

"Why not? Our technology far exceeds mankind's." Talmadge sat back in his chair and swiveled comfortably from side to side.

Hunter jerked his head up. "Ours?" he exclaimed.

"They really did a number on your mind, didn't they? I never thought that would be possible with your conditioning. Surely you know you're different from the typical human being?" Talmadge's eyes probed Hunter's being, making Hunter feel more than a little strange.

"You mean the long life, quick healing, that type of thing?" Were his abilities odder than he'd thought. And, not only that, but shared by others?

"Don't forget sensitivity to cold and low body temperature."

"Believe me, I haven't forgot that."

The senator reached into his drawer and pulled out what looked like a viewmaster attached to a cap. "Put this on and all your questions will be answered. It may seem like hours but it will only take a few seconds. Just let yourself relax and think of what you see as a movie."

Craig took the proffered device, examined it for a moment

and looked back at the senator.

"You're in no danger but you may feel a little disoriented after it's over. I'll be right here."

McCord put on the device.

A gigantic mechanical foot imitated life, with sinew like cables running up and down its structure. As it raised and lowered, it crushed houses in its path with thunderous concussions. Stepping through the dense trees, the enormous device pushed them down as easily as straws. One could only view the whole machine from miles away. Even the tectonic plates rumbled as several similar machines engaged the planet.

A once proud race was humbled by the attack. Crude offensive equipment eventually overcame otherwise daunting planetary defenses with sheer numbers and a lengthy campaign. The attack beggared the combined economies of the aggressor's worlds, yet their misguided leadership gladly paid this price for freedom. Soon now with the master race crushed they could cast off the imposed golden age of peace and resume their internecine holy wars.

A native couple witnessed the destruction of their world by those they once ruled. Atop a hill, they were less than a mile from a siege machine whose steps vibrated throughout their house. Tall and well formed, they represented the dreamy perfection the subject races had grown to hate.

A virtual planetwide paradise spawned the master race, which carefully maintained its home world's environment. A beautifully scenic inland sea shimmered at the couple's backs as shadows from the smoke of burning debris had yet to reach its shore. Water covered ninety percent of this world's surface, its warm climate propagating lush jungle, even in the northernmost latitudes. The attackers held no respect for this delicate ecology, their siege machines indiscriminately crushing all life that ran underfoot. Even the magnificent predatory lizards roared their fear as they, too, were crushed or burnt by radiation.

"What a waste of life," sighed Eroica as she surveyed the sack of a world that had ruled countless suns. "It's over, Jan. I never wanted to even think about the possibility, but

Vertropicus is defeated. You've done all you can."

In the absence of organized resistance, Jan had tried to combat the invasion on his own. Using powerful robotic servants and gravity suspension devices, he'd moved mountains of equipment to generate mighty induction fields. They fused the ferrous components of the juggernauts, but the invaders had loosed too many on them. Dejected, he had appeared at Eroica's estate, still in his near-invisible field armor.

"I can think of only one alternative," he stated now.

"You're going to take the option?" She didn't express much emotion with the question, but her eyes betrayed a grave concern.

"Yes, and I'd like you to join me." He turned from the window and sat in one of her shape-embracing chairs.

"You don't know what you'll find," she argued, although without much conviction. "We don't even know if it works... this untested theoretical miasma."

"I know it's a risk but it's less of a risk than staying here. Please come with me. We could have an exciting new life."

She paused for a moment, but Jan knew that she was thinking about how to voice her refusal.

"I've lived for almost a thousand years," she began. "I never thought I'd hear myself say this, but I'm tired. I've fought all the battles I care to fight and now I long for the eternal rest. Please go without me. You're young and yearn for adventure. You'll meet others. Don't squander your life because of me."

He smiled as a tear ran down his cheek. Jan stood again and started to go, but turned to kiss her.

"Go!" she urged, "before it's too late."

A single bright flash signaled his departure, just as an impossible weight obliterated their house. He hoped others exercised the option, as well, for existence could be very lonely on the other side if they did not join him.

Jan existed on his extra dimensional plane, oblivious to the destruction of his planet. The carnage ceased as all resistance evaporated. The invaders left the world now indifferent to their abandoned siege machines. The gigantic equipment, however, did more than just remind an empty planet of war. Their vaguely humanoid shapes defied the ravages of weather, and, in some instances, actually changed the climate. Clouds that couldn't pass them released their moisture with a rain forest effect.

Days turned into weeks and weeks into seasons. Snow covered the devices in the northern and southern extremes, but, as the temperature rose again, their metal supports revealed no damage. As years became decades, though, the monsters eventually showed some weakness. Decomposition began as the planet's natural defenses finally claimed a foothold, but the invaders' structures decayed unevenly. Inevitably the titans began to topple with cataclysmic concussions that forced great clouds of dirt into the atmosphere.

Newly airborne particles blocked the sun's rays, causing planet temperatures to drop and the seas to freeze and recede. Two of a handful of continents grew into one as the shallow sea that separated them withdrew. The recently exposed land held the promise of fertility, but the new harsh climate suppressed it. Centuries turned to millennia as permanent ice formed and advanced from the poles, claiming the former temperate zones. The moving ice carved great fissures in the main continent, allowing new access for the oceans. As this water receded, huge inland seas formed from the trapped fluid. The planet struggled to regain temperate equilibrium. An ice age passed and another replaced it, the cycle repeating four more times before stabilization.

New classes of animals, ignorant of the vanished predominant species, colonized the globe. Some creatures who made the trees their home ventured to the ground, became more aggressive and ranged far. Spreading out from their birthplaces, they encountered others of their kind and intermingled with them. Intelligence emerged anew.

The integration of groups occurred sometimes violently but ultimately well enough to create clans, then tribes, and eventually loose-knit societies. Inevitably, the societies united to fight bigger and more widespread factions. Primitive empires rose and fell, but each time knowledge was gained and development was stimulated.

Eventually, the most populous and competitive area spawned a dramatically successful republic. The culture learned to build on a grand architectural scale with mortar and stone. It expanded its socioeconomic influence to encompass the southern region of the continent it occupied and the Northern part of its neighboring continent that lay to the South. The triumphant empire expanded its political borders to make the sea between the continents its private lake, and, for all practical purposes, it ruled the known planet.

The empire lasted for a millennium before internal corruption caused its collapse. Its mark, however, was indelibly etched on the succeeding world powers in the Northern regions of the continent. Their ships formed an ever-widening circle of exploration, discovering new land masses, whereupon many of the established nations staked their claims.

New trade opportunities in the so called new world yielded mutual benefits—but also fueled a thriving growth industry, buccaneering. Some governments adopted this piracy as a covert means of support, causing friction between nations. The resulting clash between two world powers signaled the end of one and the rise of the lesser. Through naval dominance, the victor reigned over the farthest flung and most diverse corners of the globe for centuries. Then, its holdings on the new Western continent rebelled, and an old nemesis on the home continent threatened.

After fighting the empire to a standstill, the rebels obtained a reprieve, as their overlords diverted all resources to defeat the threat at home. A new nation formed on the new continent and expanded into the wilderness, but its population grew faster than its government, leading to a period of self-made justice. Not the most hospitable landscape for a visitor from a more civilized time.

Jan opened his eyes seemingly a mere moment after they were shut. With the option completed, he reacquired his physical form. The programmed instructions survived the ages, but where, or more accurately, *when* was he? He stood and stretched his legs for the first time in several millennia. His uniform still hugged the unchanged contours of his body. Equipment surrounded him, preserved in the same manner as himself. Space, microscopically curved, was the media for describing and storing his pattern for future reconstruction.

The orbital defender had only recently carved out this cavern for him, and because the cave was new, was untouched by the stirring of the restive planet. Sunlight filtered into the cavern through a small opening not big enough to allow the passage of a man. Dust particles streamed through the rays, signifying dirty air, as Jan's lungs made the temporary adjustment. Reaching into a small storage compartment, he removed a hand held tunneling device. After a few moments of tunneling, he stood at the mouth of a perfectly circular opening with smooth walls.

Instruments revealed a lower carbon dioxide level and cooler planet wide temperatures relative to the younger world he had known. His cat like eyes distinguished the outlines of various rock structures, as he looked down into a dry moonlit valley. The gentle surf no longer lapped at the rock walls and the peculiar natural beauty that was once Vertropicus had vanished. Gazing up, he noted the new position of the major moon, further away and exposing a different face than the one he was used to. He also failed to recognize the constellation, signifying that he'd been in suspension a very long time.

He turned to gather provisions from the cavern, when a noise brought his attention back to the valley. Well in the distance, ran a creature that bore little resemblance to any of its possible ancestors from Jan's time. When he put on his vision enhancers, however, he recognized it as not one but two creatures in some sort of symbiotic relationship. With great relief, Jan saw that the biped on top was not dissimilar to himself in appearance.

Eventually, the creature approached an unnatural wooden structure with symbols transcribed on it. Obviously some type of sign writing, yet the vision device could not translate the symbols. Jan stared for a few moments, trying to recognize any similarities to previous scripts. Without success, he stored the image for future study. On the device's display, the alien writing stood temporarily inert to his efforts. It read:

WELCOME TO THE TERRITORY OF
NEW MEXICO

Hunter removed the viewmaster device. The senator was right about the disorientation, but it was slight. He now remembered the past, his personal past.

"How do you feel . . . Jan?" asked the senator.

Jan stared at the device, but not really at it. He was millions of years away, contemplating his former life. The man in the viewmaster drama wasn't him, and yet it was. He gaped in wonderment as the last piece of the puzzle fell into place. What he had just learned was unimaginable, yet he didn't doubt the truth of it. The senator, waiting for an answer, regarded him with a patient smile.

"I'm feeling as well as I can. It's a lot to digest." He said dreamily.

"I know, but take your time. We do have a lot of it as you now know."

That evening, Hunter fell asleep in spite of himself. The comfortable bed welcomed him and his subconscious became active. Hunter dreamed dreams stranger than those he'd experienced even in his captivity.

He gazed out at a star field from an immense viewing port. The sheer size of it made Hunter want to stagger backward. The transparent cover was like a car windshield, only ten times his height and curving off to the left and right in parabolic fashion. The unimaginable depths of space stared back at his minuscule presence with contempt.

Pulling his eyes away from the infinite, Hunter looked behind him. Tiers of occupied seats ascended up and away from him as if in a theater. Each seat contained an instrument console for the occupant. McCord, or whoever he was, sensed that each section of seats performed a specific function different than the other sections. He also realized that the personnel were operating with a collective mind to manipulate this gigantic vessel.

He peered back out the observation glass to note a planet far beneath them. The globe was not earth, yet he felt strangely at ease with the idea of an alien world, as if he'd actually lived this experience. In fact, he felt in control, as if he were, himself, directing the situation.

Looking back at the crew, he noted that the seats were heavily padded and equipped with restraints. Acceleration couches for battle conditions, he thought. The current casual mood followed a very recent battle. He knew they witnessed their progress via computer-enhanced virtual reality, shown on what was now this gigantic viewing port. The viewing field enhanced the perception and reactions of the crew by screening out extraneous visual information. The technology also tapped the subconscious' reactive reflexes, making for immensely efficient battle coordination. The invincible galactic dreadnought had won its most recent fight. The crew expected to win; their insignia proudly displayed on the back bulkhead above the highest seats.

Facts such as this now poured into his head as a small, sleek space cruiser zoomed by the left side of the gigantic port. Hunter knew the craft came from the massive vessel he now occupied. He watched its progress toward another ship he hadn't noticed before. An unsophisticated enemy star ship, its hull breached, awaited rescue by its adversaries. He watched in fascination as the dream faded.

Hunter awoke to a familiar smell that filled him with a euphoric sensation. Recognizing the scent as perfume, he turned to see Lisa in the near darkness, standing over him in revealing nightwear. He was surprised to find he'd slept into the night. As he gazed up at her, he imagined a halo, as the moonlight lit up the exterior of her hair. Indeed, she looked the picture of health, as the senator said.

"What's the matter?" he asked, still half in the other world.

"I was about to ask you that. You were shouting something in your sleep." Concern swept across her face.

"I'm going to have to work on that habit." He smiled at his own attempt at banter.

"So you're all right?" She sat beside him on his bed.

"Of course. I'm fine." He looked directly into her face.

"Then why the hell is it so hot in here?" she complained, wiping the sweat from her brow.

"You're hot? I'm comfortable. Must still have a chill from my dip in the Tasman Sea, I guess." He was still unsure of her, though he cared for her. Despite the fact that she'd given him away involuntarily. At least he thought it was involuntarily-- or had she suspected her role? Had she intended to betray him to the Army?

"You're not over that yet? I'm afraid we won't be spending much time together, until you've warmed up completely." She blew air on her face, which continued to drip with perspiration. She got up and turned to leave.

"Wait. Put on the air conditioning if you want." He wanted her company, despite his doubts about her.

She didn't have to be asked twice. She ran over to the thermostat, adjusted it and then shut the window.

"I was hoping you'd realize I wasn't acting of my own free will back on the ship," she told him eagerly.

"I know."

"You risked your life for mine. I'll never forget that. You know, when those men . . . ." She paused in mid-sentence.

"Can we talk about this some other time?" He slid his hand along the smooth, tanned, golden skin of her arm and pulled her to him.

Jan woke to the first noises of the morning. As he looked back at the pillows, Lisa reminded him of Eroica. Incredible that his mate was still alive and vibrant in his thoughts over one hundred million years after her death.

One hundred million years. The thought was staggering. No one expected the option to last that long. No one expected that it would function after countless millennia--but apparently it did and not just in isolated instances. A fair-sized population of his kind had survived on this earth and a good bet would be that all were notables in some field or another.

Lisa started to rouse. He was reminded of their first intimate encounter in the Old West facade and its unhappy ending when he admitted remembering another-- Eroica. He also saw why Lisa reminded him of her. The memory wasn't sparked by her looks, for Eroica would fit none of today's standards for coloring. Her demeanor was similar to that of his long lost love. Lisa and Eroica had many of the same qualities: strength, intelligence and determination. Amazing that two creatures so inconceivably separated by time and evolution could be so alike.

"Good morning," he said.

"Good morning," she responded, her eyes opening to greet him.

Jan decided not to make the same mistake twice. Eroica would be his inner secret. Lisa smiled and turned over and he lay back down beside her.

Chapter 25

Jan slept late and ate breakfast after everyone else had left the table. He still hadn't recovered his stamina. Lisa, on the other hand, ran to him excitedly with something in her hand.

"I'd forgotten all about the pictures I'd taken on the sub. I just found them in my other gear. Look! I was right."

She handed the pictures to Hunter, while pointing out the significance.

"A definite dead zone exists within close proximity to the fissure. See the remains of the tubeworms and the other animals. This change just happened recently."

Hunter thumbed through the pictures, conceding her point, but not her conclusions. "I see the dead zone but it doesn't necessarily mean that all the fissures are like this one."

"What else could supply the huge amounts of toxins we saw?" she demanded.

"I don't know, but we should try to keep an open mind, and that means being skeptical of circumstantial evidence."

"You call this circumstantial?" She brandished the photographs.

"I'm only suggesting that we might find alternative reasons for this."

Lisa remained silent, choking back her anger, as Hunter continued his scan of the photos. Now he looked at the shot of the rusty old hulk.

"What's this?" His memory engaged, flipping through images of the long-ago past.

"Some old ship or something. What difference does that make?"

The shadows of this thing were familiar to Jan.

Jan opened the double doors of the senator's study unannounced and closed them behind him. Talmadge looked annoyed at the intrusion and seemed about to say something, when Jan slapped the pictures on his desk.

"Do you recognize that?"

Jan pointed to the device that Lisa took for a rusted old hulk. The senator stared at the photo, with no expression. Even the annoyance had left his face. Jan identified for him what they were viewing.

"It's a tectonic destabilizer. If you'll remember, we used to use it to keep some of our unruly subject worlds in line." He waited for some kind of reaction.

"Well, being an elite soldier, you would know more about that kind of thing than I would." The senator shrugged.

"Are you saying you knew nothing about it?" Jan glared.

Talmadge sat back and rubbed his eyes. For the first time, Jan noted the official looking papers on the senator's desk-- graphs, charts and tables, computer printouts much like the ones at his Antarctic biosphere. The senator knew exactly what was happening to the environment.

"Jan, or Hunter, whichever you prefer, didn't you enjoy your old existence on Vertropicus? I know I did and I know many others like us who want back that life. Certainly you enjoyed what would now be called executive privileges as an elite high-ranking man machine. I can't believe you wouldn't want that back."

Now Jan was confused.

"Have you discovered a method to go back in time?"

"No, of course not. Even the natives here know, thanks to their Einstein, that that's not possible. We have a different plan to regain our empire and I'm afraid mankind is not invited." Talmadge appeared unconcerned by the implications.

"Genocide?" asked Jan, without giving any indication of his reaction to the idea.

"We practiced it in the old days, after all. You remember the Pallantides? Aggressive and warlike and had just discovered star travel. I still marvel at their gall in bursting onto the interstellar stage, which they knew nothing about, and immediately starting to rape and pillage. These earth people are no different and maybe worse."

"That wasn't genocide," refuted Jan. "We merely responded in kind to one of their attacks on our worlds. When they realized the threat, their social development improved. They became our allies, when all others deserted us. In the end, they wanted peace in the galaxy as much as we did."

"Not genocide you say? Did we not eliminate the aggressive portion of their society? Anyway, it's all semantics. Our scientists tell us that a natural frequency of the earth's atmospheric gases exists where the output of toxins exceeds the input. The give and take of pollutants and natural cleansers occurs with cyclic precision. We've just presented the pollutants with an edge. Have you noticed that chronometer running backwards?"

Jan looked over and saw what the senator indicated. Hours, minutes and seconds ticked down ominously. Presently, it read:

87:14:12

"In that amount of time," the senator continued, "with the help of our tectonic destabilizers, atmospheric equilibrium will be hopelessly compromised and nobody will be able to stop the runaway greenhouse effect." To him, the idea seemed to be a matter of business, nothing unusual, nothing wrong.

"I can't believe I'm hearing this." Despite his usual sense of caution, Jan couldn't help but speak up about what he felt was a moral outrage.

"Our bloodlines will be lost forever if we stay here," Talmadge clarified, as if that would explain the matter and rid Jan of any doubt or hesitation. "Already intermarriage is diluting our gene pool. Don't you see they are a threat to us? You of all people should be painfully aware of that. I'm just thankful that they didn't capture someone without your drug resistant bioengineering." He sighed, then continued to explain their rationale.

"Our plan is to set off this ecobomb and return to suspended animation. The orbital defender will recreate the young world's clean environment and revive us to a human free planet. The increased carbon dioxide level and the greater surface area of water will produce an average temperature that we're most comfortable with. The empire will live again." Talmadge's expression was that of a man whose lofty dreams at last become reality.

"These people have a right to live!" shouted Hunter. "They are our successors. Obviously they are more like us, than not, or the orbital defender would not have awakened us at this time. The option provided that we would mate with them and repopulate the cosmos with their help. You, of all people, are in an ideal position to ensure their maturation." His obligation was at least try to convince Talmadge. If he failed, he would then see what else could be done to follow the path their own ruling species had set forth.

"What are you talking about? They're killing each other and poisoning the planet. Eventually they will exterminate themselves without our help." Talmadge shook his head and gazed at Jan as if he were a pitiable lunatic.

"If you really believe that, then why don't you put yourselves back in suspended animation now until that day comes?"

"Why are you arguing with me? Don't you see that this is best for us? Enough of us are present now to repopulate an empty planet with accelerated, out-of-womb reproduction."

The senator paused, thoughtfully.

"It's the girl, isn't it? Have you grown attached? You can take her with you, you know, although she'll have to be sterilized."

"You son of a bitch. I don't know who's worse you or Magnuson." Jan was repulsed by the senator's lack of normal compassion for other living creatures of whatever genus.

"All right, I'll spell it out for you. Yes, the plan was to repopulate the cosmos with the help of similar genetic material. The satellite probed for this material down through the ages and eventually found it in the form of man. Man is in abundance enough now to help us retake the stars in a very short period of time-- but at a cost. The cost is diluting our genetic superiority.

We are not willing to pay that price. We will wait for our own pure bred populous to proliferate." Talmadge glared, his eyes shooting flashes of anger straight at Jan.

"But man will eventually evolve to our level." Jan was the only one who could or would plead humanity's case, it seemed.

"Not as quickly as we can multiply to the necessary numbers," Talmadge countered.

Neither man spoke. Several moments passed with the two inhabitants of a younger earth staring at each other--each aghast at the other's opinion.

"Now I must ask you to either join us or not interfere in our efforts," stated the senator decisively.

Talmadge's statement was a straightforward proposal set out face to face by one of Jan's own kind. Jan could not deny that the senator had been completely above board with his intentions, misguided though Jan felt they were.

"I cannot do either," responded Jan.

Talmadge looked disappointed at the answer.

"I am not surprised, judging from your reactions. Now, I'm afraid I'll have to detain you here. You'll be allowed to enter the suspended state when the time comes, of course. I hope you'll see it our way when we reawaken."

Talmadge pressed a button under his desk, a signal that prompted several men to enter the room through the double doors. Apparently, they had listened to the whole conversation.

"None of my friends here were soldiers, but I think without your equipment we should be able to contain you," threatened Talmadge.

Jan looked around and assessed his odds. The doors closed and five men took up positions around the periphery of the room. He knew that they were all like himself and the senator. He sensed the confrontation and felt newly energized by it.

"I'm sorry," Joseph Talmadge told him.

Jan turned back around to set his eyes on the senior statesman. A cold humor crept across Jan's face. Without taking his eyes off Jan, Talmadge opened a drawer in his desk and withdrew a transmuter. "Please don't make me use this," he said. "I've neutralized my own kind before and I won't hesitate to do it again if you threaten my plans. Now please choose life."

Boldly ignoring the senator's threat, Jan set his watch alarm for the time indicated on the chronometer, then looked back at Talmadge. Their eyes locked.

"Stop, damn it! I don't want to kill you."

Abruptly, Jan broke eye contact, looked beyond the senator and stared. Unnerved, Talmadge resisted the impulse to look behind him and instead, looked at his henchmen to see their reactions. The instant his eyes left Jan, he lost. With the speed of thought, Jan wrested the transmuter from the senator's grip. Talmadge motioned to his guardsmen who fell on the young world's soldier half heartedly. Jan easily parried the five away with a technique similar to a modern martial art. All five writhed on the floor, clutching various limbs as Jan ran from the room.

"We're no match for a highly trained man machine, even without his armor," cursed one of the less seriously injured.

"Quick! Get to the girl before he does," order Talmadge. "Threaten her if you must but keep him at bay."

Since no one could move from injuries, however, Talmadge raced up the stairs himself and burst through the door to Lisa's room. She wasn't there, but he heard a car engine rev. Dashing to the window, he looked outside as Jan and Lisa pulled away.

"I knew that dead zone was not coincidental," stated Lisa excitedly. "I had a feeling that those fissures were peculiar. So the senator is part of an underground group that planted those things?" Her face was flushed as she turned to him and spoke.

"Tectonic destabilizers, yes." He drove the stolen Mercedes and worried that the senator might simply have called the highway patrol.

"That's a scary thought," Lisa commented. "That someone so high up in our government could be that radical. I don't understand why he'd want to kill the biosphere, though. Wouldn't he die too?"

"He's got some twisted death wish for humanity," said

Hunter truthfully.

He didn't tell Lisa that he and the senator weren't human and that both had personal escape plans. Best not to test his credibility yet, he thought.

"Well, we'd better rout these people out." She looked determined.

"We don't have time for that. We have to disable those devices or in a few days what we do won't matter." He drove carefully just at the speed limit, so they wouldn't attract special attention.

"Why? What happens in a few days?" She sounded alarmed.

"In a few days, enough toxins will have accumulated in the air to start a runaway greenhouse effect. The earth will become another Venus."

"Jesus Christ! What can we do?" she asked.

He had thought through a plan. "First I have to get back to the Antarctic, where I can locate these devices with my uplink. Then I'll have to physically knock them out, one by one. You can help by using your connections to line up fast transportation. I'll radio the locations from there. I just hope we'll have enough time."

This was the first time that time had become an issue in Jan's life since his rebirth. Ironically, it contradicted the senator's claim that they had all the time in the world.

"Godspeed," said Lisa, hopefully.

Chapter 26

Back in the Antarctic, Jan's computer flashed the locations of the tectonic destabilizers and printed out a corresponding map. Twelve of them had been set, roughly equally spaced around the globe. Only three operated now, meaning that the others had already done their job. At least three would be easier to get to than twelve.

His watch indicated a little over 75 hours left. *Before I go,* thought Jan, *I've got to get protection from the cold, heat and pressure, and now I think I know where to get it.* He radioed Lisa for swift transportation to his mesa. Ironic, he thought, that the place selected for his safe rebirth was the remains of one of the planetary siege machines. He wondered if the other mesas hid the same grim monuments.

To get Jan to his mesa, a supersonic fighter used afterburners and refueled several times in the air. He again marveled at Lisa's connections, as he ran through the tunnels. Time sped by, but if he was right about his protection from the elements being here, the detour would be well worth it. He finally reached his destination. Good, it was still here. Despite the interlopers, the exoskeleton remained undisturbed.

The workers below had begun to carefully dissect the guardian robot that frightened Lisa the night she'd sneaked out of the Hopi village. They would find nothing of use there, thought Jan. The real treasures were right under their noses.

Just like Caleb, they didn't perceive the holographic wall that provided camouflage for the gold power source and the exoskeleton armor. The illusional barrier could be defeated, though, by the same kind of mind trick that can make two dimensional images on paper appear convex or concave. To the unknowing, however, it provided an effective mask. Even so, Hunter felt a lot more comfortable with the armor now in his hands.

The armor represented the cutting edge of the technology of his day. Only a dozen like it had existed on Vertropicus during the final attack. If more had been available to trained people, he mused, the battle might have turned out differently. Useless wishing, he thought. The truth was that the empire's forces were, in effect, beaten by that point. The rebels had needlessly pulverized the home planet, out of an irrational fear of the Vertropicans. More suits would have made no difference. The enemy won their autonomy, but at least they knew they'd been in a fight. Even with their combined efforts, they had still taken more than a millennia to subdue the most powerful empire in the universe.

Literal ages had passed since he'd last worn the armor. Not since then had events warranted it. This time, Jan intended to save a promising species: mankind. Reason enough to don the ultimate protection a soldier had ever had.

Hunter slunk around, trying to avoid detection, but in a few minutes it wouldn't matter. He started to go through the elaborate procedure of putting on the exoskeleton. Several fasteners needed to be clasped around specific parts of the body. The whole outfit weighed practically nothing, as it was made of composite materials not yet known to man. Each clasp disappeared into a dimension of thought as it was closed. The tenuous fields, intrinsic to the armor, melded with Hunter's own aura to truly become a part of his body. Expertly, he executed the fitting procedure, which took less than half an hour to complete. The custom made device rendered itself invisible, except for the black and gray undersuit. The suit magnified his range of senses and physical abilities a thousand fold. With the current inferior technologies, he was practically indestructible, he calculated.

A government technician noted a stranger hurrying through the tunnels. The man walked with purpose, yet idly noted the various experiments the technician worked on.

"Hey you! Where the hell do you think you're going?" the technician called.

The stranger ignored him. Immediately, the technician reported this on his communicator. He was advised that a team of soldiers was on the way.

"Where is he?" asked the sergeant when the soldiers arrive.

The scientist motioned with his head. The armed party

jogged down the indicated tunnel, stopping abruptly when they caught up with Jan.

"Hold it right there, mister!" ordered the sergeant.

Hunter looked behind him at the drawn weapons with amused curiosity, but otherwise ignored them and kept walking.

"Stop now!" repeated the sergeant after firing a warning shot, dangerous to them because of possible ricochets.

They jogged to catch up with Jan, who only walked briskly. *Can't run yet*, he thought. The suit hadn't warmed up enough to allow that.

The sergeant motioned for a private to go hand to hand, when Jan was no more than ten feet ahead. The private dropped his weapon and engaged Jan who went to shove him out of the way. The private feinted, caught Jan's arm and threw him to the ground.

"That's very good," commended Jan, "but I'm sorry I can't stop and play."

Reminds me of the good old days, thought Jan. *I wish I could spar with them a while.* He stood, in spite of the soldier's efforts to stop him. The other four joined in. This time, Jan accepted no resistance, shoving them away, but carefully so he wouldn't injure them.

The stunned military men recovered their wits after being overpowered by a single man. The sergeant, red faced, gathered up his rifle, aimed at Jan's legs and shot. The intruder showed no effect from the bullet. The team leader's rage turned to shocked horror, as he scrambled for his communicator.

"This is Unit 5 to Eagle's Nest. We've got a code red emergency here. The intruder could be Hunter McCord."

Outside, several armed teams waited around the base of the elevator shaft. Some had taken cover behind crates of equipment excavated from the mesa. All eyes trained on the caged elevator car above, waiting for it to descend. They waited well beyond the time Hunter should have taken to get to the opening.

Jan accessed the suit's built in transmuter to recreate the

ground level opening that he had used to escape the Confederates now so long ago. Once outside, he grinned at the elaborate preparations for his expected appearance at the elevator. *They really know how to throw a party,* he thought. *But now, I've got to find transportation.*

The suit provided several super-technical capabilities, but the designers had omitted teleportation or flying. They'd built it for the ground soldiers' purpose of capturing land. The men machines were ferried to the battle, where they would then walk or run while annihilating the resistance. The exoskeleton armor made this task so simple and safe that people volunteered for the rush and the opportunity to enhance their social standing. They earned an extra measure of prestige for planting the conquerors' pennant on other worlds.

Circling around the still heavily populated scene, Jan found a jeep, got in and turned the key that was in the ignition. Slowly, he drove away, heedless of the tense gauntlet of soldiers. One soldier, focused on the elevator, eventually noticed the moving vehicle out of the corner of his eye. He informed his CO, who identified Hunter in the jeep already several hundred yards away. Using a bull horn the officer ordered Hunter to stop and fired a warning shot from a bazooka.

Jan flinched at the close impact. Shit! He'd been found out. He saw several soldiers pile into the other jeeps and start after him while still firing. *Why are they raining ordnance around my jeep? Don't they need me alive? For all they know, their firing jeopardizes me as well. Can't let them disable my only transportation.*

The pursuing jeeps sped along the dry ground at speeds that threatened to jar the occupants onto the sand. A lieutenant contemplated his orders not to kill Hunter McCord, although they didn't say anything about causing injury.

"Fire at will, but avoid a direct hit," he commanded.

Commencing the firing anew, the lieutenant prodded his jeeps on to greater speeds when it looked as though Hunter was pulling away. With the gap remaining constant, he knew it was only a matter of time before they damaged the escape vehicle enough to stop McCord.

Before that happened, though, a bolt of lightning lanced at them from the stolen jeep. It enveloped the pursuit vehicles in some sort of energy plasma.

"What the hell is this?" shouted a driver.

Several men jumped out of the moving jeeps, afraid of contact with the stuff. *Looks like Saint Elmo's fire the way it shoots up and down the length of the vehicles*, thought the lieutenant. The occupants, all unhurt, watched their jeeps coast to an un-powered halt. The lieutenant's car jerked to a sudden stop when his panic-stricken driver slammed on the brakes, throwing the officer from the vehicle. He hit the ground, rolled per paratrooper training and then ran toward his men who hadn't landed as nimbly. No one sustained severe injury, thankfully.

Soon, an unmarked helicopter blew away the dusty plume left behind by Hunter's jeep and picked up the wanted man.

"How much time have we got now?" Lisa asked Hunter as soon as he climbed in.

"About sixty-seven hours. You'll have to get that fighter to deliver me over the Aleutians, pronto."

Lisa got on the radio and ordered up the plane as if it were fast food. When she got off, she quizzed Hunter on the consequences of not getting all the devices.

"It seems to me that if we knock one out that should solve our problem," she said.

"That was true when all twelve were operational, but it's too late now. The atmosphere is on the verge of going critical. Knocking one out will gain us some time, but I'm afraid we'll gain only a matter of minutes, maybe even seconds. I have to get all three before the deadline or all bets are off."

The helicopter banked and took off to a private airport Lisa had access to. She became silent as one of her last shreds of hope evaporated. She didn't really believe it was possible to get all the ecobombs in the time remaining.

The fighter zoomed over the ocean with a speed that seemed

dizzying, even at forty thousand feet. Outfitted with all the cutting edge technology, it represented the fastest, best equipped transportation Hunter could want. On this sunny day, white clouds raced by beneath them, frequently exposing the vast blue Pacific. The pilot flew unerringly toward the coordinates Hunter had given him and didn't question why a jet fighter was necessary for a mere flyover. He had his orders and would follow them to the letter. The guidance system flashed, telling them that they had reached their destination.

"ETA zero, sir," the pilot stated into his mouthpiece.

His passenger made no acknowledgment. Turning his head, the flyer looked to the rear seat to find nobody there. The man's oxygen mask lay on the seat as if he, himself, had dissolved.

The instant Jan heard the locator beep, he passed through the floor. The plane roared by overhead as he plummeted seaward. *I've got to gain speed,* he thought. Unlike a paratrooper, he adopted the straight up and down posture of an Olympic diver to achieve terminal velocity. He broke through the first cloud layer and didn't bother to compensate for the momentary blindness. Now, the blue beneath him acquired a personality as he got close enough to see occasional white caps. About a mile away, Jan made out the aircraft carrier that was luckily available for his pick up after he destroyed the ecobomb. It steamed directly toward his coordinates.

First Officer Phillips stood outside the bridge and scanned the area with his binoculars. He saw nothing but water to every horizon, but then something flashed by his field of vision as he rapidly panned. Phillips jerked the binoculars back and saw something that made his mouth fall open. A man fell from the sky in a perfectly vertical attitude with no parachute. He wore nothing more than some black and gray, one-piece outfit. Phillips couldn't see the doomed man's face, but noted that he didn't flail his limbs or appear distressed in any way. It was the most impressive display of fatalism the naval officer had ever witnessed.

Now, the man passed the lieutenant's level only a couple of hundred yards away and at terminal velocity. In a fraction of a second more, the falling man struck the water. From a ten meter platform, the dive would have merited perfect scores from Olympic judges. From forty thousand feet, it should have signaled a bloody pulp oozing over the surface of the ocean.

"God damn!" shouted Phillips excitedly.

Forgetting his officer's discipline, he ran inside the bridge, shouting like a five year old.

"Did you see that?"

The captain was intent on the spectacle with his own binoculars.

"Yes, I did," said the ship's master unemotionally. "I was told to expect something like this. All right let's get to work. We've got a plane coming in that's going to pick up that man when he's done."

Phillips just stared. The man had entered the water cleanly, but he still could not have survived the impact. The captain, however, not only expected him to live, but to perform some mission.

"Now, people!" reinforced the captain.

Jan slipped through the air/water boundary and in a heartbeat experienced three atmospheres of pressure sixty-six feet below the surface. The drag of the sea water, however, considerably slowed his descent. Jan converted the water immediately below him to lighter molecules and channeled them through a gravitometric field above him for propulsion. He accelerated again.

Sunlight was lost in the depths, but now the suit compensated, allowing Jan to see an electromagnetic wavelength that sea water was more transparent to.

Continuing with his straight toe dive, he adjusted his approach to the fissure still far below him. Nothing was a higher priority than stopping the poisons spewing out of the fissure. He had to survive until all the ecobombs were destroyed. His biogenetic program forced him to focus on the task at hand.

The exoskeleton easily tolerated the pressure at two miles

deep and would tolerate a lot more before reaching the target. Jan plumbed the depths, viewing life forms that any biologist would give his right arm to see. Whizzing past a giant squid, Jan considered that he was probably the only one on the planet who had ever seen a live specimen at its natural depth. The monster looked at him with a huge curious eye, perfectly comfortable at a depth where no one dreamed of finding the creatures.

How much time remained? He looked at his watch, also protected from the pressure by his invisible armor. A little over sixty-four hours left.

When he was within sight of the bottom, the temperature increased rapidly. There it was. The ecobomb, crudely camouflaged. Ignoring the beauty and wonder of the surrounding life, Jan touched down and walked toward the large device. Within reach of his target, something grabbed him around the waist.

What the fuck? Some sort of gigantic pincer picked him up just as lights illuminated the blackness. The suit reacted immediately to protect Jan's vision from the sudden harsh brilliance. He turned around in the thing's grasp to see one of the men from Talmadge's study through a porthole in a hostile looking bathyscaph. *They've been waiting for me all along. Probably expected another bathyscaph.*

They don't know about the exoskeleton's capabilities or they'd think twice about taking him on. They tried to crush him, hydraulics increasing the pressure on Jan's middle. The exoskeleton compensated as if he were experiencing a lower depth. *Sorry, in advance, about your sub.* Jan placed his hands on the inside of the pincers and spread them apart, bursting the hydraulic lines.

He dropped in the middle of a tube worm colony and started to run back towards the destabilizer again. The sub had carried him quite a way from his original drop point. *Losing time and I'll bet that's all Talmadge is hoping for.* Other pincers came around to grab him again. This time, he didn't waste energy considering what was attacking him and swatted the appendage, crippling it. *Got to neutralize the target.* Then, more spotlights turned on and shone from his destination. *Damn! Another sub?*

I'll have to. . . Hmmpf! He found himself face down in the muddy bottom.

The first sub rammed him from behind, but as it went over he managed to turn and strike a killing blow. Out of his peripheral vision, he watched the bathyscaph strike the bottom a few times before finally resting on it's side. Through the porthole, he saw the water rise in a matter of seconds and the lights go out. The second sub was almost on top of him. He anchored himself by increasing his mass, grabbed a pincer arm and threw the sub behind him.

Propelling to the ecobomb, Jan punctured it, crushed its electronic brain and sensed its death. The second sub just hovered fifty feet away. *Bastards only wanted to delay me.* Quickly, Jan rose through buoyant force, assumed an ascending position and propelled to the surface at torpedo speeds.

The giant aircraft carrier waited on the surface, virtually unaffected by the ten foot seas. Jan saw the bottom of the vessel as he rose rapidly, immune from the bends due to the exoskeleton's protection. Breaking the surface, his sight converted back to its normal spectrum sensitivity. Men waited for him on the deck in parkas, but Jan, in his armor, ignored the frigid cold that might otherwise have threatened his life. He reached the landing deck and his admiring welcoming party. Lisa met him, while a sailor offered him a blanket. He didn't need it, but took it anyway, out of politeness.

The crew applauded as he left the deck for the hard top. They knew of his plunge from forty thousand feet and of his sophisticated armor, although they didn't know where it came from and who made it. He and Lisa had also told the crew of an impending threat, but didn't say that the danger was due in just a few days.

"Is my plane ready?" asked Jan, without even pausing for a restful breath.

"Yes," replied Lisa. "And the research ship from the Tasman Sea will be in position when you arrive. I'm afraid a helicopter will have to do after that, unless I can get some help from our naval base at Diego Garcia."

"Keep me informed."

Eager to leave, Jan consulted his map which showed the next target at a point nearly midway between the Seychelles and Madagascar. He had sixty two and one half hours left. Jan handed his blanket to Lisa who took it gratefully, as she shivered in the cold wind.

As soon as he reached the hard top, Jan took two steps and sank chest deep in runway material and metal that had turned to the consistency of jello. Instantaneously, it re-solidified, pinioning his arms to his sides. The crew stared awestruck at this display of super technology. He heard a voice and identified Talmadge. Of course. Who else could it be?

"You were making great time, man machine, but this is as far as you go. There'll be no more free rides from the military."

Jan was indeed immobilized, but considered his options. Without free movement of his arms, he was helpless. He couldn't direct the power of his armor or use the built-in transmuter. Although, he might still be able to use the enhanced strength to free himself. He started to do so, but then noticed Lisa with a gun to her head. A Navy Seal held the weapon and, ironically, he recognized the man from his rescue in the Tasman Sea.

"I've seen that these men at least have been briefed on your criminal activities, including unauthorized use of military transportation," stated the senator.

Jan looked around at the faces of the Seals and the crew of the ship. The same men who had cheered him now stared at him with contempt. He would get no help from them.

There was no priority higher than the mission, he reminded himself. Life on earth must survive, even if it meant sacrificing Lisa. Jan prepared to tear the metal from around himself, but his muscles would not contract. His genetically implanted single-mindedness was opposed by a conflicting emotion. He looked at Lisa.

"Go ahead," she shouted in encouragement. "Don't worry about me."

This is as it was with Eroica all over again, thought Jan. Can't get her out of my mind, even after one hundred million years. Talmadge must know this and is using it as his trump card. He's as much a psycho-sociologist as I am a soldier. The bastard! The pain of separation. How can I let it happen again? I can't. The conflict robbed him of his strength, but not his resolve. He would think of another way, a way to save her and complete his mission.

Chapter 27

"Remove your suit!" ordered the senator.

He stood with Jan in a room below decks monitored by a surveillance camera. Jan knew that Lisa, in another secure room, watched them on screen, while being held by a Seal with orders to kill her if Jan gave the senator any trouble. Talmadge had impressed the Seals with the idea that this was the only way to subdue Hunter.

"How did you convince them I'm dangerous?" asked Jan, as he opened the fasteners on his suit.

"I didn't have to. The show you put on for my sub's cameras was enough."

"You've really turned out to be quite the lawyer, haven't you?" Jan shot back. He moved carefully, not wanting to elicit a command that would jeopardize their hostage.

"You can't be in this human profession and not learn a thing or two." Talmadge smiled.

"If you can learn from these people, why destroy them?"

"The skill benefits me in their society only. It would and will be useless in our neo-civilization." Talmadge spoke softly and Jan wondered if the Seals who monitored the room understood at all what they were discussing.

Jan unfastened the last clasp as the exoskeletal man amplifier fell visibly away from his body.

"You know this is the first time I've ever seen one of these," Talmadge remarked. "How harmless it looks at rest when it's unoccupied. It's really only your kind that add the murderous intent to it." The senator shook his head, as if in judgment.

"Don't give me that holier-than-thou bullshit. What are you going to do with us now?" A fire of anger rose in Jan's chest and flashed through his eyes at his fellow Vertropican.

The senator leaned down, un-politician like, and scooped up the armor before speaking.

"Nothing," he said and left the room with perhaps mankind's

only salvation.

Of course nothing, thought Jan. In less than sixty hours it wouldn't matter anymore anyway. Naked except for a pair of shorts, he lay down on his bunk and fell asleep.

Now alone, Lisa saw him from her room by virtue of the surveillance camera. The guard had left her once the senator had secured the armor. *What the fuck is he doing?* she thought. *Doesn't he care anymore that the whole world's at risk?*

"Wake up, damn it," she screamed and threw her shoe at the monitor.

Although Jan's conscious mind was dormant as he slept, his subconscious remained extremely active. The electromagnetic aura of Jan/Hunter McCord changed it's attitude. Ever so slowly, it began to phase- shift with his biological frequencies, separating from his physical body. Now, an electromagnetic entity floated to the ceiling, looking down at it's own dispirited body still functioning on autonomic nerve impulses. Darkness closed around the image of Hunter's physical frame as his electromagnetic self slipped through the deck. Now, it "looked" at the floor of the cabin above, while still rising through tables and assorted furniture.

"I hope you find your quarters acceptable, senator," said the captain to Talmadge, when Talmadge came onto the bridge.

"They're fine, thank you, Captain. I'm very grateful to you and your men for helping us recapture McCord." The senator stared out to sea.

"I'm honored to be part of such a high level project, sir. Would you like some coffee?" the captain asked as he poured himself a cup.

"No, thank you. I'm excited enough."

They both smiled and looked out on the bow as it cut through the waves to their destination. Deck hands fitted and fueled one after another fighter to take off for a routine patrol.

"Looks like clear sailing, Captain."

"We forecast several days of light weather." The captain, preoccupied with something else, sipped his coffee.

"That's some suit our captive stole. I had no idea we had anything like that on the boards."

"I'm proud of the security we maintained around it," the senator lied. "The body armor is quite an accomplishment."

"How does it work? How did it keep him from being killed from the fall and then enable him to overpower those subs? That's remarkable."

Talmadge smiled before answering.

"I'm sorry, but you're asking the wrong guy for technical information. And I'm not even sure I could give it to you, if I had it. Security reasons you know." He shrugged.

"I understand, sir. Can you tell me what other capabilities it . . .?"

"Captain?" interrupted one of the bridge personnel.

"Yes, Ramirez what is it?"

"My navigation system. It just went haywire." The man sounded alarmed.

The captain leaned over and noted the LED readouts. Symbols like ASCII figures appeared and disappeared in radical patterns. The monitor screen looked like a staticky broadcast. The captain glanced at the compass he kept on the bridge as a souvenir. It was spinning wildly. Abruptly, everything returned to normal.

"What the hell was that, Captain?" asked the senator. He didn't seem happy.

"It looked like we just passed through a strong electromagnetic field but..."

"But what?" The senator's voice had a hard edge.

"But everything is shielded. An EM field should have no effect."

"Let's not take any chances. If the cause was an EM field, it may have erased some software. Go to back up systems and get the electronics guys to check it out."

"Aye, sir," acknowledged the captain. His voice was strained.

Talmadge left the bridge and went to the storage locker where the exoskeleton was stored. It was still there. Then he headed down the hall where another surveillance monitor was set up and trained on Jan's room. Jan was still fast asleep. Talmadge watched for several more minutes to ensure that he wasn't being deceived. The old elitist troops were capable of remarkable cunning. As a final precaution, Talmadge ordered the guard into the room in case Jan had pulled off some camera trick. Indeed, he was asleep on his bunk as the camera had shown. *Must be completely resigned to the situation,* thought Talmadge. *Best not to disturb him or he might start feeling otherwise.*

Jan's bodiless consciousness infiltrated the ship's computer and discovered their heading and destination. With this information, it ascended while watching the scene on the bridge. Below him, Talmadge leaned over the console and, together with the captain, tried to fathom the disturbance in the electronics. As before, the periphery of its vision closed in on the center, as it penetrated the ceiling of the bridge. Above the ship, it accelerated upward dramatically, but the bodiless being felt no inertial forces. Hovering over the radar dish, Jan saw the runway stretch from bow to stern, parts of it shimmering in the exhaust of the fighters.

Still higher, his bodiless self watched the carrier leave a white wake in the sparkling northern Pacific, as it receded from view. Then the restless seas became uncharacteristically bland, when the white caps all but disappeared after he passed the first sparse cloud layer. Jan now "saw" the Aleutians on the northern horizon. The air rarefied and the sky grew dark, while he flirted with the outer boundary of the ionosphere. Higher still, Jan was able to view a good portion of the hemisphere's land masses.

His essence approached the speed of light to arrive instantly in parking orbit. He sensed the orbital defender. Outside the visible light spectrum, it shimmered about a thousand miles to the south. Jan penetrated the ancient satellite. Incredible! It was still vital after all these eons, still defending itself against meteors, human interference and whatever else might come along. Certain mediums, subtly powered the device, mediums that man could not extract one milliwatt from.

Now, how to manipulate the satellite without the benefit of a physical form. How about an electromagnetic aura?

Mops stood soaking in buckets containing dirty water cleaned from the decks of the carrier. Cleaning fluids, rags and similar paraphernalia lined the walls of the dark closet. Everything was as one would expect except for the incongruous outfit that lay on the floor. The technology, it contained, made the most advanced fission reactor seem like the sharpened bone tools of Neanderthals. Now, it stood by itself and assumed a shape as if a man were wearing it. The brooms looked on, as if envying the animation. The closet door dissolved to air as the suit exited and strode down the corridor.

Far above, in the orbital defender, the electromagnetic entity relayed instructions to the suit. Affecting the gravitometric flow was a strain, even with the satellite, but the single-minded Jan would not give up.

The empty suit walked toward the room where Lisa was held. A bored Navy Seal guarded her door, while idly playing with his rifle. He didn't hear the suit, since no feet touched the ground as it walked. It resembled an invisible man wearing a sophisticated black and gray wet suit. Now, the Seal caught the movement in his peripheral vision, immediately aimed his gun, but hesitated when he saw what stalked him. He struggled to focus his eyes on the nonexistent head, desperately trying to will something there.

Within arm's reach, the phantom exerted some force preventing the Seal from squeezing the trigger. He felt the impact of where a hand might have been on his jaw, though, and collapsed into blackness. The suit picked up the gun and dissolved the door to Lisa's room. She was pacing the floor when the thing entered holding the rifle. Like the guard, she strained to see a head where no one existed. Lisa recognized the exoskeleton and thought briefly that Hunter had escaped using some advanced personal stealth capability, but abruptly the thing collapsed and the gun slid toward her. She quickly caught on to what had to be done.

The captain had just fallen asleep in his bunk, when someone frantically came knocking on his door. In shorts and tee shirt the captain rolled out groggily to answer the call.

"The woman has escaped, sir," reported a crewman. "Her door has disappeared and the guard says he was attacked by a wet suit with nobody in it." Puzzlement and confusion sounded in the sailor's voice.

Carrying the high tech wet suit and rifle, Lisa slunk down the corridor toward Hunter's room when the alarm sounded. Damn! She heard shouts and the sound of running feet. She had to make tracks. She ran toward Hunter's room, when a voice made her turn.

"Freeze!" commanded a crewman.

Wheeling around, she hit the ground rolling and fired the rifle. She missed, but the shot made the man retreat around the corridor as she got up and crouched, gun at the ready. When she backed toward her original destination, something hard jabbed up against her spine. A gun.

"Don't move a muscle ma'am," ordered a Southern accented voice.

At that instant, the suit's arm rose of its own accord, startling the man into pulling the trigger--but his gun did not fire. Taking advantage of his confusion, Lisa caught the stupefied man on the chin with the butt of her rifle. He folded up, but the others who'd been in front of her had rounded the corner and were taking careful aim. Intending to disable, they shot at her legs, yet despite their combined marksmanship Lisa was unharmed. She looked at her knees. What had happened? The bullets disappeared into a transparent barrier that suddenly appeared in front of the men. Turning around, she noted others held at bay by a second barrier at the other end of the corridor.

It must be the suit. But where had it gone? Distracted by the confusion, she didn't notice that the suit had reanimated and was now sitting up with it's back against the wall. As she watched, it waved its arm and collapsed into lifeless clothing once again. The door to Jan's chamber dissolved and Lisa saw him still sleeping on the cot. Picking up the suit, she entered the room, while the crewmen watched, helpless to stop her.

"Hunter," Lisa called, gently shaking him.

No response. He was still breathing, but refused to wake up. She sensed that his unconscious state had something to do with the animated suit trick. Now, she felt guilty about cursing him from her locked room. He had been implementing a plan all along. Finally, his eyes opened slowly, tiredly. Lisa could see that he was exhausted.

"Once or twice in a lifetime is enough for that maneuver," he stated.

"With the suit? Was that your second time?"

"At the academy, they made us do several drills but none more than one hundred seconds long." After he spoke, he realized he should have been more careful with his words.

"It's been at least ten minutes since I was let out of my room," volunteered Lisa, assuming he meant the U.S. Military Academy at West Point or another military academy.

"No kidding." His eyes were bleary and he yawned.

"Do you want to put it on now?" She offered the armor to him.

"As soon as I can move. Give me a few minutes." Hunter, with Lisa's help, eventually managed to suit up for the second time. Since he had worn it so recently, no warm-up period was necessary.

"You look a little better now," she judged.

"All I needed was a few moments of rest. Of course the suit helps by taking the weight off my muscles."

She just shook her head in amazement.

Hunter checked his watch. Only fifty-seven hours left. "We'd better move if we can't rely on military assistance," he told her.

"How do we get out of here?"

Hunter looked at the ceiling and dissolved a hole in it near the bulkhead. A chair fell across it as two of it's legs dropped into the hole. Jan then punched hand and footholds in the bulkhead to make a ladder.

"Climb on board," he invited.

Lisa secured her arms around his neck, and he ascended the

wall like an insect. Once they got to the launching deck without incident, she let go and sought her pilot momentarily, forgetting he would be denied to her.

"I'm afraid my connections are useless to us now," she said somberly.

"Can you fly one of these things?" he asked.

"What are you, nuts? I can barely drive a car."

Despite their situation, he laughed. "All right, I guess I'll have to."

"You mean you know how to fly one?" She shook her head in further amazement.

"How hard could it be? Besides I have an insurance policy," he said, as he pointed to his outfit. "Come on."

"Oh no, you don't. I don't have any such policy and Mrs. Peterson didn't raise any suicidal children." She backed away from the hand that reached out to take hold of her.

"You've got to trust me. Didn't I protect you when you were outside my room just a little while ago?"

While she was thinking that over, he grabbed her by the wrist and hurried her along with him. She didn't resist. After all, the whole world was at stake. Some men ran up on deck, took positions to Hunter and Lisa's right and fired. Lisa noted the bullets were simply not getting to them. Hunter, despite the commotion, never took his eyes off the plane. They boarded it and tried to figure out how to taxi it to the start of the runway. After several false starts that nearly plunged them over the side, he got the plane rolling. Lisa had her eyes closed. Meanwhile, the crew placed barricades in front of them, but Jan dissolved the impediments more quickly than they could be replaced.

"I think all we do now is give it full throttle and release the brake." He gave her a `what the hell' expression.

"Just do it," said Lisa, still with her eyes clenched tightly closed.

The engines roared and they were off. They dipped a little bit just off the end of the ship, normal for a takeoff, but the drop still caused Lisa to yelp. They gained altitude very quickly before leveling off at about twenty thousand feet. Lisa opened her eyes and looked around, visibly relieved that she hadn't been killed instantly on takeoff.

"We're home free now," she said. "Where are we headed?"

Just at that moment an alarm sounded in the cockpit.

"What's that?" she yelled.

"I don't know. No, wait, I think I do. A missile is homing in on us."

"A missile?" Her voice squeaked.

Looking around, Lisa spied several pursuing fighters immediately behind them. The missile never hit, however, as it was sent to oblivion just like the barricades on the carrier. Beyond that, she noticed that all the planes were now falling behind and losing altitude.

"What's happening to them?"

"They're caught in an electronic damping field. No circuit can function, including their ignitions. They might be able to make it back to the carrier. If not, they'll have to bail out. They should be all right, though."

"With all this sophisticated magic going for us, whether or not we can get to those destabilizers is still up in the air?"

"I'm afraid the designers of the man amplifier didn't provide for rapid transport. The suit is strictly a ground war tool." He focused on trying to learn how to fly this complicated jet.

"Then how are we going to get to the Seychelles and the north coast of Ireland in time?"

"*We* aren't! You're staying in Oahu. I would have left you on the carrier if I thought you'd be safe. I'll get a flight from Honolulu. In about two hours, we'll be at Pearl Harbor."

Lisa didn't argue. She would be more than happy to stay on terra firma for a while--or maybe she'd finally decided that she really would be in his way.

They saw the Hawaiian chain of islands on the horizon as Lisa suddenly spoke up again. "You know, now that I think of it, a friend of mine said the hardest part of flying was the landing."

"I don't doubt it," he agreed.

"Any idea how you'll handle it?" She licked her lips nervously.

"I won't," he stated.

"What do you mean, you won't?" Her color began to turn a little whiter under her tan.

"Just what I said, now trust me."

As they flew over land for the first time in several hours, Hunter reached back and took Lisa's hand. Mistaking the gesture for affection, she was unprepared for what followed. Without warning, they slipped through the bottom of the plane, where no opening had been before. Finding herself in free fall, she began to scream until Hunter forced her to look into his face.

"It's all right," he shouted in the rushing air.

As soon as the words left his mouth, she sensed that they were starting to decelerate. The wind rush ceased to blow her hair straight up.

"We're gliding down on an invisible disk about two hundred feet in diameter. It's got stabilizers and air vanes so we won't simulate a piece of paper rolling over itself."

"What's the disk made out of?" she heard herself say.

"The aether."

Under a different name, Lisa stayed in a hotel room paid for by yet another of Hunter's aliases. He departed an hour later than planned, due to a flight delay. That left only fifty three hours from the time of his departure.

Chapter 28

The boarding passengers stared at Jan's costume but he didn't care. He knew the impression he made on curious travelers would be irrelevant if he failed his task. Looking forward to finishing his work, he fidgeted in his seat, a state very uncharacteristic for such a master of self discipline. Jan willed himself to mentally practice his upcoming chore and ignored the expected aggravations of making his flight connections. The lack of efficiency of this world's airlines would be quite abhorrent to the old empire, he thought.

He allowed himself a last look out the window where a thriving Vertropican city had once stood, a location where now only ocean reigned. Jan lamented how much the active planet had changed. The land masses of his home were almost unrecognizable in this much later age.

"And here's a picture of my house in Surrey. That's my wife touching up some paint near the drain pipe. She loves to putter around outside."

For the last leg of the trip, Jan tried to fend off the unusually talkative Englishman who sat beside him. Giving up the battle, he realized he had mentally prepared all he really needed to. Eighteen hours had gone by since he had taken off from Honolulu and this diversion was now almost welcome. Very soon, however, he would make the drop.

"Wait, I think I have some more of the kids' pictures in my carry on."

The man bent over to pull the bag out from under the seat in front of him. Shoving in his hand, he started to feel for the photographs, when he realized his audience had disappeared. Bewildered, he dropped the case and looked around. He knew that Hunter didn't slip by him. *Must have climbed over the seat*, he thought. *Was I carrying on that much?*

Jan didn't have the luxury of being flown directly over the ecobomb, as before. When he left the plane he fashioned a glider from the aether and soared to within a couple of hundred yards of his coordinates. Plunging through the water, he accelerated toward the bottom as he had done near the Aleutians—except this time he had to angle his descent slightly to hit the target. Jan expected to encounter resistance at the bottom, but this time he resolved to dispatch it quickly. He adjusted his vision to search the depths.

There it was. The same type of underwater oasis as in the northern Pacific. There had been nothing like this on the younger planet, thought Jan as he descended toward it. An unlikely and surprising evolution, but then again the living Vertropicus had been the most dynamic planet in the galaxy. Perhaps being born of this volatile world predisposed the inhabitants to their aggressive imperialism. The human race also showed this tendency, though sometimes to its detriment, but mankind was still young.

Indeed humans could even boast a steeper evolutionary curve than their sentient predecessors. Between both intelligent races, acting in cooperation, great accomplishments could lie ahead. He had to save them.

Nothing opposed him as he smashed the second ecobomb. He now had thirty-three hours and change to get the last one.

"He just got the second one, Joe," said a technician as he looked up from his screen.

"Damn! This is getting too close. Find out all the possible commercial airline routes he could take to get to the last one. We know we can't stop him but I think we can slow him down enough so it won't matter."

Hunter swam for about ten hours before he had the opportunity to get off a signal flare to an over-flying plane. A half hour later a helicopter picked him up and flew him to the African mainland, saving Jan another two hours.

Finally, on a plane heading north he noted he had slightly more than eighteen hours left. Jan relaxed, confident that he was making progress--just before a terrible explosion rocked the plane. A hole appeared in the floor near the rear lavatories. The cabin depressurized and the oxygen masks fell in front of the passengers. Shrapnel sprayed those near the blast, leaving grisly evidence of the bomb's impact. A stewardess, scared but exercising self control, admonished Jan to put on his mask. Jan didn't need it, but did so, anyway, so as not to cause further stress on the crew.

They just started to get some semblance of order when another bomb exploded at the front of the plane. The nose pointed downward and the whole fuselage began to spin. Pandemonium ruled. Jan could not save them, so he exited to try and save their kind.

The African veldt, a sparse wilderness, rarely obstructed one's view of the horizon. Jan started to run north, pacing himself at thirty-five miles per hour, but then stopped short. What he really needed, he thought, was the closest airport. Time for another out-of-body experience. He chose a spot to lie down. Since he would not have to manipulate any satellites, suits or tenuous fields the strain would be minimal.

With the speed of light, his conscious rose to an altitude that would allow effective reconnaissance. A pocket of civilization lay to the northeast but their standard transportation consisted of oxen. He scanned further by going to a greater altitude and after several more sightings of primitive villages he saw a city due south. Positioning himself directly over the city he couldn't believe his luck. A military air base lay waiting for him with several fighters on the ground. Here was a nation unable to educate it's own people, yet found enough money for sophisticated weaponry. He thanked the spirit of the old empire for providing these war planes. Now he could continue his mission. He re-inhabited his body.

After two hours of running he reached the base and promptly stole a jet standing near the runway. Fending off some attacking aircraft, he idly conjectured that they were either protecting their airspace or pursuing his stolen fighter. He didn't care which. His contrail streaked the Mediterranean sky over the Spanish coastline before he noticed his waning fuel supply. Jan soared to one hundred thousand feet to get the most horizontal glide out of the vehicle. When the engines blanked out, he leveled off the plane and glided toward the northern coast of France.

Over the French coast, Jan exited the plane, landed unseen and bullied a ferry ticket from a passenger going to England. Reaching the British countryside he stole a car and broke several speed limits and police automobiles getting to London. Finally, he found himself on a small twin prop headed to Belfast.

"Who's got the fastest boat on the dock?" asked the stranger with an American accent. A grizzled fisherman looked up from the rope he was handling in his dirt blackened hands.

"That would have to be the Scotsman's," he replied suspiciously. "But he's not in the habit of giving rides to strangers."

"Do you think this would change his mind?" inquired Jan as he exposed a wad of Irish pound notes.

Somewhere nearby, a rich tourist would find his wallet lightened by the same amount now in Jan's grasp--but the theft couldn't be helped. The man looked at the roll in awe before slowly answering.

"My boat is almost as fast, mister," said the Irishman as he gestured toward his dilapidated trawler.

Jan came over and deposited a hundred pound note in the man's pocket.

"There's another one of those for you if you'll quickly point out this Scotsman. And help convince him to give me a ride."

The man led Jan down the dock almost before Jan could withdraw his hand. They stopped at a shack and went inside. The place turned out to be a smoke-filled bar although one could not tell from the exterior. The low level din inside, however, was typical of a crowded barroom in any corner of the world.

"Jock MacPherson, are you in here?" yelled the guide suddenly enough to startle Jan.

A hush came over the bar as everyone stared at the oddly paired duo. Eventually, a pathway opened among the unwashed fishermen and a young man came out. Jan thought the youth looked out of place, relatively clean-cut.

"What's all the yelling for?"

"This bloke would like to hire out your boat. He seems to be in a big hurry, so he wanted the fastest," said the old man stroking the youngster's ego.

The young man smiled at the compliment. The others in the bar realized they weren't going to witness a fight and went back to their drinking and fish stories.

"I don't give rides, Yank, but there's a place down the coast that can. . . .."

"I don't have time for that, Jock. I am willing to pay for the service though. Would this be enough?"

Jan showed Jock five hundred pounds, while hiding the bills from the eyes of any of the other bar's patrons.

"It'll take me an hour to get it ready. How far are you going?" Jock blurted out nervously.

"I need to get here."

Young MacPherson looked at the map Jan held.

"Then I'll have to get gas, too."

"You'll just need enough for one way. You can radio for a tow back. Do you have enough for one way now?"

"I think so," Jock said haltingly, "but I still need an hour."

"Make it a half hour and I'll have another two hundred pounds for you."

Jock ran off to get his boat prepared, while. Jan remained behind with the fisherman. "Here's your other hundred and thank you. Is there a phone around?"

"There's one in the back."

Lisa fidgeted with her hair while absentmindedly watching television. For two reasons, she didn't dare leave her room, first, she didn't want to be recognized by Talmadge's men and, second, she didn't want to miss any phone call that Hunter might make to her. Finally the latter occurred. She sprang out of the chair to answer the phone.

"Hello!" she said eagerly.

"It's me, Lisa."

"How are we doing? Did you get them?" Her pulse raced with anxiety.

"There's one left and I've got a shot at it."

"Then why the hell are you wasting time talking to me?"

"I've got a few minutes before the boat is ready. It's an hour and a half out and I've got two hours to go." His voice sounded strained. "I'll give you a call in either case. Wish me luck."

"Good luck, Hunter."

Despite jarring impacts, the boat crashed at full throttle through the waves. Hunter motivated Jock for more speed by offering him still more money for every minute taken off their travel time.

During the trip Hunter found out that the young man's father was a fisherman no different than the ones on the dock, except that he'd had high aspirations for his son. Jock attended the best schools available and was now the proud owner of a dockyard business. Hunter hoped he'd have the opportunity to make it grow and prosper.

Due to the choppy seas, they got to the spot in a little more time than Hunter would have hoped. Still, he should have just enough time to do his job. He paid his fare and jumped into the cold waters before hearing Jock's exclamation of astonishment.

Plummeting like a rock, Jan looked at his watch to find he had exactly four minutes to find this last bomb. He increased the rate of his descent by adding mass and streamlining his force envelope. The temperature rose and the water ahead became very murky. Even his keen suit-assisted vision could not penetrate it very well. Jan eventually spied the bottom, however, and, decelerating rapidly, he still hit with a thud. He had sixty-eight seconds left, but he couldn't see the device. Jan ran in a spiral until finally he made it out in the murk.

Twelve seconds left now. Twelve seconds to either shut it down or bid adieu to all of mankind. Drawing on the suit's extra reserves, he ran toward the device as fast as he could, but his progress was still maddeningly slow, due to the deep water currents and the soft bottom. The thing was still operating. He still had time. Within arm's reach, he reared back for the killing blow. Then, abruptly, it stopped with a silence that had a ringing finality about it. The ecobomb had stopped on it's own. If it had had a personality, it would have gloated, content to have fulfilled its purpose before heading off to oblivion. Refusing to believe he'd failed, Jan struck uselessly at the blasphemer over and over until he was forced to recognize defeat.

His watch displayed all zeros now. Zeroes, the number that tried to define the concept of null. The same concept that now described humanity's future. Conflicting thoughts ran through Jan's mind, muddying his reasoning, inducing delirium. He stood there staring numbly at the device. Irrationally, he tried to invent a scheme for turning back time. He desperately needed to go back and make everything right. *If only I'd acted a few seconds sooner*, he thought as he replayed the events of the last few days in his mind. Eventually the reality hit home and he resigned himself that he was too late. A few seconds had meant the difference between mankind's survival and its extinction.

Humanity, he smiled grimly to himself. They were so worried about inflicting a nuclear holocaust on themselves. They could at least be proud of the progress they'd made toward peace. A very poor epitaph, he thought, but, then again, he didn't know of any good memorials to an entire species.

He had nothing else to do, now. He reluctantly considered his preparations to go into stasis again. Jan would prepare, but only after taking a few more moments to deal with his grief. Sinking to his knees, his next thoughts were of Lisa.

Chapter 29

Talmadge drew loud applause, as he descended the stairs. With a cigar in his mouth, a drink in one hand and a beautiful woman on his other arm, he appeared every bit the conquering hero. Awaiting him at the bottom of the staircase were all the senior officials of the Vertropican exodus. He nodded regally at his well-wishers and stopped at the tenth step from the floor.

"Thank you all," he started. "Truly, thanks to all of you we're now in position to realize our shared dream. The rebirth of Vertropicus and the empire."

The remark was greeted with hoots, hollers and the ancient Vertropican salute, a fist held in front of the heart.

"It isn't exactly the plan of the original architects, but, like you, I believe in the purity of our race. And I believe that the new galactic civilization will be better served by those who've administered it before. To mix the humans into our genetic heritage puts the upcoming civilization at risk from their violent tendencies. The humans can take heart, though, that they've ushered in a new age... only one with us at the helm. So, now celebrate, for soon we sleep and when we awake the world will be new again and completely at our disposal."

After some applause the senator continued down the stairs to shake hands, when he froze at the sight of Hunter in the crowd. Dressed in his formal wear, Hunter casually sipped on what looked like a martini. Regaining his composure, Talmadge made his way over to the former man machine soldier.

"I'm surprised to see you here, Hunter. You struck me as the kind of man who'd stoically go down with his planet."

"I enjoy a good party the same as the next man," chided Hunter.

"You seemed so crestfallen after failing to save the planet. But I'm glad you've decided to join us." But Talmadge didn't actually feel pleased.

"Oh, I'm not going anywhere," Hunter said as he took another drink.

The senator didn't like Hunter's demeanor. Something was up.

"You're going to die here? Along with your human friends?"

"I'll have plenty of company... human and Vertropican."

The senator stared at him, trying to digest the comment.

"You'd better go with your aide," said Hunter as he nodded to a man who approached. Talmadge turned as Hunter indicated. The aide whispered something into the senator's ear. Both men headed for the senator's study, the room with the device that had educated Hunter about his past. Hunter followed. Inside the room, the aide noticed Hunter had followed them in, as did the senator when he turned around.

"That's all right, Krebs. Please close the doors."

With the doors closed, the senator grilled the aide.

"What's the problem?"

"We can't access the option, sir. The overseer won't respond."

The senator was looking at Hunter the entire time.

"What have you done, Hunter?"

"I eliminated the pathways for the escape option. I erased the computer file in today's language. And no one living today can recreate it." Hunter seemed quite at ease with what he had done.

"I don't believe you," declared Talmadge harshly. "I can't believe that you'd sentence your people as well as the humans to certain death."

"Certain death? Is that what I've done? Don't tell me you have no contingency plan."

Hunter's tone was entirely sarcastic.

"You son of a bitch," said a red- faced Talmadge.

"I thought you'd feel that way. Although wouldn't it be wiser to schmooze the only man machine alive that could help you?"

The senator laughed.

"Your kind are a dime a gross. If we can come up with a

contingency we will find hundreds of others like you available to help."

Now Hunter laughed.

"Nice bluff, Senator. If that were the case why didn't you employ them to stop me earlier? No soldiers were given the escape option when Vertropicus fell. At least no soldier who wasn't also a consul. As you know, my fellow politicians, those like you, were far too afraid of a military coup in a new world without a political system. No, Senator, if you're to have a chance you'll have to deal with me."

Talmadge sat back in his chair, pondering deeply. But what could he come up with? Jan was right.

Several years later

The day was crisp, like October in New England, except this was January in Washington. President Talmadge cut the ribbon for yet another of the skyscraper- sized CO_2 scrubbers, amid loud applause. Hunter McCord, the owner of the corporation that had built the giant machine, looked on in pride. The task of cleaning the atmosphere was a fight, at first, against the overly complacent political right, but then Talmadge was able to muster a powerful environmentally concerned coalition.

Even some of the Republicans yielded to the incontrovertible data in the face of obvious climactic changes. No guarantee could be made that this basic twenty-first century technology could reverse what the mighty Vertropicans had wrought in their destructive zeal but the world had hope. Lisa grasped Jan's hand firmly and he couldn't help but smile. His heart sang at the revival of the elders' original plan.